GISELLE

Charles lifted her chin and told her to look. When she did, she saw the other man. His towel was gone and his sex was thick and hard.

'Help yourself,' Charles told him.

The man smiled and presented his sex to Giselle's mouth. She didn't want it but it slipped in as easily as a knife. The man's paunch rested against her forehead.

'Is that just a toy?' he growled. Giselle didn't understand what he meant until the whip came into view, Charles's hand delivering it to the questioner.

'Get the girl to use it.'

By the same author:

SISTERS OF SEVERCY
EXPOSING LOUISA

GISELLE

Jean Aveline

This book is a work of fiction.
In real life, make sure you practise safe sex.

First published in 1999 by
Nexus
Thames Wharf Studios
Rainville Road
London W6 9HT

Copyright © Jean Aveline 1999

The right of Jean Aveline to be identified as the Author of
this Work has been asserted by her in accordance with the
Copyright, Designs and Patents Act 1988.

Typeset by TW Typesetting, Plymouth, Devon

Printed and bound by
Cox & Wyman Ltd, Reading, Berks

ISBN 0 352 33440 1

Contents

1

Caravans

They came into Briere like an exotic Eastern caravan, but instead of camels and robed men there were strange cylinders of polished aluminium and four-wheel drives. The creatures that descended from these machines were no less astonishing. Perfect women, tall, slender and dazzlingly beautiful, suddenly filled the old, cobbled square. The villagers stopped and stared. The wrinkled faces of the old men outside the café came alive, as if the invasion of youth had relit their souls.

In the back room of the pharmacy, Giselle had no idea of this sudden invasion. She was stretched out on an old leather examination couch, her dress a pool of cotton on the chair beside her. Whenever she was left in charge of the little shop, her thoughts drifted to sex. Perhaps it was her youth, perhaps it was her history in the south, the history that she must conceal and that cut her from ordinary relationships. Perhaps it was the sterility of her present life in this tiny northern village. For whatever reason, memories, dreams, the potency of her imagination, drove her relentlessly into the storeroom where the sun burnt through the grimy skylight like a divine fire. If the bell on the shop door rang, she would hurriedly make herself decent, serve the customer and then return to her makeshift bed. She could spend the whole day touching herself, climaxing from time to time, resting with her dreams for a while, then starting again.

1

Outside in the square one of the strangers was asking the way to the coast, questioning the old men about the best beaches and enjoying a glass of wine offered by the café owner. Everyone knew from his accent that he was an Englishman and from the voices of the others that they were from Paris. They asked if the circus – that is what the old men called it – had driven down that day; they asked the Englishman if he had been to Brittany before and where he had found such beautiful girls. He smiled and said they were on a shoot for a fashion magazine – *Femmes Parisiennes*. 'Have you heard of it?' he asked in excellent French, teasing them. '*Mon Dieu*! We are country people but we are not ignorant peasants!' the waitress exclaimed, her voice rising above the chorus of protest. Everyone had heard of it. Only *Vogue* was more famous. The photographer said that he had worked for that magazine too. They asked his name but, unlike the magazine, they didn't know it. He assured them that they would hear it again and often – he was the best photographer in Europe. They laughed. He was from London and his arrogance was to be expected.

In the storeroom, Giselle was remembering a dream that she had had a few days before. It had been so vivid, so involved, and so unlike any of her other dreams, that it seemed to come, not from her own mind, but from some external agency. The dream began in a familiar place, a building that she should have known. She explored it as she tried to place it. There was a sitting room with an old man reading a newspaper. He didn't look up as she passed through. There was a kitchen with an old, iron range, rusty and grease stained. There was a hallway, gloomy and stone floored. The air was stagnant, fetid. All of these places were familiar but she couldn't remember their significance. Then, turning a corner, she found herself in a corridor that was different, entirely unfamiliar, frightening even, in that it

2

shouldn't have been there. Underfoot there was a plush red carpet and the lighting was low so that the ceiling was shadowy.

As she walked down the corridor she passed a series of doors and heard sounds from each. From one came laughter, from another, murmured conversation. There was music and the sound of dancing from somewhere. Behind one door it seemed that there was a menagerie of wild animals. She wanted to open the doors but she was afraid. The tension became unbearable as she went on. Curiosity and fear contended fiercely. At the end of the corridor there was one final door, larger and older than the others. She had to press her ear to the oaken surface to hear the sounds in this room. Something was being dragged across a stone floor. Then, there were soft words, a woman's tones, importuning and needy. There were long silences punctuated by groans and cries. The cries were very sexual but there were notes of protest too and agonised frustration. The words came again, a pleading rendered inarticulate by sobs and gasps. Men's voices could be heard occasionally, low, laconic, patient. Giselle pressed herself more closely to the door. The desire to know what was happening was overwhelming, strangling her. Then there was a series of sharp gasps followed by a single loud cry, half of pain, half of excitement. The cry was like a hand reaching through the door and penetrating her sex in a rush. The arousal made her feel feverish and she rubbed her whole body across the cool oak. It was in this position – pressed to the door, aroused, lost in her imaginings of what those sounds meant – that the man found her. At first, she was aware of him only as a presence, as a warmth behind her. Then there were lips at her neck and hands on her hips. Now she was very afraid; now the arousal was acute.

In the storeroom, as she remembered the dream, her heart raced and her hand worked rapidly in the wetness

3

of her groin. The man was invisible but so real. The dream was more real than anything in the dreamy village. His teeth, when they sank into her shoulder, were like the teeth of a lion holding its mate. The hands that lifted her dress to her waist were large and powerful. She wanted to turn and look at his face but he whispered to her, told her to be silent, told her to close her eyes. The sounds from behind the door were louder now, the woman's cries more plaintive, the men's voices more insistent. Giselle's dress was torn from her shoulders and she was pulled from the embrace of the door as the rent fabric was drawn down and off her shaking body. She was naked and the man lifted her into his arms. As one hand wrapped around her shoulders, the other slipped under her behind, the fingers seeking her sex and entering her there.

She knew that the door was being opened – there was the sound of iron grinding on iron as the hinges yielded. The sounds ceased and she opened her eyes. She was inside a large windowless room, softly lit. A woman was sitting on the smooth stone floor looking up at two men reclining on an ancient couch. Giselle gasped as the fingers inside her suddenly opened, spreading her sex wide. The figures turned. The woman's eyes were large and bright but troubled. One of the shoulder straps of her dress was pulled down her arm and a breast, smooth and taut-nippled, quivered as she breathed. The perfect flesh of the breast was reddened, as if it had been slapped. The men seemed very much at ease. Their postures were casual and they were smiling. Giselle wanted to ask what was happening. She wanted to know what she had disturbed but no words would come from her mouth. The hand at her sex worked and she groaned. The woman smiled now. The men leant forward to watch. Giselle wanted to look too. She wanted to see the man who held her.

'Is she for us?' asked one of the men.

'Later maybe,' replied the man holding her, then turned and carried her out of the room and down the corridor.

Without hurrying, without speaking to her again, he opened each of the doors successively. He showed her the rooms and he showed her to the people within them. In the room with music and the sound of dancing, she saw her sister in the arms of a boy from the village. The girl laughed when she saw Giselle. In another room there were only men, playing cards. She was presented to them and they cleared the table where they sat, allowing her to be laid there. Her legs were drawn apart. She was examined and commented on. Giselle turned her face away as she was touched. Then she was lifted again and taken from the room.

There were no more doors now, only the corridor. She was taken back to the familiar part of the building.

'Where is this?' she whispered.

'Nowhere,' he replied as he set her down on her feet.

As soon as she felt the stone of the floor, cold beneath her feet, she realised that she was in her father's house. This was the overfamiliar hall, with the crooked steps leading to the upper floors. Through an open door was the kitchen where she had laboured for so long.

The stagnant, fetid air made her feel nauseous and she clutched at the man behind her. He disengaged himself, pulling his hand from her sex, leaving a void.

'Another time,' he said. Then, abruptly, he was gone.

She turned but saw only a shadow disappearing down the hall. The arousal faded. The familiarity of the surroundings bled it from her. There was a chill despair seeping through the stone floor. In the storeroom too, Giselle's arousal was fading, but she had come, three times in succession, as she remembered being carried and presented to those mysterious rooms. Then her dreams were shattered by the sound of the shop bell ringing.

It was impossible to hurry. She rose unsteadily, wiped

her flooded sex with tissues from a box that always lay ready and pulled up her underwear. Her breathing was still laboured and she had to work hard to compose herself. At her first step she felt dizzy and wanted only to sit, return to her dreams and enjoy the languor of her body, the floating sensation as if she lay in a warm salt bath. The moisture between her thighs was a distraction as she made her way slowly to the front of the shop. Through the curtain that separated the shop from the storeroom she heard women's voices and the rustle of packaging.

The sight that met her eyes as she pushed aside the curtain might have been from one of her dreams. The women that had dazzled the old men in the square were equally dazzling for Giselle. A tall blonde, shoulders bare, breasts pushing through the thin fabric of her camisole top, stood at the counter, her hands full of suncream and baby wipes. Behind her, half a dozen girls were rifling the shelves of the tiny cosmetics section. The blonde glared at Giselle as if she had been waiting for hours to be served.

'Is this the only brand you have?' she said, waving the suncream in Giselle's direction.

Astonished by the apparition, Giselle could only nod.

'You have no Etemis?'

'No, Mademoiselle. I'm sorry.'

'Very well.'

The woman dropped the cream and wipes on to the counter and took a purse from her shoulder bag.

'This is the place to come if you have corns, piles or fallen arches,' said one of the girls.

'Or varicose veins and warts,' said another, reading from the back of a large bottle of greenish liquid. There was general laughter.

The blonde smiled, then glanced at Giselle, softening when she saw the girl's confusion.

'Bitches,' she said. 'One and all. Be glad that you aren't one of us.'

6

Giselle took the money and turned to the till. It was only then that she saw the man. He was standing near the window, staring at her intently, and, as her eyes met his, she felt a sudden charge. He might have been the man in her dream. There was an indifference to her feelings as he stared so rudely and an unconcealed calculation as he scanned her face and body. She quickly opened the till and made a fuss of finding change, avoiding those eyes. In her confusion she forgot how much the blonde woman had given her and had to ask, blushing as she did so.

The man approached the counter and leant across it, looking up into her face. When she kept her head resolutely lowered, he took hold of her chin. She pulled back abruptly.

'It's OK,' he told her, with an accent that she didn't place as quickly as the old men had done. She looked at him and saw a great gentleness, so different from the quality of his gaze when he had stared from the window. When his hand reached for her again, she allowed him to take her chin and tip her face to the light.

'Look to the side,' he told her. She did. 'And upwards a little.'

As she followed his instructions, his thumb stroked her cheek. It was the gesture of a father with a nervous child.

Giselle was aware that the shop was quiet now and realised that everyone must be looking at her. Her blush deepened.

The man released her and stood back.

'Pull the dress tight about your waist,' he told her.

'Leave her alone, Charles. She's only a baby,' said one of the girls.

The man swung round abruptly.

'Shop!' he told the girl, savagely, then turned back to Giselle. 'The dress,' he reminded her.

Giselle hesitated, but then, as she had in the dream, she complied.

7

Her waist was very slender and as she pulled the dress tight about it she was aware of the fabric pressing into her breasts, outlining them clearly. His eyes took in everything. She felt herself becoming heated within, as if the blush had transferred to her sex, inflaming her there.

'Turn round.'

She turned slowly. The cheeks of her behind felt his gaze and tingled. She found herself pressing back a little, presenting herself more fully. Her legs parted without her conscious consent and there was a dizzy feeling as she realised what she was doing. She flushed from throat to groin but held still, controlling the rising panic.

'OK,' he told her after a moment.

When she turned back he had moved away and was talking to one of the girls at the cosmetics counter. He didn't look at Giselle again as she served her customers.

It was only when the shop had emptied that he came back to her.

'We are staying at L'Atlantique, in Pleneuf-Val-Andre,' he told her. 'Come tomorrow morning at ten o'clock.'

'Why?' she asked.

'I might be able to do something with you.'

Before she could reply he had pressed a card into her hand and was heading for the door.

'Remember,' he said, 'L'Atlantique, and be punctual. I won't wait.'

Giselle looked at the card in her hand, stunned. It had only a name; no address, no telephone number. The lettering was thin, slanting as if written by hand. Charles Mannay, she read aloud, pronouncing it first in French and then in schoolgirl English. The card held her mesmerised until the square was filled with the sound of car engines, then she ran to the door and out on to the pavement to watch the cavalcade pull away and disappear down the hill towards the coast.

* * *

8

That evening, as she was making dinner, she told her sister what had happened. Nana listened in astonishment as Giselle described the invasion of the square and the man who had stared at her.

'You must go!' cried Nana, dropping the cloth that she had been wiping the table with.

'I should work.'

'That job! It's nothing. A fashion photographer from Paris! Does he want to photograph you? He must! If he saw you he would want to. You are more beautiful than any girl that I've ever seen in a magazine.'

'Nana! Those other girls were so different. So elegant, so . . .' Giselle ran out of words. Nana put her arms round Giselle's waist and hugged her.

'My sister is the prettiest girl in France. I hate to say it but it's true. And when I am older I will be as pretty.'

Giselle finished chopping the onions and turned to her sister. The young girl's eyes sparkled and her cheeks were flushed with excitement.

'Prettier. But first you must get to be older. And for that you must eat; we all must eat.'

Nana looked uncomfortable, obviously aware of Giselle's sacrifices for her sake. Giselle was the only one working. Her father was past trying to find a job. Nana was still at school. The girl pulled away from Giselle and leant against the table.

'I'll work in the shop instead,' she said.

'If a teacher saw you, you would be in trouble. Besides, you aren't old enough to work in a shop.'

'Old Renais won't care as long as his smelly shop stays open. I'll say that you're ill. Anyway, I know that he fancies me. He'd like the chance to come on to me again.'

'He came on to you?'

'When I was in the churchyard picking flowers.'

'You should have told someone.'

'He's harmless. Doesn't he try it on with you?'

9

'Only once. I said that I would tell Father Hierre.'

'What about this photographer? Is he good-looking?'

Giselle flushed.

'Very.'

'Very, very good-looking?'

'Like Alain Delon. Better-looking even.'

'*Alors*! You aren't going to fall in love are you?'

'Of course not.'

There was a shout from the sitting room.

'Giselle!'

The two girls stared at each other, aware of their beauty, ignoring the ugliness of the voice from the sitting room. There was another shout, louder and uglier.

Nana wrinkled her nose. 'I'll go. I know what he wants,' she said, a sudden weariness in her voice. She fetched a glass from the cupboard and filled it with a cloudy red liquid from one of the bottles on the floor. Then, holding it to her sweet mouth, she spat into the drink. 'One day I'll lace his wine with rat poison,' she said, vehemently. Giselle laughed and watched her sister carry the sullied drink through to the sitting room. There were the usual words, the threats of the father, the contempt of the daughter. After a few moments Nana came back with a face of thunder.

'As soon as I'm old enough I'm leaving this place. Go tomorrow – and if you never come back you have my blessing.'

'Never come back!'

Giselle laughed at the impossibility of such a thing. Yet that night was the last that she ever slept in the old, crumbling house. On that final night she dreamt of the flooded quarry, as she had dreamt of it on so many other nights. She dreamt of the jewelled dragonflies that swept across the mirrored surface and the fish in the clear waters, exposed by the bright southern sun. She dreamt of Giles, who rowed her out to the fishing hut

10

where the gang spent its days. She dreamt of the taut, tanned bellies of the boys and the cool, Jesuitical smile of Xavier, who presided over them like a king. There was a new element now though, an Englishman with his own gang: beautiful women fighting like a squall over the calm waters.

2

L'Atlantique

The following morning at ten o'clock Giselle arrived at the Hotel L'Atlantique. The grand baroque facade faced a grey-green ocean across a boulevard dotted with palm trees. Pleneuf-Val-Andre was quiet at that time of the year; autumn was in the air and the wind was cool. A row of carriages waited near the pier, the horses shuffling and snorting, the cab men in antique livery hoping to catch the last of the tourists.

Giselle made her way into the reception nervously, feeling very much the country girl. A black-suited man at the reception looked at her sympathetically as she gazed across the marbled floors and panelled walls. After a few moments she gathered her courage and approached the desk. The man knew who she was looking for without being told.

'The English photographer?' he asked.

Giselle realised that she was one girl amongst many and flushed with the embarrassment of thinking herself so special.

'I have a card,' she said, fumbling in her bag.

The man waved his hand.

'There is no need. Fifth floor, room 5005. Take that lift.' He pointed to an ornate wrought-iron cage that seemed to be made for an oversized bird of paradise.

On the fifth floor, Giselle found herself in an endless corridor. The carpet was red and plush beneath her feet,

12

the ceiling shadowy in the light of the discreet lamps. The series of doors that she passed, anonymous as they were, seemed to possess a life and she was aware of the interiors of the rooms, the dramas that they staged. With each step forward she was entering into her dream. With each step she was leaving her father's house.

The door to 5005 was ajar. Girls' voices could be heard, a hubbub, the ebb and flow of laughter. Giselle knocked tentatively and was startled when the door was flung open immediately. A tall brunette glanced at her briefly.

'New flesh?' she asked.

Giselle didn't know how to reply.

The brunette looked at her pityingly. 'Wait over there,' she said, pointing to a chair near the window. The room was filled with girls in various states of undress. The couches and floor were littered with clothes. One of the desks on the far wall had been turned into a makeshift dressing table and girls fought for space in front of an ornate, gold-framed mirror that must have been taken from one of the walls. Giselle could see other girls in the rooms that led off from the sitting room. The tall blonde that she had met the day before was sitting on a bed smoothing stockings on to her legs. She caught Giselle's eye and smiled wearily. Before Giselle could respond, the woman's face was consumed by an endless yawn.

At the window, Giselle stood and looked over the esplanade to the ocean. The calmness of the great vista of water was a sharp contrast to the mayhem of the room. She took some of that calmness inside herself before sitting and looking around. From one of the bedrooms there came a man's voice, raised and angry, and a moment later a girl clad only in briefs ran into the sitting room, tears running down her face, her small breasts shaking. Giselle stared at her in alarm. Her

13

short-cropped hair gave her a pixieish look. The rage twisting her face made her seem ready to cast an evil spell.

'I hate him,' she screamed. One or two of the other girls looked at her sympathetically for a moment before resuming their varied tasks. Charles emerged from the room and slapped the weeping girl on the behind.

'Hush,' he told her with a scowl, 'I have a hangover.'

'I don't have to stay here. I can work for anyone!' the girl cried.

Charles waved his hand theatrically.

'Go then. Work for anyone! When you want to work for *someone*, it will be too late!'

'You have such a high opinion of yourself and you aren't even that good!'

Charles took hold of the girl's shoulders. Giselle watched him transform himself from angry ogre to benign father in a moment.

'Mimi, I love you, but you are a baby.' He kissed her cheek. 'Now stop crying and get ready. We are late.'

The girl, bathed in his smile, calmed herself and Charles turned to the rest of the girls.

'Everybody! We will leave in ten minutes. If you aren't ready you will go as you are. If I have to carry you naked through the hotel, I will!'

There were giggles, and renewed haste.

Charles saw Giselle as he swept his eyes across the room and made his way towards her.

'Who are you?' he asked, as if he had never seen her before.

Giselle, intimidated, stammered that he had told her to come, that he had seen her in the pharmacy in Briere the day before. Recognition dawned.

'You are the same girl?' he asked, examining her.

'Of course,' she said in surprise.

He pulled up a chair and sat down opposite her. He was very close. His knees, spread wide, encompassed

14

hers, which were pressed tightly together. When he smiled it was like being bathed in a shaft of sunlight after many days underground. She had seen this ability to transform himself several times now. He could move from rage to sympathy, from distance to intimacy; he could be any number of people it seemed. However, such knowledge did nothing to prepare her for the effect of these changes, her susceptibility to them.

'I saw something very special yesterday,' he told her, 'but now I am less sure. Forgive me if I sound cruel. But you showed something of yourself in that shop which is hidden today, as if a cloud has obscured the sun.'

She didn't know what he meant. She was the same Giselle that she had always been. He took her hand gently.

'But I'm glad that you came. I want to make some images of you. Perhaps the cloud will pass.'

She thanked him, although she wasn't sure why. Perhaps it was the caress of his eyes, the warmth of his hand. The world receded as he spoke. The din of the hurrying girls was muted as if he had constructed a special bubble around her, a bubble that only he and she could occupy.

'Are you shy about your body?' he asked.

His hand still held hers and he responded to the tightness that the question produced with a quick, reassuring caress.

'No,' she said, lying because she wanted to please him.

'I need a mermaid.'

He laughed when she saw her puzzled reaction.

'It's for a shower-gel ad. It isn't part of the *Femmes* shoot – it's just a little thing that I want to do whilst I'm here. If we use you, you will get paid. At least your journey won't be wasted.'

'OK,' she said tentatively.

'I will need to see you first.'

15

'See me?'

'Your breasts.'

She froze.

'If you don't want to, it's no problem,' he said, as if it really were no problem. She looked around the room. Mimi was still wearing nothing but her briefs as she fixed her make-up at the mirror on the desk. One of the other girls was pulling a white cotton top over marvellously full and creamy breasts. It was so ordinary, an everyday thing for these girls to be topless. Giselle would go topless at the beach herself with hardly a thought.

'It's fine,' she told him, colouring a little and reaching for the zipper at the side of her dress. It should have been easy but it wasn't. The problem was the man before her; his eyes were not like the eyes of others; his presence was quite different. Perhaps she was afraid of what he would draw from her. Perhaps she was afraid of what he would see in her eyes.

Finding her courage at last, she unzipped the dress and pushed the shoulder straps down until the top of the dress rested in her lap. Her bra was a natural silk, very plain and soft. She looked at him as he examined her.

'Very beautiful,' he told her.

She unclipped the bra and slowly let it come forward, releasing its burden of flesh. She flushed and looked down as she eased the bra completely off.

'Pull your shoulders back.'

Forcing herself to look up, she did as he said.

'Oh yes, those are the breasts of a mermaid. Those are the breasts that would lure sailors on to the rocks of misfortune and count themselves lucky to have seen such things as they sink into the icy depths.'

Her self-consciousness eased with his approval and she smiled shyly. Mimi, seeing that the new girl was topless, came over and draped her arm over Charles's shoulder as if to demonstrate a degree of ownership.

16

'Isn't she beautiful?' he asked.

Mimi shrugged. 'We are all beautiful until we won't do what you want us to.'

Charles laughed.

'Mimi is angry with me because I have forbidden her sex for the duration of the shoot.'

'He thinks that I will look sexier if I am in heat,' Mimi explained. 'He chased away such a nice boy at the bar last night. He is a monster. He thinks that he owns us.'

Charles laughed again.

'Dress now,' he told Giselle. 'We have to go.'

3

The Shoot

Giselle shared the back seat of a Citroen with three other girls. Mimi was the smallest and the lightest and lay across the laps of the others. When the suspension kicked in and the car lifted, it felt to Giselle as if she was beginning a trip to the moon.

The convoy pulled away and soon they were in the flat Brittany countryside. After a while they joined the coast road and followed it as it looped through tiny villages built in the severe local stone – grey and matt. Each collection of houses seemed like a military outpost facing the power of the Atlantic. Leaves were already falling from the plane trees that lined the road and the sunlight had that sad, cool quality that signals the end of summer.

The girls were quiet after the chaos of the hotel rooms and Giselle guessed that they had had a late night. The blonde woman, Arsene, was still yawning and Mimi had settled her head on the shoulder of another girl, Selene, as soon as the car had started off. Mimi's eyes were closed and her lips were parted, giving her the air of a beautiful infant.

The driver, a young man whom Giselle hadn't seen in the hotel, was struggling to keep up with Charles in his Range Rover. Behind them was an old American Jeep towing the first of the gleaming aluminium caravans. The further they went, the further it fell behind. The second caravan was nowhere to be seen.

The countryside became wilder and hills would suddenly rear up in front of them, hawthorn and pine pushing out from their sides like bad haircuts. Then, quite suddenly, they slowed and Giselle looked ahead to see Charles's Range Rover pulling through a gate into one of the fields. The Citroen slowed.

'He's mad,' said the driver. 'Even if we get across that field, the caravan never will.'

They could see Charles gesturing wildly through the windows of his car for them to follow. Then the Range Rover plunged down the slope, scattering a herd of pure-white Charolais. The grass was firm enough for the Citroen but the girls were still thrown around like dolls in the back seat as they followed. Mimi woke up and cursed at the top of her voice.

'I am a professional,' she declared. 'I am not an animal to be loaded into a cattle truck and driven through a field!'

She glared at Giselle, as the car hit another bump and her head was dashed against the roof.

'Why does she get a seat? She's a nobody!'

The other girls nodded diplomatically as they tried to keep their own balance. Looking back, they could see the Jeep edging the caravan through the farm gate.

Giselle wanted to be somewhere else – anywhere else – as Mimi dug a heel into her thigh.

'Tell her to get out! Make her walk!'

The Range Rover had disappeared behind a pine copse and when the Citroen reached it and slowly skirted the dark trees they saw the sea, very close. There was a track now, roughly paved with granite chippings, and they took this since the Range Rover was no longer in sight. The going was a little easier but still steep as they plunged into a gully between two high cliffs.

'It is probably one of his jokes,' Mimi declared. 'He will make us drive to the bottom, to a place where the car will get stuck, and then he will leave us, laughing like the madman that he is.' Mimi wound down the window as she spoke and pushed her head and shoulders outside.

The girls told her to be careful and tried to pull her back in but she resisted.

'I want to see the hole that is going to kill us all. I want to spit in Charles's face as he watches us plunge into the abyss.'

The blonde woman had Mimi's elbow in her face and, losing patience, bit it. Mimi screamed as if slashed by a sword. There was a brief struggle, undignified and frightening for Giselle but hilarious for the driver, who had trouble concentrating on where he was going. Then the car slid on to the sand of a broad beach. The blue-green of the water was a hundred yards away. Sullen waves slopped fitfully on to the rocks of the headland to their left.

Suddenly, the car doors opened and they fell out on to the sand like squabbling children. Charles stood photographing them as they bitched and struggled. When they saw what he was doing they turned on him and he ran, laughing, to a rock jutting from the sand, scrambling up its jagged sides before they could catch him. He kept taking the photographs as they shouted and threw seaweed and handfuls of sand at him. He seemed like a demented king to Giselle, a sovereign in a madhouse. The girls started to enjoy the assault and Arsene picked up a long whiplike wrack of seaweed, flicking it at the behinds of anyone who came within her range. Then everybody turned to watch the caravan arrive. The driver had reversed down the steep slope and the engine of the Jeep screamed as it held the shimmering monster.

'Another new gearbox,' said the boy who had driven the Citroen.

The rear end of the caravan gouged a broad, smooth path as it ploughed into the beach. Finally, the Jeep's engine gave up and stalled. The man behind the wheel jumped out with a smile and the girls applauded.

'We will probably have to leave it here, of course,' he said apologetically.

Charles clapped his hands. 'Let's get set up,' he shouted.

The two men and one of the women started to haul gear out of the caravan. The models wandered down to the water's edge as the preparations were made. The second caravan arrived, also reversing through the gully. Most of the crew were in the Spacewagon that pulled it. The preparations went much quicker with their help. Giselle was left watching as tents were erected and directors' chairs were set out. After seeing her standing alone, looking awkward, Charles went to her.

'It's always chaos,' he said. 'At the beginning of every day on location I wish I was a painter or a sculptor. I wish I had a comfortable studio in London, with a coffee shop next door and fresh bagels across the road.'

'Is that where you live?' she asked. 'In London?'

'When I can.'

'I lived near Avignon in the south. I miss it. Do you know Avignon?'

'Where the heretics were burnt?'

'Yes, and at Alibi. I get very homesick.'

He took the camera from around his neck and took a few shots of her as they talked. She was self-conscious and he told her to forget the camera, but it was impossible. He got her to talk about her family and about Avignon. Perhaps he thought it would relax her but it didn't. There were too many things that she had to keep from him.

'Do you love your father?' he asked unexpectedly.

'Once maybe. I don't remember.'

'Not now?'

'No.'

'A pity. Some people say that the camera is a penis

21

and that a girl who wants sex will always look good through a lens. I think it is the girl who wants to be loved – who expects to be loved – who will look best through the lens.'

She was unsettled by the conversation and he stopped shooting for a moment. Before he could start again, a woman called from the door of one of the caravans. 'Make-up is ready.'

Charles turned away from Giselle and she had the feeling that she was instantly forgotten.

'OK, get the girls,' he called.

The woman nodded and trotted across the sands, shouting as she went. Eventually, the knot of girls returned, dragging their heels as if summoned to an execution.

'You will be last,' Charles said to Giselle apologetically. 'They have a pecking order.'

Giselle took a chair and watched as the girls crowded into the caravan. Charles stood at the door shouting out which dress each girl should wear, dealing with the deluge of complaints, soothing injured pride and alternating compliments and insults with practised ease. Nothing seemed to throw him. Only Mimi seemed able to get under his skin and then only briefly.

Finally, the girls started to emerge, dressed in the season's colours – subdued reds and golds, like the leaves of the plane trees. It astonished Giselle to see them, more of a surprise even than discovering them in the pharmacy at Briere. The clothes welded them together into a pack, outrageous in their beauty. As they walked across the fine yellow sand, with the green sea behind them, they could have been members of another, altogether superior, species. The rabble of the hotel had disappeared. Panther-like, they walked in silence, legs long, backs straight, heads high.

Charles followed. When they reached the rock that he had climbed to escape their alter egos, he started to

22

arrange them. Selene was chosen to drape across the pinnacle of the outcrop, her blonde hair streaking the jagged surface like a vein of gold. Mimi was pressed into the side wall, hands clinging like a shipwrecked mariner in a storm. The other girls were arranged around these two, like angels around divinities. Giselle was beginning to understand the pecking order.

When he had finished directing them, Charles took a series of Polaroids. The drivers were now his assistants and brought reflectors to catch the autumn sun and direct it across the girls' bodies. Everything took a long time. A blanket had to be fetched for Selene to lie on; the rock was tearing at her dress and flesh. Mimi became quarrelsome when the delays grew and grew. Finally, the Polaroids must have showed that the composition worked and that the lighting was OK. Charles fetched a Hasselblad, huge and cumbersome, and set up the tripod himself. The shooting proper began. Giselle watched in fascination as he took shot after shot, minutely varying the position of the girls, subtly altering the lighting, pulling the Hasselblad back through the sand and to left and right to gain a series of perspectives. When he had finished, the girls padded back to the caravan, where coffee and tiny breakfasts of croissant and cereal had been made. Giselle came over when she was called and took a coffee, strong and black.

Arsene smiled at her sympathetically.

'There is a lot of waiting. That is why the girls all smoke. We can't eat so we just drink coffee and smoke.'

'I'm not bored,' she replied. 'I've never seen anything like this before.'

Giselle was watching Charles as he chatted to Mimi. The girl was revelling in the attention, swinging her hips softly as she spoke, leaning over and touching his arm to emphasise her points, smouldering like a firework ready to go off.

Arsene followed Giselle's eyes. 'Charles has slept with

23

all the girls,' she said. 'It helps their careers in the beginning. Mimi is just the latest. She is shameless, as we all were.'

'Did you?' Giselle asked.

'Sleep with him? Of course.'

'And was it just for your career?'

Arsene smiled.

'Mostly, but I liked it too. Or I liked it at the beginning. He can be cruel: a girl must be careful. Some men want a girl only so they can break her.'

Charles turned at that moment and called for their attention. He was going to do some individual shots and he wanted Arsene and Mimi first. Giselle thought about what the girl had said as she followed Charles out to the rock. She wondered how he could break a girl. It sounded like a cowboy breaking a horse so that the animal would do whatever he wanted. Mimi didn't seem to be broken. Quite the reverse. She was as wild as any mountain lion as she leapt on to the rock and crouched with her mouth wide and teeth bared. Charles shot her like that – bottom high, hands clawed and raking at the air.

Giselle wondered if Arsene was simply trying to warn her off Charles as a rival would. Giselle didn't even know if she wanted the Englishman. She knew that she wouldn't refuse him but that was a different thing – between not refusing and truly wanting lay a gulf that she found hard to cross. She hadn't wanted so many of the boys at the quarry, but refusal hadn't been an option, not after the first time anyway. In time, she had even come to prefer it that way. They had adopted her as they would have adopted a dog and they were as kind or as cruel as their mood dictated. If they hadn't broken her it was because there was nothing to break or because they had never found the thing that could break. Jean had said something like that to her. He had said that even after all those evenings at the quarry she was still

24

his little sister, still a virgin in everything but the fact. 'Nothing really touches you,' he would say. 'Every time you spread your legs for a boy, it seems to be the first time – you flush and you tremble. Do you know how much that makes a boy want you?' Then, invariably, he would undo his trousers and she would kneel and suck him as he poured scorn on her compliance. But Jean was dead now. He was dead and her father crippled because the boys had wanted her so much and she had never refused them.

Charles had begun photographing Arsene. He was telling her that she was too angelic. No man wanted an angel. No woman reading *Femmes* wanted to identify with an angel. Arsene tried to appear more severe.

'No,' he shouted in English. 'Nobody wants a schoolteacher either.'

He strode across the few feet of sand that separated them and Giselle saw fear in the girl's eyes. Charles raised his hand and Arsene shrank from him. Instead of the expected blow, he took her chin and kissed her hard and deep. When he stepped back, Arsene was flushed and her eyes were bright. Charles looked at her for a moment. 'OK, keep that,' he told her and, while stepping back, he began to shoot, shouting instructions all the time. Arsene had the breathless look of a girl struggling with an overwhelming impulse, although what that impulse might be Giselle couldn't decipher. Her intense beauty was intensified further by the ambiguities that shaded her features.

'We might be able to use one of those,' Charles said as he finished up. He squeezed her shoulder as she passed him on her way back to the main group. Giselle's ears caught a soft apology from Charles and a hiss of anger from Arsene. Giselle saw that the girl was almost in tears.

Later, after a very unglamorous lunch of soup and bread rolls, it was Giselle's turn to enter the make-up caravan. Racks of dresses and shelves of cosmetics made the interior tiny but there were still three other girls being worked on as Giselle entered. A woman introduced herself as Odette and took Giselle to the rounded end of the aluminium tube, squeezing past the others as they went. Even Odette, a make-up artist and never destined to be on the sharp side of the camera lens, exuded glamour and beauty. Her very short, very black hair framed a pale, oval face in which eyes of an astonishing emerald blazed. Her lips, when she smiled, were gentle and teasing and mocking all at once. There was a strength in her as she took charge of Giselle, directing her to her seat, examining her face and hair, commenting on her colouring and praising the perfect smoothness and richness of her skin.

'I once had skin like that,' she said as if she were impossibly old, when Giselle could see that she was only in her thirties and still very beautiful.

When the examination was finished, Odette brought several costumes from one of the clothes racks. Each was a froth of silk that ended in a fish tail of grey latex. The colours ranged from blue to green. Odette laid them in turn against Giselle's face, finally choosing a violet-green confection and laying the others aside. Giselle stripped when she was told to, leaving only her underwear.

'You can leave the bra for a moment if you want to,' said the woman kindly, aware, it seemed, that this was Giselle's first time, 'but the pants will have to go. This fabric is so sheer. A mermaid with a panty line just won't work.'

Giselle took the waistband of her pants in her hand. She hesitated for a moment and one of the girls from down the caravan laughed. 'Perhaps she has terrible scars.'

Giselle slipped the underwear down her legs swiftly, silencing those who were laughing with the sight of a perfect behind.

'Mie, you have nothing to be embarrassed about,' Odette told her, taking the silk costume from its hanger.

Giselle had to lie on the floor and put her legs in the air so that she could be fitted. It was undignified and the wooden floor was cold. Odette kept apologising as she hurriedly drew the fabric over Giselle's feet. The basis of the costume was an extraordinarily thin, tight, Lycra sheath, which pressed Giselle's legs together as it was drawn downwards and clung to thigh and calf with the tenacity of honey. When it was finally in place, Odette smoothed the layers of silk down from the waist. These were even more transparent than the sheath so that Giselle's legs were still apparent, as if covered by layers of brilliant, violet-green water. The latex of the fin was the only solid colour and form, uncompromisingly alien as it encased and hid her feet. Once the costume was securely in place, Odette helped Giselle to a seat in front of the mirrors and began on the make-up. Giselle had to remove her bra because the make-up was an all-over effect, more of a body paint in fact, transforming her skin to a subtly shaded green with blue and violet highlights. Her skin was blended smoothly into the tail so that there was no sudden change where the girl ended and the fish began. After a time, Giselle was obliged to stand so that her back and belly could be worked on. It was only then that she realised how low the sheath was. It covered her to the top of her mound at the front and the beginning of the divide of her buttocks behind. A fine line of blonde hair was visible running from the front of the costume to her navel.

As Odette smoothed the body paint across her slightly domed belly, she asked if Giselle worked out. It was a strange question for a country girl. Giselle knew what working out meant: it meant gymnasiums with weights and running machines. She had seen these things on television but not in Briere.

'I swim,' she replied. Last summer she had swum

27

regularly in the blue waters of the quarry. The puppy fat had dropped from her and left the lean, athletic frame that Odette seemed to admire so. These days, it was a long bus ride into Rennes and the doubtful pleasures of the ancient, algaed, municipal pool. For Giselle, swimming there was an exercise in dulling the flesh, reducing desires that had been too keenly honed, rather than a conditioning of muscles.

'A little more weight here,' Odette suggested with a smile, smoothing her hand across Giselle's belly. 'A woman's stomach should expand with the promise of fertility.' She cupped her hand to indicate a full womb and her face danced with pleasure.

Giselle smiled. Fertility had never crossed her mind. She a mother! It was inconceivable. 'It turns men on like nothing else, even if they don't know why they are turned on,' Odette told her and laughed.

She had Giselle sit and returned to her breasts, adding the final touches there, blending and smoothing the colours with the heel of her hand. It was strange to be touched so by a woman. The touch was firm but intimate, sensitive to the structures within.

In the mirror, Giselle could see the marine creature that she had been made into while accepting the caresses. Her nipples hardened as Odette highlighted them with a glossy mauve. She blushed beneath the make-up and Odette's smile grew wider and warmer. 'Not that a girl always needs a boy,' she whispered, making Giselle flush even more strongly as she gave a delicate twist to each nipple with thumb and forefinger. Giselle hunched her shoulders defensively but her hands stayed in her lap, palms upwards. Encouraged, perhaps, by this quiescence, Odette trailed her fingers away slowly, following the line of each perfect breast over the ribcage. For a moment, Giselle waited to be touched again and, seeing herself in the mirror, wondered at the glow of her skin as she waited. To be the object of

28

another's gaze, to sense the surprise that her passivity produced, then to see the other's desire, a palpable rush from groin to eyes – these things made her feel alive. But Odette didn't touch her again. Instead, Giselle saw the woman make an effort to compose herself, saw her smile then frown and shake her head as if shrugging off a spell.

Now that the make-up was finished, Odette opened a cupboard over the mirror. From a row of extravagant wigs she chose the most extravagant and started to fit Giselle's hair inside it. Long blonde-brown curls cascaded over Giselle's chest and halfway down her back. She wasn't sure that she liked the effect – it reminded her of the patently false wigs that American country and western singers wore.

'Now we have to get you out of here,' Odette told her, helping Giselle to her feet, or at least to the large latex fin that was now a substitute.

'Can you hop?' Odette asked.

The other girls turned to watch Giselle, as she hopped gracelessly down the caravan. 'Don't mind them,' Odette said, glancing at the girls sharply. 'They are just grateful that they aren't going to be mermaids today.'

Giselle hopped past the laughing girls, laughing herself at her clumsiness. One hand clutched the wig, which threatened to come off at any moment; the other clutched at shelves and chairs to steady herself.

Finally, she was at the door. Odette slipped past her and helped the hobbled girl down on to the sand. Giselle, truly a fish out of water now, looked around herself uncertainly. Charles was far away by the sand dunes on the other side of the bay. Giselle could hear his shouted instructions as they carried on the faint breeze and see the flashes as he fired off the camera. Then, to her astonishment, Odette leant over and plucked her from the ground, lifting her easily, obliging Giselle to drape her arms around the woman's neck. She was carried towards the directors' chairs like a child. Odette, the mother, smiled at her every step of the way, her face close, her breath warm on Giselle's lips.

Giselle accepted the attention as if it were to be expected, as if to be carried – and courted – by such a beautiful woman were an everyday thing.

'You are shy but you certainly aren't innocent,' Odette said, as she sat Giselle securely in one of the chairs. She stepped back to look at her creation in the full light of the September sun. The hair of the wig covered Giselle's breasts and Odette took the heavy locks and lifted them away, holding them wide for a moment, eventually laying them down the sides of the girl's arms.

'If I were a man . . .' she began, then laughed. 'Even if I were a fish you would have to swim very fast!'

Giselle smiled. 'You like girls?'

'Some girls. You?'

Giselle shrugged, her shyness returning.

One of the models emerged from the caravan. 'Odette,' she called plaintively, and Odette went to her.

Giselle could hear the woman complaining that her eyeliner wasn't right and begging Odette to redo it. The two of them returned to the caravan.

Giselle made no effort to cover her breasts: they had been uncovered by another and would remain uncovered. The sun was strong enough to lull her as she sat bound and prepared for the lens. Her eyes closed and she remembered the other times that she had waited, bound by the presence of the boys, her will absent when they were near her, her wishes secondary as soon as the quarry enfolded her in its stony arms.

If she had had sufficient insight, sufficient perspective, she might have seen the events of the previous summer as a virus that had invaded her and penetrated every organ of her mind. The events of that place never left her. They coloured each new experience so that no experience was truly new, merely a continuation of what Jean and Giscard had begun and what Xavier had taken to the inevitable, still shocking conclusion. They had transformed her to the point that nothing was without a sexual meaning. The very shoes on her feet as she had walked home from school in that summer had been a holding, a touching. Her clothes were the bodies of the many, pressing into her, claustrophobic, exciting. Leather and cotton, silk and nylon – every texture suggested something that they had done to her. Even the fantasies that she might have were fantasies that they had made for her, distilled from her girlishness, strengthened by their maleness – an immature maleness that knew neither restraint nor guilt nor responsibility.

Yet she had no insight, only a crowded room of memory – overheated, impossible to organise and impossible to escape from. It was always Xavier in the centre of that room. Xavier beckoning her. Xavier in boxer shorts, hard already, calling her to his side. She saw the flat, tanned belly, the tattoo on his biceps, the shining blackness of his ungoverned hair. She was aware of the eyes that watched her go to him, the boys that waited for him to be finished with her so that they could have their turn. She slipped into that crowded room of memory every night – the door could never be fully closed and the fantasies within had a siren's power.

Perhaps she slept for a while. Certainly, when she opened her eyes everything had changed. Dense white clouds scudded across the sky and the wind had freshened. She was no longer alone. Charles was standing over her, looking at her costume. Odette was by his side. They were talking rapidly in English – too rapidly for Giselle to keep track. It was obvious that Odette was pleading a case and that Charles was losing patience. Finally, he raised his hand to silence Odette's protests and walked away. Odette turned to the bemused Giselle.

31

'We need to take you back inside,' she said.

'Is something wrong?'

'Only if your name is Charles Mannay. For him the sea is the wrong colour, the sky is too high and the air is too thin.'

She bent over and picked Giselle from her chair.

'If I was your mother I would make you eat,' she said. 'I swear a seagull will steal you to add another twig to its nest.'

Once inside the caravan, she set Giselle on the couch.

'He says that your pubic hair will show as a dark smudge and ruin the effect. He wants me to shave you. It is unreasonable. I told him that it was. He said that if you objected you should simply get dressed and forget it.'

'Why is it unreasonable? I mean, if it ruins the photograph?'

'The hair will not show, not even with the flash. It is a game. We all know him. He plays with us. Everybody knows that I like girls. He gives them to me naked to embarrass them and me. He wants to have you shaved so that you go away a child and remember him as the man who took away your womanliness. He will get off on that.'

'I don't mind,' said Giselle. 'I mean, I don't mind that you like girls and if he wants me to be shaved . . .'

Odette frowned and Giselle was aware that the woman's anger was something strange, something possessive. It was as if she, Odette, had staked a claim to the flesh in front of her first and resented Charles's interference.

'Very well, if that is what you want. Stand up.'

Giselle stood and Odette unceremoniously tugged the costume down. Giselle stepped clear of it as soon as the sheath was bunched about her ankles. Then Odette pressed her to the couch, so that she lay facing the door. Her ankles were seized and spread wide. Odette rested one of Giselle's legs on the back of the couch and the other on the floor. A cushion was pushed under her behind. As Odette disappeared down to the far end of the caravan, Giselle was very aware of the strip of light that was the doorway. Outside, the figures of Charles and one or two of the girls were visible. Giselle knew that the interior of the caravan was in shade and that she wouldn't be seen easily, but she still felt exposed. From time to time, Charles would turn in the direction of the caravan and gaze intently in her direction. The desire to close her legs was intense, but there was something else, a frisson of excitement that made the hairs of her pubis rise. Odette took her time, finally returning with a bowl of wax and a hairdrier. She plugged the hairdrier into a socket near the couch and used it to melt the wax in the bowl. Giselle was aware of the woman's eyes on her body. She certainly didn't seem to be embarrassed. Her gaze was cool and appraising.

'You certainly have the body to be a model,' Odette told her. 'You have as good a body as any of the girls out there. All you need is a little fire in the eyes. You are like a neon light with no power. When you look at me, I feel only my own reflected energy.'

The wax in the bowl began to melt and a scent of beeswax filled the caravan. Odette was still angry when she sat on the couch between Giselle's widespread legs. 'When I kiss a woman between the legs I like to feel her hair on my tongue,' she said suddenly. 'This is a castration.'

She started to pour the wax over Giselle's sex. It was warm, like a hand, but set almost immediately without penetrating to the roots. Odette used the hairdrier to melt it again, smoothing the viscous fluid through the brown curls with her fingertips. It was a luxurious feeling and Giselle was stirred against her will. Odette saw the pleasure straight away and grinned, softening at

33

last. She poured on more wax and used the hairdrier to keep it fluid as she worked it around Giselle's mound.

'It will hurt terribly when I take it off,' she said. 'Another thing that Charles will enjoy. I'm surprised that he hasn't come in to watch. But perhaps he doesn't know you yet. Perhaps he doesn't know that you wouldn't send him away.'

Giselle's eye's shot to the woman. The smile told her that she was already known. The hand between her legs was unmistakably caressing her now, seeking the most tender parts, finding the clitoris, heating her inside and making her belly inflate with arousal.

'You shouldn't,' Giselle told the woman weakly.

'Do you want me to stop?'

'Yes,' Giselle groaned.

'Then stop me.'

Giselle wanted to. Her eyes pleaded but her hands didn't move. She was like a bee that has blundered into a spider's web and spins helplessly on the invisible gossamer. The heat of the hairdrier, as it played across her belly, made all of the muscles relax. She felt a ballooning outwards and, for a moment, thought that she might wet herself. A tiny involuntary gasp left her lips. The heel of Odette's hand pressed hard at the top of her pubis then softened and span over the clitoris in light, cruel circles.

'He'll want to fuck you if he sees you like this,' Odette told her. 'Shall I call him?' Giselle shook her head abruptly, suddenly afraid. The fingers took her clitoris more firmly and worked it quickly in its moist, protective sheath. The thought of the photographer standing over her, watching, reminded her of Xavier and the quarry and tipped her over the edge. She bit her lip and groaned loudly. Odette leant forward. She watched intently as the orgasms came, following the movements of the sex as it rose and fell with her fingers, never losing contact with that burning blister of

34

pleasure. Then, as Giselle lay breathing heavily, her belly still full, Odette picked at the edge of the wax with her thumbnail. When she had pulled away enough to grip firmly, she tore downwards sharply and without warning. Giselle screamed. Odette held up the hideous mass of wax and hair for her to see.

'A castration,' she said, then leant down and kissed the denuded skin lightly. For a few moments, she gazed intently into Giselle's eyes. Giselle could read surprise and even awe in those eyes, as if the woman was seeing something that she hadn't seen before. 'Now you are alive, castrated or not,' she breathed.

Giselle frowned in puzzlement, watching as Odette reached for a hand mirror on the dressing table.

'There,' she said, holding it so that Giselle could see her face. 'A transformation.' Giselle saw a girl with a face so open, so transparent to feeling that she was almost afraid of her own nakedness. Then she looked again and saw the sensuality of the eyes, the easiness of the mouth, and knew why men wanted her. Every feature said, 'Fuck me if you can.'

It needed two more applications of the wax to render her completely bare but these were businesslike and quick.

'Ready for the master,' Odette said ironically. 'You make it too easy, you know. Men will do terrible things to you.'

Terrible things. Giselle knew that the terrible had already happened. There would always be fear when a hand reached for her, the fear that came from her own culpability. Yet she also knew the joy of the terrible.

Odette helped her to stand and refitted the costume. Giselle could see Charles pacing the sand outside and glancing at his watch. 'He's getting impatient,' she said.

Odette laughed. 'Good. If he wants me to make you into a little girl he will have to cope with a little girl's slowness.'

35

Odette had to apply fresh body paint to Giselle's lower belly. Since she was now shaven, Odette had fitted the costume lower, so that it covered her only to the very top of her sex. When she looked down, Giselle could see into the valleys on either side of the mound. Between her legs, the Lycra pulled her unprotected sex open. There could be no mistaking her condition.

Finally, Odette stepped back and checked every inch of her, front and back.

'To die for, as the Americans say.'

Giselle hopped to the door of the caravan on her own. Odette had no intention of carrying her for Charles and Giselle had to call for help. Charles motioned for George, the driver of the Citroen, to fetch her and began to walk along the beach to the headland. George picked Giselle up with courtly aplomb, as if it were a normal part of his job to ferry mermaids to the sea. With her arms around his neck and the hair of the wig trailing in the wind, they followed Charles and the crew out on to the rocks that thrust seawards. Charles chose a place where the waves broke fiercely and shot spray high into the air. It was cooler than the beach and goose bumps rose on Giselle's exposed skin. George halted just short of carrying her into the area where the spray fell. They waited as Charles set up a tripod and his crew unfurled reflectors, opened cases and set out lenses and flash units. After a while, George set Giselle down on a boulder. Gallant to the last, her escort undid his leather jacket and draped it around her shoulders. 'Rock and roll mermaid,' he said laconically. Giselle smiled.

When Charles was ready he came over and took a few shots of her with the 35 mm around his neck. These shots seemed to be his equivalent of holiday snaps. Then he told George to take away his jacket and got her to strike pose after pose. As soon as he had one that he liked he used the Polaroid to gauge the composition and arrange the reflectors for maximum effect. Finally, he settled for a shot on the boulder where George had first set her. She balanced precariously on her behind, tail lifted into the air, arms back so that her breasts were lifted high. Crouching low, he shot so that the sky was the background and the spray of the waves would seem to explode about her. He had her look this way and that, had her smile or seem pensive, angry or sad. He was shooting almost continuously, changing from one camera to the other. The girl at his side could hardly load the films quick enough.

'This suits you,' he told her. 'Something suits you anyway. Keep giving me that look and you will work every day.'

When they had exhausted the possibility of the boulder, Charles had George carry her to a rock pool back along the headland. Pink and orange anemones in the still, clear water formed vivid counterpoints to the sombre rock. George laid her on a bank of olive seaweed, dried in the sun but still slimy within. The bladders of the weed popped beneath her. The shots here were more intimate. The rocks formed a wall around her, keeping away the wind. He concentrated more on her face. She gazed into the mirror of the pool like a female Narcissus. She lay back on the bed of weed as if they were crisp sheets and the man with the camera was her lover. Her eyes invited and teased.

Charles picked some of the long strands of bladderwrack and trailed them across her belly. She shivered and he shot her while she was hunched over and giggling with the slimy, tickling sensation. He transferred the wrack to her shoulder and trailed it over her breasts, pulling it this way and that to get the right effect, brushing her nipples to make them erect. As he leant over her, she expected to be kissed and she was ready to be kissed. He had made her forget the crew completely. It was just she and him on the rocks and she was bound and helpless. He brushed her hair out into a long spume across the rocks behind her and fussed with the costume when it slipped down to reveal the pink skin of her mound.

He touched her everywhere, arranging her for the penetration of the lens, but he didn't kiss her. He had her lying on her belly, her breasts in the soft slime of the weed. She smiled as if she were being held by a lover. He had her support herself on her long slender arms so that her breasts hung down in inverted cones, her blue-tipped nipples so very obviously aroused. The slime of the seaweed oozed across her belly and she felt like a puppy in mud. It excited her – like wetting her pants had excited her when she was little. She pushed her sex into the slime and moved slowly from side to side. He kept shooting, capturing the shades of light and dark, the pleasure and the dirtiness.

When he had her turn over, most of the green on her belly was the green of the seaweed, the natural juices overlying the fakery of Odette. He leant down and drew his fingers in a circle around her navel. When he examined the tips, she saw the gleam of the mucous-like alginates. 'They make jellies from that,' she said, 'for children's parties.'

He shook the slime from his fingers and had George lift her again and carry her back to where the waves broke. This time she wasn't spared the cold of the spray. Charles had her placed on the very point of the headland. It was scary at first. If she had fallen in, she wouldn't have been able to swim in the restrictive costume. When the waves broke she could see nothing but spray all around her. She cried out with the first dousing. He caught her with her mouth open, gulping air as her body convulsed at the ocean's touch.

The fabric of the costume, where it became wet, also became transparent. He may not have planned this but, as soon as he saw it, he used it. Her legs were pinkish columns now and the costume had the appearance of a binding, the binding of infants, the binding of the insane. He had her turn away and then look back over her shoulder. The waves continued to break, soaking her more and more thoroughly. She could imagine the costume transparent behind, the divide of her behind clearly visible, her thighs taut ovals as she pushed back.

The coldness had shocked her out of the mood of the rock pool. This wasn't a place of intimacy but an arena of extremes. Her look was the look of the siren. She wanted him to be wrecked on her flesh. Then he had her push out her behind as far as she could. She felt her sex contract as it pressed itself to the wet fabric behind. He had her push harder still so that her sex, as it thrust back between her legs, was the part of her closest to the camera. She imagined the pinkness as it split and opened.

Xavier came into her mind. He had liked to pose her on the sand of the island. Not for the camera, though – for the switch, the slender bough that she would have fetched from the willows by the water's edge. She would be posed so that he could demonstrate his power while the other boys watched. The switch was always moist – fresh wood, still alive as it burnt her behind and her thighs. If she cried he would wait for the sobs to subside. If she wriggled away from him he would be furious and force her back to the place that he wanted her. There was no tactic for avoiding the blows. Her tears, her running away, only postponed what he would do to her. Afterwards, she would be posed so that he could fuck her or so that he could watch while one of the other boys fucked her. Those other boys! They slithered over her flesh like eels, restless and rushed. They entered every opening, seeking only for them-selves. When they had left her limp and exhausted, and the marks on her thighs were darkening into bruises, Xavier would take her for himself and give her such savage pleasures. The memories fired in a vivid

39

sequence. As the cold Atlantic waves hit her she wanted to scream in sympathy with the impersonal power. The great explosions of water towered over her, as sex had towered over that island. The explosions of the waves were like the explosions of the boys inside her and her own explosions too, later, at the hands of Xavier. Only he had ever made her come. She wondered if Charles would. She looked at him with the question in her eyes.

Charles had stopped directing her. He simply photographed what she gave him. The curling of her feet, the glances behind, enigmatic and cool while her body rang with a profound desire. She revelled in the gaze of the lens, was a lens herself, focusing the power of the waves. The ocean gave her life. Sex gave her life. Xavier had opened her to extremes, scooped out false modesty so that she was a basin to be filled with the violence of desire. All of this went into her form; all of it was available to the man who photographed her.

Finally, Charles called a halt and handed the camera to his assistant. For a moment, he stood staring at Giselle and she gazed back from the clouds of spray. There was the same surprise in his eyes that she had seen in Odette's – the same surprise she had felt herself when she had looked in the mirror of the makeshift dressing room. Then he turned his back and walked quickly away. As soon as he was gone, cold penetrated to her bones and she began to shiver violently. George rescued her from the spray, wrapping her in his jacket again and carrying her back to the beach. The wig slipped from her head and hit the rocks with a wet thud. They left it where it had fallen, like a blonde octopus.

Odette was motherly when she saw the shivering girl that George dropped into the caravan. She quickly stripped the waif and towelled her fiercely until pink returned to her skin. Then, as Giselle stood wrapped in the towel, the life slowly returning to her limbs, Odette kissed her full on the mouth. It was not the first time

40

that a woman had kissed her and she opened her mouth wide to let the strange tongue take possession. It was more intimate than the earlier caressing of her sex and so tender that Giselle began to weep. '*Ma chère!*' Odette said softly, embracing the girl and pulling her head to her breast. 'What is it?' Giselle shook her head. The tears kept coming but she didn't know why. Odette helped her to a seat and sat with her, holding her hand and stroking her hair. Giselle hadn't cried for a long while.

'You are so kind,' she finally managed to say.

'And that makes you cry?' asked Odette.

'Yes.'

Odette laughed and took the girl in her arms again.

At the end of the day, a long day – evening was well advanced by the time all the shots had been completed – it was a matter of waiting while the crew packed away the gear into the caravans. The girls drifted across the beach in small groups, chatting and laughing. Giselle walked on her own amongst the sand dunes dotted with seagrass.

As she drew nearer to the cliffs, large boulders blocked her way and she was forced to scramble over them. Then she heard a woman's voice, muffled and indistinct. It seemed strangely familiar and she stopped for a moment as she tried to place it. The voice came again and the memory with it. It was the woman in her dream, the voice behind the oaken door. Steeling herself, she rounded the rock boulders and found herself staring at Charles as he leant back against a rock. Mimi knelt before him, his sex in her mouth. She was groaning out obscenities, telling him to fuck her mouth, telling him how good his cock felt in the back of her throat.

Giselle's first impulse was to turn and run, but Charles's eyes caught her and held her. She stood quite

41

still as he smiled and ran his hand through the hair of
the girl before him. Then he raised his hand to his
mouth and laid a finger to his lips, bidding her to be
silent. Mimi was kneeling up, her pushed-out behind
working with the rest of her body as she sucked. The
clinging fabric of her light summer dress lay in the
widely spread space of her buttocks and revealed the
backs of tanned thighs as they flexed and tightened in
sympathy with the greed of her mouth and lips. Giselle
felt the softness of those perfect lips at her own sex. The
day had left her starved for such a sensation and she
found herself staring at the side of the girl's mouth
where the thick sex penetrated. Her eyes flicked
nervously from that sight to Charles's eyes and back
again. Her own lips opened a fraction, as if offering
themselves. She blushed, almost turned away, looked
again, felt a surge of wanting and let him see that
wanting in her eyes.

Charles leant forward and pulled Mimi's dress on to
her back, exposing the girl's naked behind. There was a
cruelty in his expression as he did this, as he exposed his
lover to a stranger and, again, Giselle was reminded of
Xavier, except that with Xavier it would be her that was
exposed. She watched as he pushed his fingers into
Mimi's mouth and carried moisture to the space
between her thighs. The girl's body tensed and she
groaned as Charles penetrated her sex. Giselle felt
herself tense and then go slack as the fingers slipped
inside, as if those fingers were now inside her. She
looked into his eyes as he fingered the girl and drew
gasp after gasp from her.

Then, Charles stood and ran his hand across his chest
while gazing at her breasts. At first she didn't
understand but then realised that he wanted to see her
breasts. She shook her head. He took hold of Mimi's
hair and twisted it in his hand making the girl struggle
against the pain. He looked at Giselle again, insistently,

42

a threat in the line of his mouth. She surrendered, undoing the buttons of her blouse and pushing the fabric aside so that he could see her. He stroked his hand across his chest again and she saw that he wanted her to caress herself. Hesitantly, she ran her hand across her breasts, self-conscious and blushing even more deeply. He groaned and thrust hard into Mimi's mouth so that his sex was completely buried and the girl gagged. When he pulled back a little he pushed his fingers into her mouth again as she gulped air. He reached for her sex again, thrusting three fingers into the tight opening. Clear liquid oozed from the opening as if he had pushed his hand into a ripe peach. Mimi began to groan continuously and Giselle sensed the approaching orgasm.

Charles withdrew his fingers and ran them into the valley of her behind. Giselle saw the fluttering of the anus as it relaxed and pouted outwards like the whorl of a flower. Charles circled and stabbed at that opening. Only the very tips of his fingers penetrated her as they passed but, each time, the girl grunted. Then he went back to the sex and took the protruding clitoris, working until Mimi was bucking and moaning spasmodically. He pushed her until she could stand it no longer and, withdrawing from his sex, she threw her head back and howled as the orgasm ripped through her.

Giselle felt herself shaking with the power of it and her legs almost buckled. Charles was watching Giselle all the time that she watched Mimi shuddering at his feet. Then, while the orgasm still had her in its grip, he seized her head and pushed into her mouth again, seeking the depths of her throat. She gagged and came as he fucked her fiercely. Without realising it, Giselle was pinching up her nipples and grinding her thighs together obscenely. When his gaze went to her thighs, she checked herself and froze. He motioned for her to lift her dress. It seemed impossible to say no, but her hands wouldn't comply. Mimi had gone entirely slack and allowed herself to be pushed this way and that as he worked his hips and fucked her mouth relentlessly. Finally, with shaking hands, Giselle lifted her dress. Her sex was naked. Odette had said that none of the girls ever wore underwear and that it would excite her to know that Giselle didn't either. Charles's eyes darkened as he saw the naked, hairless sex and, almost immediately, he began to come. She watched him fill Mimi's mouth with a series of savage grunts, then hurriedly covered herself and stumbled away.

Later, when the gear had all been stashed away and the girls were all gathered around the cars, Charles and Mimi emerged from the sand dunes hand in hand. Mimi looked blissfully happy. Even Charles looked relaxed and easy in himself. He barely glanced at Giselle as they piled into the cars and headed back to the hotel.

Giselle almost fell asleep on the short journey and, when they arrived at the grand facade, she found Odette opening the door of the car for her and taking her hand. Charles, standing by the revolving door to reception, looked at the woman questioningly. Odette smiled first at Giselle, then at him. 'I have a spare bed in my room. I assume you want her for tomorrow's shoot?' Charles nodded and looked at Giselle with an amused smile. As he disappeared into the hotel, the two women giggled.

'He's jealous,' Odette said, 'and so he should be.'

As soon as they got to Odette's room, Giselle was sent to shower and five minutes later Odette joined her. They washed each other in silence. Their smiles – shy and nervous on Giselle's side, strong and warm on Odette's – were the only communication that was needed. Afterwards, in bed, Odette was gentle, demanding little for herself. She caressed Giselle until she came, then masturbated against Giselle's thigh while whispering

44

fierce endearments. By eleven o'clock they were fast asleep in each other's arms.

In the morning, Giselle felt wonderful, as if summer had just dawned in her soul. Or as if she had suddenly found a new home.

That day, Charles took them to a resort about twenty miles from the hotel. It was a cheesy town, full of amusement arcades and dominated by a large funfair. In the autumn light and with the crowds gone it had a melancholy air. He shot the girls in elegant evening dress as they walked down the shabby main street. He had them in impossibly exotic confections on the dodgems and the big wheel. They were stared at. They had fun behaving badly. The local paper sent a photographer and reporter. Mimi mooned at them from the top of the big wheel. 'That'll make the front page,' the photographer said as he snapped the perfect cheeks of her pale behind.

Charles used Giselle as an extra only: as a figure in a doorway far behind Selene as she modelled a Givenchy; as a pair of long elegant legs emerging from the door of a car while Arsene strolled along the street in a Westwood.

Giselle slept with Odette again that night. This time there were toys, things that Odette put inside Giselle. She was rougher and Giselle came harder. Giselle realised that she could get used to a woman as a lover.

In the evening of that final day, Charles booked a restaurant in Rennes for a private party. Somehow word must have got around. A crowd of twenty or thirty people had gathered at the door when they arrived. Giselle gave her autograph to a teenage girl who told her that she was beautiful.

Inside, the manager of the restaurant had to pull down the blinds so that they weren't stared at all evening. The wine flowed. They pulled the tables out of the centre of the room so that they could dance. George got drunk the fastest and kept picking up the girls on his shoulders and trying to run off into the night with them. Fortunately, the manager had locked all the doors.

They managed to behave while they ate, but afterwards they paid the manager to turn up his sound system and leave them free to help themselves at the bar. It quickly got rowdy. Mimi did a striptease on a table that George had dragged into the centre of the room. She swayed her hips like a snake, hypnotising the men and drawing whistles from the girls. She went naked for the rest of the night, like a naiad in the house of Bacchus.

Charles was quiet. He seemed like a man at a theatre, enjoying the spectacle but remaining detached. When he saw that Odette had left Giselle alone for a while, he came and sat next to her.

'So, what do you think?' he asked.

'Of what?' She was a little drunk.

'Of the circus.'

'It's great,' she told him, looking around the room.

'So you want to join?'

She was surprised. He had hardly spoken to her since the shoot on the rocks.

'Could I?'

'Oh, yes. There are stars and there are superstars in every profession. All these girls are stars but, with the right programme, you could be a superstar.'

'Are you saying this to get me into bed?' she asked, laughing. She felt his hand settle on her thigh and looked at him seriously. 'I came with Odette. She has been very kind to me.'

'Odette won't get you on to the cover of *Vogue*.'

'You don't have to do that. Just wait until another time. Let Odette have me this evening.'

46

He removed his hand with a look of disappointment, nodded and stood up.

'Come to Paris with us tomorrow.'

She nodded and he kissed her on the cheek before heading for the bar.

4

Greta

The next morning, the girls went their separate ways, some heading south and some returning to Paris. Giselle accepted a lift in Arsene's Peugeot. Mimi and Charles drove together in the Range Rover.

Arsene chattered all the way and, for the first time, Giselle began to get an idea of what the life of a model was like. The images that she knew from glossy magazines, and had always seemed so unreal, had their counterpart in the actual. Arsene described the parties and launches, the circuit of shows and presentations. She let slip the names of the famous and described their houses and yachts. She hinted at the darker side, the money-men at the edges of the fashion world who preyed on young girls, the stress of endless travel and the temptations of drugs and alcohol.

When Giselle asked if she ever regretted becoming a model, Arsene looked at her as if she were mad. 'Never! It is the centre of everything!'

Giselle wondered. She was just a country girl. The life that Arsene described seemed as rushed and urban as crack cocaine.

It was early afternoon when they reached the suburbs of Paris. Arsene drove with a reckless abandon through the narrowing roads as if youth and beauty conveyed immortality.

Charles had given Giselle the name of a hotel in the

48

Latin Quarter and Arsene dropped her off there, with a flurry of kisses to the cheeks. Giselle watched the Peugeot pull away at speed and wondered if Arsene would remember her name the next time that they met.

There was an envelope for her at reception. She opened it to find a wad of thousand-franc notes and a note from Charles: 'Everything is paid for, courtesy of Shiva. Call you later.' Shiva was the company that made the shower gel. Apparently she was still on the payroll. A bellboy appeared to take Giselle's luggage but she had none. She had arrived in the capital of fashion with the clothes she had left home in three days ago and only one change of underwear.

The woman behind the desk seemed to sense her embarrassment and told her that, if she needed anything, the hotel had its own shops and she could simply charge it to her bill. Giselle had the impression that Charles, or the girls that he sent there, were well known. The woman had pointed to the far end of the reception area when she mentioned the shops and Giselle wandered away in that direction once she had completed the registration formalities.

Through glass doors with huge chrome handles there was an Aladdin's cave of cosmetics, clothes, accessories and underwear. She bought basics: toothbrush, moisturiser, shampoo, three pairs of white cotton briefs with matching bras, and then, because she felt a little homesick, a purse for Nana in the softest tan leather.

From the clothes boutique, she bought a pair of Ralph Lauren jeans and a practical dress for travelling. The blouses were overpriced but she bought two, one cream and one black, plus some T-shirts. On the shoot, she had more often been naked than clothed during the day and, in the evenings, Odette had dressed her in clothes from her own collection. She was on her own now and struggled away with the glossy carrier bags and a faint feeling of guilt after charging it all to Shiva. It

49

would be a while before she could squander money the way that the other girls did.

Her room was on the third floor, spacious enough for a sofa as well as a bed and with a grand ensuite bathroom in malachite green marble. She showered and then watched TV as her hair dried. Room service brought her coffee and a slice of lemon torte once she had discovered how to use the telephone. Lemon torte was one of the few things that she had ever eaten in a restaurant – that in Rennes with a middle-aged man who had propositioned her at the swimming pool. He had dined her and then taken her to his flat for sex, which had left her cold. The cake she remembered with affection though, and the hotel version was even better. She wondered how models ever kept their figures when room service was so obliging.

The TV bored her so she tried on her new clothes in front of the mirror. This, too, soon bored her and, as she always did when time lay heavily on her hands, she ended by masturbating. She lay on the bed with a pillow between her legs and the memory of Charles filling Mimi's mouth.

At about eight o'clock there was a knock on the door. She was dressed only in T-shirt and briefs and, thinking that it must be Charles, answered the door like that. Charles had seen her in every state of undress possible. Besides, she didn't expect to stay dressed for long once he arrived.

Instead of Charles though, Giselle found an immaculate blonde woman smiling at her from the hallway.

'I'm Greta,' she said, as if the name should mean something. Giselle blushed, feeling absurd in the T-shirt, which covered her only to the waist.

'Charles didn't tell you to expect me, did he?' the woman asked.

Giselle shook her head.

'Were you expecting him instead?' she asked, glancing

at the length of Giselle's bared legs and tight whorl of her navel as it peeped from beneath the shirt.

'I wasn't expecting anyone,' Giselle stammered.

'Can I come in?'

Giselle stepped aside and let the woman enter. The woman moved to the sofa and sat, seeming entirely at home. Giselle hurriedly picked up the clothes that were scattered around the room, then, taking her new dress, said that she would change.

'There's no need,' Greta told her. 'Charles wanted me to see that you were OK, that you were comfortable. If I force you to dress up or embarrass you if you don't, I'm not doing very well, am I?'

The woman's tone was gentle and her smile unassuming. There was an alluring fullness of warmth in her eyes, something that Giselle wasn't used to, a selflessness that she didn't associate with the fashion world.

'I'd prefer it,' Giselle said.

The woman nodded and allowed Giselle to go into the bathroom to change. She was smoking when Giselle returned.

'Do you mind?' she asked, holding up the cigarette. 'A terrible habit; worse than heroin, they say.'

Giselle shook her head.

'So, Charles didn't tell you about me?'

Giselle shook her head again. 'We haven't talked very much.'

'Charles doesn't really talk – except with his camera. But he usually mentions me,' Greta said in surprise. 'I'm Charles's wife, Greta Mannay.'

She held out her hand and Giselle overcame her surprise to shake it.

'Is he still with Mimi?' Greta asked.

Giselle didn't know what to say.

'You aren't betraying anyone if you answer,' Greta assured her. 'We don't have the kind of relationship where betrayal could be an issue.'

'He drove her back to Paris,' Giselle said diplomatically.

Greta nodded. 'I assumed when he rang and mentioned you that you were his new lover,' she said without animosity.

Giselle shook her head and sat on the edge of the bed.

'Later perhaps,' Greta breathed, smiling.

Giselle blushed.

'How old are you?'

'Twenty.'

'Can I look at you in the light?'

Giselle was too surprised to reply. Greta came to sit beside her and switched on the table lamp by the bed.

'Don't be nervous. I'm entirely harmless.'

Giselle smiled, almost believing the woman. She could feel the heat from the woman's face on her own as she was examined.

'He is one of the great photographers, you know,' Greta told her. 'He can make a girl. Not many photographers can.' She turned Giselle's face towards her and gazed into her eyes. 'Yes, I think I see what he wants from you,' Greta said finally. 'And it is more than just sex.'

Greta switched off the lamp and went back to the sofa.

'How well do you know Paris?' she asked.

'Hardly at all.'

Giselle had been only once before, when she was still living in the south. An aunt had taken her on a Christmas shopping trip. All that Giselle could remember were the crowded pavements and the endless vacillation of her aunt as she tried to choose presents.

'Then I'll show you the sights. It is best at night.'

They took a taxi to the Pont Neuf and from there walked along the left bank arm in arm. Greta asked about Giselle's home town and her family. She seemed

52

to realise quickly that there were secrets, events that Giselle wanted to hide, and she was careful not to press the girl. Notre Dame loomed above them as they walked further, its floodlit face like an old priest: severe, noble and arcane. They stopped at a café for a drink. Giselle was aware of the elegance of the women there and again she felt like a country cousin. When she told Greta, the woman laid a hand on her arm.

'Elegance can be bought. What you have is something else. Grace – no, more than that. Something that comes from inside. Spirit perhaps.'

Giselle was embarrassed but Greta refused to allow her any false modesty. She raised her glass. 'To your beauty and . . . to the artist and his model – this is the Left Bank after all.' She laughed, a cadenza of warm notes that washed through Giselle with the wine.

When they had drunk, Greta leant forward and spoke more seriously. 'Let him mould you. Enter into the fantasy for a few years. Make some money then walk away and live your life however you want to. Don't forget, though, that it can be an addiction. And don't forget that none of it is real. Only a surface shine. Think of yourself at every turn. Think what it is that *you* want.'

Giselle nodded but it had always been the thing that she couldn't do. It was always the desires of others that moved her. Her own desires were triggered and she tripped after her tempters with a schoolgirl's willingness.

They crossed the river and Greta showed her the Tuileries, full even at that time of night with skateboarders and tourists.

'This whole city could be yours,' Greta said, as they walked down the long avenues arm in arm. 'Your beauty will open every door. Men will fall at your feet. You will be a queen.'

Even if it were true, Giselle wondered if she wanted any of those things. A week before, she would have said, unequivocally, that she didn't. She would have said that she wanted peace and quiet and a place to feel at home. Yet, in the centre of that great city, with its elegant women and expensive cars, its sumptuous restaurants and grand houses, there was an appeal: fame, money and entrée into those places denied to the ordinary. It tugged at her vanity.

'I feel as if the devil is at my shoulder,' she said.

Greta laughed. 'He is offering you the whole world if only you will renounce your soul.'

'Yes.'

They laughed together and walked on arm in arm.

It was late when the taxi got them back to the hotel. Greta took a card from her pocket and pressed it into Giselle's hand.

'Charles is expecting you tomorrow morning. Ten o'clock.'

As the taxi sped away, Giselle looked at the card. It was the address of a studio in Montmartre – Chemin de Fer.

The next morning, early, Giselle rang Nana for the first time since she had left Briere. There was a dread that her father would answer the phone but it was her sister's voice.

'You did it!' said Nana when Giselle announced herself. 'You got away.'

'Are you angry with me for leaving you?'

'Of course. But I'm also glad. I will go too. The day that I am sixteen, I will pack my bags and leave. Is it wonderful? Paris. Celebrity?'

'I'm not a celebrity yet.'

'I said that you were the most beautiful girl in France. I knew that they would want you.'

'How is Father?'

'Angry. Impossible. He hasn't stopped shouting since you left.'

'No change, then?'

Nana laughed. 'No. I told him that I would go too but it just made him worse. I think he wants to drive us all away.'

'Maybe.'

'He said something about you and Jean.' Nana's voice dropped as she said this, became serious. 'He called you a whore. He said, "Even with her own brother," then stopped himself.' Nana paused and there was an uncomfortable silence for long moments. 'Is it true?' she asked eventually.

'We shouldn't talk about this on the phone,' Giselle replied softly.

'When will I see you?'

'Soon. As soon as I get a break in the shooting, I will come down and find a hotel in Rennes for a few days.'

'You will tell me, though? I'm not a baby.'

'I'll tell you everything,' Giselle assured her solemnly, wondering if she ever truly could. 'Look, I must go, I have to work.'

'Lucky you. I have geography, maths and English this morning.'

'I miss you,' Giselle said, then hung up before the tears could come.

5

The Studio

Subdued after speaking to her sister, Giselle hardly noticed the streets as the taxi took her to the address on the card.

The studio was a large, ugly, nineteenth-century building, the brickwork still covered with soot from the steam trains that once plied the railway tracks that lay next to it.

An iron banner, with lettering burnt through, identified the building and beneath this was a steel-and-glass door. The contrast between the inside and the outside of the building couldn't have been greater. The interior walls had been encased in brushed stainless steel, smooth and aggressively clean.

A receptionist sat behind a desk of sculpted pink acrylic. Her stockinged legs and patent leather heels were visible through a series of subtly refracted distortions. The girl smiled from beneath crewcut hair and shaven eyebrows – alarmingly androgynous. She might have been an extra in a sci-fi film. Odette would have liked her, Giselle thought as she explained who she was.

'Stage 3,' the girl said when Giselle asked if Charles was there. She checked a screen in front of her. 'Yes, Stage 3,' she confirmed. 'That way.' A carefully manicured finger pointed through a cagelike door of gleaming, heat-blued mesh.

The spaces inside were vast and thronged with people in a hurry. The corridors were wide enough and high enough to accommodate a speeding lorry.

There were signs for sound studios, video suites, mixing rooms and even a cinema. It was clearly more than a photographers' studio, more a factory for fantasies of all kinds. Giselle followed the signs for Stage 3. They took her through a restaurant filled with the scent of coffee and breakfast cakes and across a steel catwalk with an auditorium below where the banks of seating reached to the distant ceiling. Through thick glass windows, she could see into studios whose floors were strewn with snakelike cables and whose sound-proofed walls seemed to have been carved by Saharan winds. In one, a gang of Arab boys played and sang soundlessly; in another, a string quartet rehearsed beneath the rheumy gaze of an unshaven conductor.

Stage 3 announced itself with a sign of blinking red neon. The door was locked and she had to press the button on the answerphone. A squeaky voice asked who was there. She gave her name and then waited. There was silence for a few minutes and she thought that she had been forgotten. Then a buzzer sounded and she quickly pushed open the door.

The space inside was void of human beings. She looked around herself in surprise. She had expected to find the same circus that had formed the shoot in Brittany. Instead, there was only a large empty space with a high ceiling and a polished wooden floor. Sunlight came through a series of doors, which were open to one side, and, hearing music, she headed in that direction.

Finally, she saw Charles. He stood in the middle of a lawned area outside, surrounded by the high brick walls of the building and directing a group – no, a pack – of vampish girls in black leather. They were crouched like wolves when she first saw them, menacing even in sunlight.

There was music coming from a speaker set out on the grass and a second group of girls in soft pinks – chiffons and silks – sat in chairs along the prison-like walls.

It was a strange mixture and Giselle felt hopelessly out of place until Charles's assistant, Mary, came over and told her to go to make-up. For this, Giselle had to go back inside and cross the studio to a door that she hadn't noticed when she first came in. She had also failed to notice the fine wires that hung from gantries on the ceiling and the banks of lights along the walls, almost invisible in the gloom. The wires made it feel as if she had blundered into a spider's web and the lights were like the serried eyes of spiders waiting for their prey.

On the far side of the studio there were several doors and she chose the one marked MAKE-UP. Odette was leaning against one of the dressing tables, flicking through a copy of *Vogue*, when Giselle entered. She dropped the magazine and hurried over, smiling broadly.

'Am I allowed to kiss you?' she asked. 'On the cheek at least?'

Puzzled, Giselle nodded and accepted a soft brush of the lips to each cheek.

'I've been warned to be businesslike with you,' Odette explained as they stood smiling at each other. 'Charles seems to think that he owns you now. Does he?'

Giselle shrugged. 'He's taken a lease, I think.'

Odette laughed. 'Well, we must abide by the rules, I suppose, for now.'

She took Giselle's arm and led her to a seat.

While Odette attended to her hair and face, consulting the notes that Charles had left, Giselle looked through the tiny window to the gardens. Charles was photographing the girls in pink. She recognised Arsene and Selene amongst them. Charles had them standing close together, embracing, exchanging kisses and caresses like kittens preening each other. As always, their bright bold beauty intimidated Giselle and left her feeling small and mousy. All the reassurances of Greta and Odette counted for nothing in the face of those girls' astonishing assurance.

When Giselle's face was finished, Odette asked her to stand and she then helped her out of the robe. She began to powder Giselle's back with a huge powder puff. As Odette worked down and across her hips and behind, Giselle realised that Charles must be intending to use her naked. There could be no other reason for the clouds of powder that surrounded her.

'Do I have a costume?' she asked.

'Costumes were fitted an hour ago,' Odette told her, 'so I guess not.'

She moved around to the front and worked on Giselle's shoulders and breasts. Giselle wondered if she would be the only one to be left naked. She was angry that he hadn't asked her, that he had simply assumed she would comply. At the same time, the attentions of Odette lulled her. To be made up, to be transformed by colour and texture was to be inducted into a dream world. It was another's dream of course – Charles's dream – but there was still that magical sense of reality being suspended, of time slowing and possibilities being created.

When the powder had covered her entire body, Odette applied a translucent pink colouring to her nipples, the same colouring that she had applied to her lips. Looking in the mirror, Giselle saw a tall, pale creature – almost an albino, except that her hair was dark and her eyes blue. The powder not only made her skin very pale but also very smooth, so that the lips of her sex stood out as crenellations of soft pink in the otherwise perfect planes of skin. She wondered at the power of such simple things to transform – she might have been a shade from Hades.

Odette allowed herself a brief kiss to the side of Giselle's neck as she examined the reflected image. 'I haven't given up with you, you know. We hardly began.'

Giselle smiled. 'Don't give up,' she whispered. 'I still think of you.'

As she said this, she became aware that the garden had emptied and that there was the sound of mayhem from the studio. Odette also heard it and opened the door to reveal a scene from Dante's Inferno. A number of the girls were suspended in midair, some were slowly spinning in place and others ascended into the gloom of the high ceiling like souls migrating heavenward. It took a moment for Giselle to realise that the figures were suspended from the wires that she had seen earlier. It was only then that she noticed the men who were securing Arsene, who was dressed in pretty pink chiffon, by hooking one of the wires into the harness that the dress concealed. As soon as she was secure, one of the men gestured to another at a console near the doors and Arsene, too, slowly ascended. Giselle watched the air of the studio gradually fill with girls in black leather and pink silk. They seemed nervous at first but after a while began to call to each other excitedly and swap jokes. Every movement made them sway and spin like badly controlled puppets. There was a stack of thick safety mats in the far corner of the studio but nobody seemed concerned to use them except for a black-and-white cat that had wandered in through the open door and sat preening itself, oblivious to the chaos.

Charles demanded a few last-minute changes to make-up and Odette left Giselle to watch the circus arrange itself on her own.

Once all the girls were hooked in place, Giselle saw that there was a sort of pattern. They were in pairs. Each girl in black had a girl in pink within touching distance. The pairs were arranged in a slowly ascending helix that narrowed towards the top to leave one figure at the apex – Mimi, diabolical in black-and-red make-up, her hair short and severe.

Charles went over to the console and the lights powered up, bringing the three-dimensional construction of black and pink into focus. Giselle leant against the wall and watched as Charles worked with the engineers to perfect the positioning of the girls and the lighting. The banks of lights swivelled as they picked out their targets and the colours were changed experimentally until Charles had what he wanted. With the lights on, Giselle no longer had the protection of the darkness. She was acutely aware of her nakedness and of the eyes that examined her. Charles glanced at her once or twice but didn't speak or acknowledge her presence directly. There was an impulse to retreat into the make-up room but she knew that Charles would send for her immediately. That is the way that men are. They like women to wait for them; they like to show others that they have the power to make women wait.

Charles finally seemed satisfied with the positioning of the girls and came to the centre of the studio. He shouted for the first pair of girls to be lowered down to him. There was a faint hum as winches on the gantry responded to the console commands. A pair of girls, the pair that included Arsene, descended smoothly on the invisible wires to remain suspended a foot or so above ground. Charles gestured for Arsene to be raised a little and, when she was, he picked her up and delivered her into the arms of the girl in leather. As Giselle watched, he arranged Arsene so that her arms hung down behind her head and her long blonde hair cascaded across the thighs of the girl in black. She looked as if she were dead or unconscious and was being carried to hell by a demon whose tight skin of leather shone in the lights like black fire.

Then, to Giselle's astonishment, Charles produced a

knife from his pocket. For a moment she thought he was intending to slash the girl's throat but instead he took a handful of the material that encased her belly and, pulling it from her skin, made several long gashes before stepping back to judge the effect. Arsene's taut belly could be seen through the jagged gashes but it was not enough for Charles. He stepped forward and tore at the cuts, opening the dress so that the girl was naked from the lower part of her breasts to her navel. Still not satisfied, he worked on her skirt, cutting it from hem to hip so that the fabric hung straight down and revealed the backs of her thighs as they curved gracefully under the force of gravity. He pulled what remained of the tattered fabric on to her belly so that the swell of her sex was exposed. Still not satisfied, he tucked the fabric between her legs so that only the leg nearest to him was naked. Finally, he settled for allowing the whole of one leg to be seen along with most of her belly. Her sex he left discreetly covered with only a suggestion of its fullness as it pushed out the pink satin. When he stepped back, Giselle could see what he had created and felt a charge of arousal. The dreaminess of Arsene's face, the implication of force in the tight hold of the demon, the sense of innocence at the mercy of such a demonic figure – all these things combined to arouse. But it was the fact that Charles could do these things, could imagine them at all, that most stirred her. She wanted a demon for herself; she wanted to be lifted in Charles's arms.

When the girls had been returned to the place that had been selected for them, he allowed the leather girl to release her charge but told her to memorise the pose exactly for the time when he would photograph them. Arsene swung back to being upright, the tattered pink fabric about her waist making her look like a flower whose petals have been ravaged by a storm.

Charles worked on each pair in turn, varying their positions, ignoring the protests of those who waited endlessly on the ends of their wires. When he came to Selene, dressed, Giselle realised on closer inspection, in black PVC, not leather, he had her hold her slender, angelic victim around the thighs. The girl in pink seemed frozen in a struggle to escape, reaching upwards with her arms, as if she would fly if only her legs were released. Her sweet mouth was wide in a silent scream, which became real when Charles tore open the bodice of her dress to reveal perfectly rounded breasts and the deep shadows of her armpits. She laughed in embarrassment at her cry before her pretty face resumed its portrait of despair.

Finally, every pair had been given their directions and the shoot could begin. The demons each picked up their victims and arranged themselves as they should. The lighting went into overdrive. Red and orange beams swept wildly across the back wall, mimicking the flames of hell. The brightest light was saved for Mimi, who towered above everybody. Her pose was militant, with arms stretched wide, hands extended and face twisted into a mask of frenzied pleasure.

It took Charles another hour to complete all the shots and satisfy himself with the result. Finally, he allowed the technicians to lower the girls and switch to normal lighting. The girls were unhooked one by one and allowed to walk on solid ground for the first time in two hours. Those in pink looked as if they were survivors of a war in Fairy Land. The tatters of their clothes gave them a cartoon appeal, sweet and sexy but unreal. The stuff of fantasies.

As the chattering girls passed her on the way to the changing rooms, Giselle thought that she had been forgotten.

It was only when the studio floor was empty that Charles gestured for her. He had kept her waiting for over three hours, naked before the eyes of the girls and the technicians. She should have been angry and might

63

well have been if the process hadn't been so fascinating and if the final image – apocalyptic, sensual and debauched – hadn't been so striking.

He looked tired when she reached him.

'They'll hook you up now,' he told her, yawning, then asked Mary to bring him a chair and a coffee. Giselle expected the technicians to produce a harness of the kind that the other girls had worn but, when one of them approached, he was carrying a pair of leather straps instead. Firmly sewn into the end of each was a thick steel ring clearly designed to slip over the hooks at the ends of the wires. Her heart missed a beat when she imagined that they would loop the devices around her wrists and that she would be suspended in that way. The reality was worse than her imagination. The technician asked her to sit on the floor and attached the straps to her ankles. She realised with a further shock that Charles intended to suspend her upside down.

'Why?' she asked, looking at him angrily.

'It will complete the tableau.'

He described how he would superimpose a pair of images of her on to the group work so that it appeared that Mimi was holding two naked girls – twins – aloft by their ankles, one in each hand.

'Trust me,' he told her.

Giselle remembered Mimi's pose, arms thrust out and face savagely triumphant, and saw in her mind's eye the power of the image that Charles would create. This muted her protests but didn't calm her anxieties. The wires were obviously strong enough but what if the ankle straps slipped? What if the leather tore? What if . . .? There were a lot of what-ifs.

'These guys are professionals,' Charles said reassuringly when he saw her nervousness.

One of the technicians smiled at her. 'It is as safe as crossing the road in Paris,' he told her, then laughed sardonically. She was aware of the man glancing obliquely at her sex and breasts, as if it were forbidden but he couldn't help himself. She was glad that she had used a depilatory cream that morning – that she was as smooth between the legs as the surfaces of the eyes that slid over her.

At least the anklets of kid leather were comfortable. They gripped her flesh like the hands of lovers. As the technicians returned to the console, Giselle was aware of the girls emerging from the changing room in little knots and drifting to the exit. Some openly stared at her as if she was mad to allow such indignities. Arsene waved. Odette blew a kiss then disappeared with the others. There was the whirr of an electric motor and Giselle's feet were pulled slowly from the ground. As soon as she was completely clear and her fingertips were a hair's breadth from the floor, the winch stopped. One of the men came over and checked the anklets again as she hung upside down, her legs pulled wide apart and her breasts feeling heavy in the reversed gravity. This time, the man stared at her sex openly, obviously emboldened by her helplessness.

When they were satisfied that the ties were safe, they hauled her higher. At five metres or so, images of falling broke into her consciousness. There was a moment of panic and she struggled. The winch stopped. Charles pulled one of the crash mats beneath her and assured her that even if she fell she would come to no harm. From that height, the crash mat looked much smaller and much thinner than it had looked on the ground. She closed her eyes and tried to wipe away images of catastrophe. The winch started again. The next time she opened her eyes she realised that she was as high as Mimi had been.

Charles was seated now and drinking coffee. Mary was adjusting the camera position and peering at Giselle through the viewfinder.

'Try to relax,' he told her from the comfort of his chair. She almost laughed.

'We are going to let one of the wires ease down,' Charles shouted after a few moments.

Almost immediately, Giselle felt one foot being lowered and all of her weight being transferred to the other.

'It must look as if you are being held by one ankle,' Charles called, 'so just let your leg find its own position.'

Giselle's leg splayed wide as it was lowered further and her thigh came to rest against her belly. There was a feeling of stretching and lengthening, as if her body were elongating, growing moment by moment. The lights suddenly came on. These were the lights that had previously played across the wall to create an illusion of hellfire. Three spots lit her mercilessly. Charles took half a dozen shots of her in this position, hanging passively as if dead or unconscious, and then told her to look as if she were struggling to escape. She didn't want to struggle. She was afraid that any movement could push the wire or the anklets to breaking point. She struck a few poses, but they were too static, too stagy, for Charles.

'Move,' he shouted. 'Struggle. Make it real.'

She began to move tentatively. He kept shouting at her. Suddenly, there was a real panic, a combination of the danger and his threatening tone. She span like a fish on a hook.

He stopped shouting and the camera clicked. When the shot was right he was silent and only the camera spoke. Finally, she felt herself being lowered. She had probably been aloft for only ten minutes but it could have been for ever. She was breathless and disorientated.

Charles hadn't finished with her, though. When she was three or four metres from the ground he told the technicians to leave her there. He wanted some close-ups, in case they were better for his purposes.

'You never know what will work until you're in the darkroom,' he told her when she protested.

'We'll be a while,' he told the men at the console. 'Take a break. Come back in an hour.'

'An hour!' Giselle exclaimed.

'Think of the money,' he said helpfully.

She had not even been told what she was earning. Greta had made her sign a contract and the sums seemed enormous, but what she would earn for hanging from a wire for an hour she couldn't imagine.

When the technicians had disappeared, she thought that they were alone. Then a movement to one side caught her eye. She swivelled so that she could see in that direction. Mimi was lying full length on one of the crash mats. The movement was a leather-clad leg, swinging slowly from side to side.

'Do you really think that she has it?' Mimi asked. 'That look that you want so much, that you always imagine but never realise?'

'Maybe,' Charles replied, gazing through the viewfinder.

'Is this a way to find it? Hanging her like meat in an abattoir?'

When Charles ignored this remark, Mimi rolled on to her side and stood.

'You could stamp a mark on her bottom. Prime cut. Produce of France.'

Mimi circled the hanging girl.

'Out of the way,' Charles told her angrily. 'I don't need your shadow in the frame.'

Mimi pouted and retreated a few paces.

'Is it just lust?' she asked. 'Are you fooling yourself and her that you will make her a star when all you want to do is make her?'

'If I want to fuck her and she wants to fuck me back, you'll be the first to know.'

'Third,' Mimi corrected him. 'And I don't like being third.'

The door to the studio opened at that moment and Greta poked her head in.

'Is it OK to come in?' she asked.

Charles glanced at her and gestured impatiently for her to enter.

'Fourth even,' Mimi said, watching Charles's wife walking towards them.

'Poor Giselle!' Greta exclaimed when she recognised the inverted figure.

'Poor Giselle's suffering would be over more quickly if I was allowed to work,' Charles said in irritation.

Greta apologised and smiled at Mimi.

'He's caught a big one today.'

The two women looked at Giselle and laughed.

'Boys will be boys.'

Charles finished up quickly and then strode over to the control console. He pushed the down switch then strode back as Giselle was slowly lowered. He was in time to catch her as she approached the mat and turned her gracefully into a sitting position.

'So, has it been as glamorous as you expected?' Greta asked ironically.

'There's a lot of hanging around,' Giselle said with a smile.

'Like the girls in the Place Pigalle, then,' Mimi interposed tartly, drawing an angry look from Charles. Greta seemed ready to speak in Giselle's defence when Charles leant forward and kissed Giselle full on the lips. Perhaps it was a reply to Mimi's sarcasm, a punishment for the girl's possessiveness. Perhaps it was a message to Giselle about his relationship with Greta. Either way, Giselle was so shocked that she didn't even try to withdraw. When Charles pulled away, he turned and looked pointedly at Mimi.

Her face was thunderous. 'Pig!' she spat and, turning on her heel, strode to the make-up room. Greta watched her leave in amusement.

'I never did like her anyway,' Greta said, and turned to Charles. 'You never seemed right as a couple.'

Giselle shot an astonished glance at the woman. Charles laughed. 'She'll be back. If I want her. Who else could match her egotism?'

'True,' Greta said in agreement. 'You were a real couple in that department.'

Charles helped Giselle to her feet.

'I think that Giselle should come and stay with us for a while,' Greta said. 'What do you think, Charles? We can't leave her in that lonely hotel with no friends in Paris.'

'Fine.' Charles was packing away his cameras in their aluminium cases.

Giselle was still shocked by the kiss. To be invited home by the woman that the kiss had betrayed was even more surprising. Greta took her arm. 'Come on, I'll protect you from Mimi in the changing room.'

Giselle allowed herself to be led away meekly. Greta seemed to be securing her for Charles. At least she was easing the seduction that would soon come, giving it her blessing. She wondered if she was like Odette, if she also wanted to share in the spoils. But nothing in Greta had ever suggested a sexual interest. There was only the warmth – sisterly, motherly. Before they reached the changing rooms, Mimi burst through the door and strode away with no more than a contemptuous glance at those who watched her.

An hour later, Giselle was approaching a luxurious house in the Huitième Arrondissement. Charles had stayed behind to finish up in the darkroom. Greta had driven fast and gravel spat from the wheels as she swung up the driveway to the house. The baroque facade was set back from the road and surrounded by trees. Greta parked opposite the ornately stuccoed portico and smiled at Giselle's surprise.

'Like it?' she asked.

Giselle nodded.

'You could have one just like it, one day.'

Giselle shook her head in disbelief.

Inside, the hall was dominated by a marvellous staircase, which curved upwards around the rounded walls. The wrought-iron balustrade was ornamented with peacocks and fleurs-de-lys. The marble treads gleamed in the light of the central candelabra.

'My father's house,' Greta explained. 'When Charles and I married, he gave it to me. He lives in the country mostly these days. Don't let it awe you. It is just a place to live.'

She took the dumbstruck Giselle by the arm and led her through to the kitchen. This was a modern room and the scale was human. The hall had a museum quality, a sense of 'look but don't touch'.

'Coffee?'

Giselle nodded. 'Are you sure that it's OK for me to stay?'

'We have plenty of room. As you saw.'

Greta laughed self-consciously as she stood before a large coffee-making machine and ran her fingers over the various buttons and levers.

'All the staff are off tonight and I'm not sure that I can operate this device. Would instant be OK?'

Giselle nodded. She saw in a moment how out of place Greta was in her own kitchen. She remembered the slavery of the old range in Briere and her father's refusal to buy a modern cooker.

'The house is wonderful when we entertain of course –' Greta continued, then stopped herself abruptly. 'Have you eaten? I didn't think to ask.'

Giselle had had a very modest breakfast but that was all. 'Not very much,' she admitted.

Greta looked concerned.

'We could check the fridge.'

This was a giant American affair. There would have been room to step inside if it hadn't been stuffed with every kind of food imaginable.

'What sort of thing do you like? I usually just help myself to yoghurt or some salad things.'

'Salad sounds good.'

There were plenty of cooked meats and cheeses and Greta eventually found a cupboard with plates. The knives were in the last drawer that they opened.

While Greta made coffee, Giselle helped herself to food.

They sat at a table near French windows that gave on to the garden. Greta switched on the external lights so that a brilliantly lit shrubbery became their backcloth.

'I'm glad that you're here,' Greta said. 'I'm even more glad that Mimi is out of the picture for a while.'

'Don't you mind, I mean about . . .' Giselle didn't know how to phrase it.

'He has his toys. I have mine,' Greta said sharply, then, realising what she had said, looked at Giselle apologetically. 'I don't mean that you are a toy. I just meant . . . Well, marriage is something else.'

'I haven't done anything with him.'

'Nothing?'

'Almost nothing.'

Giselle remembered the beach, the way that she had pulled aside her skirt as Charles had come in Mimi's mouth.

'You let him kiss you,' Greta reminded her.

'I couldn't stop him.'

Greta smiled.

'That is one excuse. I usually say that I couldn't stop myself.'

They laughed together.

Since Giselle's belongings were still at the hotel, Greta lent her a pair of pyjamas – beautiful cerise silk, crisply pressed – and provided towels and toothbrush, soaps and lotions. Charles was still not home when Greta showed Giselle to her bedroom. It was at the back of the house and through the ornate floor-to-ceiling window she could see the lights of the city. In the distance, a red light shone atop the Eiffel Tower. It was a long way from the damp of her bedroom in Briere and it felt good to fall into the soft warmth of the ornate bed. She ran her hands across the intricately carved eighteenth-century headboard and decided that whatever happened she would go with it.

Towards the middle of the night, she was woken by the sound of the door to her room opening and through sleep-hazed eyes she saw Charles standing in the doorway to the hall. She tried to speak but was too sleepy. The next thing that she knew was being woken again by the sensation of someone sitting on the bed beside her. This time she didn't open her eyes. It was easier to remain still as a hand stroked the hair from her face.

She heard the bedside lamp being switched on and then felt the bedclothes being lifted away.

Hands undid the buttons of her pyjama jacket and pulled aside the silk. Lips grazed along her neck and descended, slowly, lingering at her breasts. She sighed as her nipples were taken in long, sucking caresses.

The ties to her trousers were undone and a hand searched, pressed for access. She was wet and the fingers went into her easily.

She groaned and her lips were lightly kissed. The fingers that had dug into her sex opened like scissors. Pleasure cut her, like a wound opening her belly. Cutting and opening, opening and cutting. It had been so long since another had touched her. She wanted to scream. Wanted the whole hand. She was all softness, ready to be the toy that Greta had denied she would become. A tiny kiss followed for each of her groans.

The fingers quit her belly and presented themselves to her mouth. She opened and took suck. He told her to play with herself. There was only a momentary hesitation. As his fingers explored her mouth, her own explored her sex. It wasn't long before she started to come but he seized her hand quickly and laid it on the bed. For a while there was nothing – no touching, no commands. She knew that he was watching her. Perhaps he was touching himself, although she sensed no movement. She was aware only of her belly as it rose and fell in long, deep pulses. The desire was acute, painful, as she waited. Finally, he spoke and told her to take off the pyjama bottoms completely. Still with her eyes closed, she complied, raising her legs high, reaching and stretching to pull the silk over her ankles. As her legs came back to the bed a pillow was pressed between her thighs. He held it firmly and told her to make herself come. Part of her rebelled: it would be undignified, doubly so because he was a stranger. He had kissed her once only, and that before his wife. Now he wanted her to abase herself as if they were intimates. She reached for her sex but he slapped her hand away. The silk of the pillow lay against her wetness, tempting her. She surrendered and began to move, grinding her pelvis into the slippery surfaces. He let go of the pillow and she was obliged to hold it herself as she fucked. Her head rolled from side to side and she began to groan again. Her thighs grasped and ungrasped the pillow rhythmically.

She forgot Charles and thought of Xavier, thought how good it would be to show him this. She imagined what he would ask of her in that elegant room. The acts that he would expect to be performed for his pleasure and the joy for her of being handled and directed by so sure an authority. The pillow became one of the boys and she was masturbating against a smooth slender belly, forcing her sex into the bone of the boy's hip, running her wet membranes across the tautness of a slender waist.

She began to come and a mouth took her breast

firmly, reminding her that she was not alone. Teeth held her all the time that she writhed and cried out. As soon as she was quiet, the teeth quit her. She reached out a hand blindly but found only empty air.

'I have a wife to fuck,' she was told as the lamp was switched off.

The bedclothes were lifted to her chin and she received a final kiss at the corner of her mouth.

In the morning, the memory of the visit was like the memory of a dream. It was only as she showered and saw the faint marks on her breasts that she knew it had been real.

Greta was drinking coffee when Giselle went down to the kitchen.

'Did you sleep well?' she asked with a mischievous smile.

'Fine,' Giselle replied, feeling awkward.

'He wants you to leave the pyjama bottoms off in future.'

Giselle looked at the woman in amazement.

'It will be easier for him,' Greta explained, matter of factly, then laughed when she saw Giselle's shocked expression.

'He told you?'

'Of course, though he had no need to,' Greta replied. 'I know Charles, and I know the things that he will want from you, things that I can't give him any more. Why do you think we let each other take lovers?'

'What things?' Giselle asked after a moment.

'It would spoil the pleasure for both of you if I said. Besides, it is a question of what you are willing to do for him. How far he can make you go. That is the excitement, isn't it?'

Greta smiled broadly and pulled out a chair so that Giselle could sit beside her.

'Doesn't it upset you?' Giselle asked after she had settled into the chair.

Greta shook her head. 'It is my way of keeping him. This way I give him everything that he needs. There are things that only young girls will do for a man. There are things that are only exciting when the man knows the girl has never done them before. Charles is a man who likes to corrupt – if that is posssible. He likes to see innocence spoiled. It is his revenge.'

'Revenge for what?' asked Giselle.

'For being born of a woman. For wanting a woman.'

Giselle laughed. She thought of Xavier. It had never occurred to her that he had been born of a woman. He seemed to have come from the stone of the island, fully formed and indestructible.

'I must be a disappointment,' she said after a moment.

'To Charles?'

Giselle nodded.

'Because you are less than innocent?'

Giselle nodded again.

'Don't worry. Charles is creative. He will find new ways of corrupting you.'

Before Giselle could reply, a young woman in a black dress entered the kitchen.

'Marie, this is Giselle.'

The girl smiled and said hello. Giselle was still thinking about what Greta had said and responded only vaguely. She gathered that Marie was the maid.

'Just tell Marie what you want to eat and she will get it for you. I have to go,' Greta told her before rising from her seat and making for the door.

'Oh, and Charles wants you at the studio at one o'clock.'

She waved from the door, accompanied by a flurry of smiles.

Charles was just finishing up a shoot when Giselle arrived in the studio. Two girls that she didn't recognise

75

were draped over a white chaise longue. They both wore long evening dresses but one dress was as white as the chaise longue and the other as black as pitch. A giant chessboard formed the backdrop.

Giselle watched as Charles composed the last few shots. His attention to detail always impressed her. She watched as he arranged not just the overall poses of the girls but the exact contours of hands and feet and the exact folds of the dresses. Even Giselle's untrained eye could see the beauty in the stark patterning.

Afterwards, as the studio emptied, he took Giselle into the darkrooms attached to the studio. There was a strong chemical smell that reminded her of the pharmacy in Briere. The red light was strange to her and a little frightening. She watched as he took rolls of film from his pocket – presumably the shots of the girls she had just seen – and set them out on a bench.

'I process all my own stuff,' he told her. 'Commercial developers are too unreliable.'

He showed her some of the shots from the previous day's work. The large prints were pegged out on lines of string like washing hung out to dry. She saw several of herself, her naked, white-powdered body rendered in shockingly intimate detail. Most were of the pyramid of girls in black and pink. A small number had her own image superimposed on that intricate construction.

'These are the images I will send to *Femmes*,' Charles said, handing her a collection of large prints. 'They will make the final choice.'

The images were entirely convincing. At the top of the pyramid of girls, Mimi held a naked Giselle in each hand. Even the leather-clad fingers, as they clasped her ankles, were believable.

'Sexy,' he said. 'You photograph well.'

She smiled.

'The ad is for the shoes that Mimi is wearing. The punch line is a pun on souls.'

76

Giselle looked at Mimi's shoes. They weren't the most eye-catching part of the photograph.

'It's for a two-page spread. They'll probably have somebody shoot a collection of their footwear and present it on the opposite page. My images are just to catch the attention,' he said, as if reading her mind.

As she leafed through the various prints he stood behind her and, reaching down, took the hem of her dress in his hands. Her heart began to beat fast as he rolled her dress to her waist.

'Why do you never say anything?' she asked.

'I'll tell you what I need,' he replied coolly. 'Besides, there is nothing to discuss. You want sex. I'm giving it to you.'

She couldn't deny this. She was wearing no underwear and she was wet again. Once the dress was perched on her hips he ran his fingers into the divide of her behind.

'I might want other things,' she said.

'Kindness? Love?'

She didn't reply; his tone was too mocking.

'Greta will give you kindness, if that is what you want. Love is something else. Maybe somewhere in this city you will find it. In the meantime, I think you want this.'

His arm circled her waist and the hand delved between her thighs. She parted her legs as he explored her sex. Her clitoris was swollen and, as soon as he touched it, she doubled over. The prints fell from her hands on to the bench, sliding into the rolls of film.

'Sorry,' she said quickly, as she felt him stiffen.

He let her go.

'Not here. Take off the dress and wait for me in the studio.'

She turned and looked at him in confusion.

'Kiss me,' she said, wanting something from him, something other than mere commands.

77

He smiled. It was the charm that he used with difficult models, practised and smoothly efficient.

'Wait for me on the couch and I will kiss you. Let me develop these films first.'

She didn't want to go but he pushed her gently towards the door. In the studio she walked to the couch, still lit by powerful lamps, and slowly pulled the dress over her head. As she lay down, she was aware of the inflammation of her sex. Her hand went to the denuded mound and pressed briefly to feel the pulse of desire. Then, with an effort, she lay back and waited.

After twenty minutes of waiting, restless and aroused, she thought of leaving. It had been this way with Xavier. She had always been made to wait, made to feel insignificant. Charles had made it clear that he was interested in the same things that Xavier wanted – her breasts, her mouth, her sex. But Xavier had wanted more. Xavier had wanted the surfaces and membranes but he had also wanted her soul. Yet, at the same time that Charles's indifference hurt her, it also stirred her. Perhaps he was right: it wasn't his love that she wanted. Xavier had used love to shock and bewilder her, to colonise her mind and mark her indelibly as his. There could be no successor, except in things physical. That was the rub, that was what held her, kept her from rushing from the studio. She wanted those physical things, wanted them very much as she lay naked and waiting on the long couch. With an effort, she curbed her impatience. She would wait, would be another's creature again, if only superficially.

Finally, Charles emerged from the darkroom. He smiled as he saw her laid out on the couch – lines of pink on white, the black and white of the chessboard behind her.

'There's a painting by Ingres,' he said, 'a woman looking at her face in a mirror. We see her from behind. Do you know that painting?'

78

She remembered it from somewhere and nodded.

'Do that for me.'

She turned away from him and lay on her side so that her hips were presented at their broadest. The twisting of her torso emphasised the narrowness of her waist. The white of the couch emphasised the length of her legs.

'Bend your knees a little more.'

He went over to her and arranged her hair so that it fell across the paleness of her back in the way that he wanted.

'The power of the male gaze,' he murmured.

Wet fingers slipped into the divide of her behind and explored the tightness of her anus, lubricating her, then withdrawing. She thought he was going to penetrate her and waited tensely.

For a moment he was silent, then he told her to turn over. His voice had changed. There was a note of dissatisfaction.

'I spend all day arranging women for the camera. It isn't difficult for me to create image after image. Yet when I have a woman to arrange for myself, all I want to do is destroy her.'

She looked up at him, puzzled.

'I create beauty and desire for others – but for myself, that is more difficult.' He laughed bitterly. 'Get dressed. I'll take you for lunch.'

Giselle didn't know what to say. She had waited for him. He had moistened her behind as if preparing her for penetration. Part of her had anticipated that pleasure. Now he was rejecting her and she didn't understand why. She was surprised at the strength of the disappointment. He must have seen it in her eyes and clasped her by the wrists as she rose.

'Has a man ever beaten you?' he asked.

She averted her eyes; she couldn't answer.

'Shall I take that as a yes?'

'If you want to,' she murmured.

'That might interest me. There is something in you that begs it . . .'

He let her wrists go. Giselle was aware of him picking something out of her. It felt as if fragments of her time with Xavier were in the air between them.

'When you were tied yesterday, did it turn you on?'

She looked at him directly for a moment. There were too many words and she was annoyed. She had asked him to kiss her and had been mocked. She had decided to give her body and had been rejected. It was too late now: her desire had faded.

'You said that we were going to lunch,' she reminded him tartly.

'I expect an answer.'

She sighed. It was only the memory of his visit the previous night that prevented her from leaving. That visit had had a power. He had made her do things that she had wanted to do.

'Of course it turned me on,' she admitted, remembering the sensation of being supended naked under the eyes of strangers.

He looked at her for a long time as if weighing her in his mind, weighing her and weighing his desire for her.

'Perhaps I should fuck you now.'

She shrugged. His ambivalence further reduced her desire. She no longer cared. Seeing this, he was suddenly angry.

'Bend over the arm of the couch.'

An unfamiliar feeling of rebellion stirred her and she refused point blank. He caught her wrists again and pulled her to the end of the couch. When she remained standing, stiffly, her hands formed into fists, he pushed her forward and down. She resisted but he was strong enough to pin her torso to the white surface. The back of the couch pressed into her thighs and hurt. He kicked open her legs and she stopped struggling, but as soon as his hands quit her she started to rise. He slapped her hard across the behind.

'I'm paying for your time,' he reminded her.

'That is not enough!' she shouted suddenly, surprising herself.

He dropped to his knees so that his mouth was next to her ear.

'You are a bitch in heat. If you could see your cunt . . .' His hand slipped into her sex then wiped wet, slippery fingers across her cheek. 'You want me all right – at least, you want somebody.'

And that was it, she realised. As long as Charles fitted her fantasy, as long as he was Xavier, she wanted him. When he was determined to be himself, the bubble burst and she was left cold.

'Xavier. His name is Xavier.'

Charles sat back on his heels and looked at her in surprise.

'Tell me about him.'

Suddenly, she burst into tears. It was the first time that she had spoken Xavier's name since she had left Avignon.

Charles stood up and, putting his arms around her shoulders, helped her into a sitting position on the couch. He would never be Xavier. Xavier had enjoyed her tears, had provoked them, then deliberately provoked more. Charles offered comfort and somehow it felt wrong, incongruous.

'Tell me,' he said again gently.

'He was just a boy I knew.'

'A boy who used to beat you?' he asked incredulously.

'There were other things.'

'What other things?'

It was impossible to explain. Nothing about Xavier could ever have been thought of as good, but he made a virtue of evil. And he was always more than a single

81

person. He carried all of the island inside his broad frame. She tried to explain about the quarry – how very beautiful it had been: the blueness of the water that filled it; the reed beds alive with birds and dragonflies. It had never been just Xavier. It had been her brother, Jean, and Giscard who had seduced her and taken her to the island as well. It was the other boys. When they weren't inside her, she was a sister and a mother to them, outcasts like herself. At least, that is how it had seemed. On the island in the middle of the lake they were like castaways. No one else ever went there. There were no adults to interfere or condemn. If she was a toy for them, at least while she was there, she wasn't a slave to her father – his maid and housekeeper.

She was too upset to explain clearly and gradually subsided into silence. Charles was patient and held her in his arms. Despite the strangeness, it was comforting.

'When you climaxed last night,' he asked, 'were you thinking of him?'

She confessed that she had been, that she always did. It was the anonymity of the touch and the commands last night, the fact that her eyes were closed, that had allowed her to come so easily. In the darkness, the fingers could have belonged to anybody.

'Perhaps I could arrange some of that for you,' he suggested.

'What?' she asked.

'Anonymous sex.'

She shook her head and smiled through the tears. 'It's never a problem finding a stranger.'

'But I want to find your strangers,' he told her.

Taking her hand, he laid it on his groin. His sex was hard.

She smiled again.

'At least I've been able to give you something,' she said.

'Make me come with your mouth,' he said, stroking her hair.

It seemed the least that she could do. She unzipped his trousers and took the hard flesh between her lips.

'I'll be your pimp,' he said as she sucked him. 'If I can't be Xavier – and I don't want to be – I'll find men who will treat you like Xavier.'

She released his sex for a moment. 'Please don't –'

He pushed her head on to his sex again. 'If sex is just sensation . . .'

She hadn't allowed herself to think of it like that. She had liked it when Odette caressed her; she had liked it when Odette had used the toys inside her. There was the warmth of another's body, the softening that comes from another's touch. But it hadn't been Odette who had made her come. Odette had just been a stand-in, as Charles was.

'Well, I have the place for you,' he continued, 'a place where no one will ask you your name. Where there will be no need for pretence. Where strangers will fuck you without you having to ask.'

'No –' she began.

'I'll take you there tonight.'

She tried to protest but he cut her short by driving deep. Once he had decided something, it was a settled thing. She gagged as he came and pulsed in the depths of her throat.

6

The Labyrinth

Charles's words – his threat, it seemed to her – preyed on her mind for the rest of the day. Greta was out when she returned to the house, but laid out on her bed was a collection of dresses. They were all new and in Giselle's size. Greta must have spent a great deal of time in choosing them. Each was beautiful, but Giselle looked at them in a sort of horror.

She imagined Charles and Greta discussing her as if she were a child or a pet. No, neither of those – as a sort of project. Charles she could understand. The pleasure that a man had from controlling a woman, that she could understand. The fact that Greta, kindness personified, was a willing accomplice was harder for her.

Giselle was determined not to fall in with their plans but at nine o'clock she started to get ready, an automaton programmed by their expectations. When Charles arrived home punctually at ten o'clock, she was dressed in a short, turquoise, beaded dress, backless and open at the front. He complimented her but made her redo her make-up. She had chosen cool colours. He made her use bold.

In the car, he told her that they were going to a club and that they would go in separately. He would tell the doorman to expect her, so there would be no problem with entry. If there was a queue she was to push her way past it and give his name. Once she was inside she could do anything that she wished, but she couldn't leave until he did. She sat in silence listening to this, wondering why she was there at all, wondering why, beneath the fear, there was a feeling of something comfortable, something familiar.

The club was in the district to the east of the Champs Elysées. The facade was discreet. A small neon sign gave the club's name – Labyrinth. Above the front door was a red-and-black striped awning. Beneath this, an impossibly broad-shouldered man in a dinner jacket stood guard. Charles got out of the car first and told her to follow in a few minutes. She watched as he spoke to the doorman and pointed in the direction of the car. Then he disappeared inside.

Giselle had the same choking feeling that she had had when Xavier motioned for her in some public place. The feeling that comes from not being in control, of fearing exposure and worse.

Still, after a few moments, she stepped out of the car and crossed the busy road. She was annoyed with herself for complying so easily and her mind wasn't on the traffic. A taxi cab appeared from nowhere and skidded by with blaring horn and locked wheels. She saw the fear on the driver's face as he narrowly missed hitting her and only just avoided a car parked on the other side of the road. Giselle watched the car disappear with her heart in her mouth then hurried to the safety of the pavement. The doorman seemed to have noticed nothing and waved her by with hardly a glance. Giselle was shaking as she pushed her way through the revolving door.

Inside, there was a reception area and a girl behind a counter asked her if she wanted to leave her bag. Giselle shook her head.

'Where am I going?' she asked.

The girl laughed and shrugged.

'The club is down there, if that's what you want.'

She pointed to a corridor opposite her booth. Giselle turned slowly on her heel and entered. The light dimmed the further that she went, as if it were a tunnel into the bowels of the earth and soon there would be only blackness. Then, opening a red lacquered door, she found herself in a bar. The music was loud and on the other side of the bar she could see a dance floor.

Charles was standing at the counter, a drink already in his hands. He watched her coolly as she entered but, when her eyes went to him, he turned his back. For a moment she simply froze, feeling entirely out of place, and entirely unaware of what was expected of her. By entering the club alone, she was setting herself up as prey for any man who wished to approach her. She remembered what Charles had said – it was a place where strangers will fuck you, without ever asking your name. Not knowing the rules, being unaware of the expectations, was strangling her. Deciding that she needed a drink above everything else, she sat on one of the high bar stools and glanced along the line of bargirls. A tall blonde, very young, came over. The strong overhead lights made her skin shine and revealed a mass of freckles that reminded Giselle of Nana. She stifled a pang of homesickness, ordered a white wine, then turned with a conscious effort to survey the club. Overhead there were batteries of lights, the sort that spin and flash. At that moment, they were switched off; only the uplighters that lined the walls like metallic mushrooms were on. Bronze pillars supported the high ceiling and gleamed like the brazen legs of angels. There were mirrors at regular intervals and as she scanned the dance floor she was aware of many eyes scanning her. Some of those eyes were her own. It was unnerving to suddenly confront her own image after it had been bounced several times around the room. In the multiple reflections she looked stiff and nervous.

To the side of the dance floor there were tables in a raised area, enclosed by a billowing bronze mesh. It reminded Giselle of the nets fishermen hung out to dry on the beaches in Brittany. She half expected to see metal fish trapped in its folds but there were only men and women, scattered at intervals amongst the tables. Nobody was dancing. There was an air of boredom but also expectation. It felt as if something was expected to happen and that, until it did, there would be a tension.

Charles crossed to the tables and sat down opposite a dazzling girl in blue. Giselle wondered if he knew her, or whether he was just trying his luck. The girl leant forward as Charles spoke, clearly struggling to catch what he said above the sound of the music. Through the mesh, Giselle saw the expression in the girl's eyes, the balance of boredom and possibility. Charles would have to work hard if he wanted her.

Giselle's wine came and she drank it immediately. She felt herself relax. The club was plusher and the clientele more elegant than anything she had seen in Rennes but there was nothing extraordinary. Perhaps Charles had been playing a game with her, deliberately making her nervous, teasing her by making her wear the short dress and the provocative make-up.

At about eleven o'clock the club started to fill up. At first there was a trickle of people, then a flood. A DJ appeared on the stage at the end of the room and the lights kicked in as the music started. This was the real beginning, Giselle realised; the piped music had just been a sheet of sound to cover the emptiness. Soon the dance floor was full and Giselle joined them. Within a matter of minutes a man approached her, smiling, touching her lightly as they danced. He was about her age and handsome in a nondescript way, but not her type. When he asked her to join him at the bar she shook her head.

No sooner did the man drift away than another took

his place. This one was older and exceptionally tall. Dark, serious eyes examined her as they danced. His long, muscled arms seemed always ready to enfold her. She was nervous of him. The turquoise dress suddenly seemed too short, too open, too much of an invitation to such a predator. When the track ended, he took her arm and pulled her from the dance floor. She was reluctant but he had his arm around her waist firmly and was smiling broadly as if they were old friends. As she was led to the bar, the familiar feeling of letting go came. She was his now. A stranger had put his arm around her and now she belonged to him. Her will faded to a tiny, faraway point. When he kissed her, she moulded herself to him as easily as water moulds itself to a cup. He released her to order drinks and she glanced at Charles. Charles was staring at her from his table and his eyes softened into a smile as the man took her in his arms again like a great bear. He told her his name – Gerard – but didn't ask hers. She wondered if she should volunteer the information but it seemed that she was already giving enough.

'Do you want to go into the labyrinth?' he asked.

Giselle couldn't hear him at first and he had to repeat what he said with his lips against her ear. She shrugged, not knowing what he meant.

The drinks arrived. He was in a hurry and swallowed his scotch quickly. Before she had drunk half of her wine, he led her away.

Beside the bar was a black door. Gerard opened it to reveal a long, dimly lit corridor. There was a strong smell of lavender, as if other smells were being concealed. She was reluctant but he pulled her inside and kissed her again.

'Have you really never been here before?' he asked.

She shook her head, nervous again now that they were alone.

'I'll show you,' he said, and pulled her down the

corridor by the hand. There were several sharp turnings and at intervals passageways led off to the left and right.

The further they went, the further normal reality seemed to be left behind. She had a sense of being somebody else. The fact that she was with a stranger, a man who had never even asked her name, heightened the feeling. Even so, when Gerard stopped to kiss her and ran his hands across her breasts, she protested. The protests were feeble and he took no notice. When she stopped trying to push him away, he opened the front of her dress and sucked on her nipples. There was a delicious sense of falling and a wash of arousal across her whole torso. She didn't try to stop him when he pushed his hand under her skirt and grasped her sex. His hand felt huge as he squeezed her mound – as if she had been captured by a giant. When she tried to do up her dress, he laughed and pushed her hands away, then tugged her further into the gloom of the labyrinth.

They had passed several closed doors before they came to one that was ajar. There was the sound of a woman groaning and Gerard pushed the door open further so that they could see inside. The room was tiny. A double bed could be seen in the light cast by a single red bulb in the wall. The bed itself was empty, but pressed against the wall was a couple having sex. The woman was still clothed but the man was naked. Giselle nervously took in the man's taut buttocks as he worked his way back and forth inside the woman. She was embarrassed and wanted to leave but Gerard took a breast firmly in the fingers of one hand and pulled her close. She uttered a little gasp of surprise and the couple in the room turned, as one, to look at her. The man smiled when he saw how Giselle was being held. The woman's face was dissolving with pleasure and she seemed too distant to truly register the intruders. The man turned back to his task, pushing harder and faster. Gerard mauled Giselle crudely as the woman groaned

89

and began to throw her head from side to side – sharp movements, as if the man were injuring her with each thrust. Giselle felt weak as the woman cried out, then strained her body into a taut arch and thrust her pelvis hard against the man who impaled her. Gerard pulled Giselle closer and grasped her sex again, his hand engulfing her so that her entire belly seemed to flow into the cupped palm.

The woman came in a long series of cries. She jerked rhythmically and tossed her head from side to side like a fish dying on the floor of a boat. The room was so small that Giselle felt they had fused together. Her own orgasm began as she closed her eyes and remembered Xavier fucking her in the tiny space of the fishing hut on the island. She saw her brother masturbating on the camp bed that was always strewn with pornographic magazines. She heard him telling her he would come in her mouth.

She pressed herself hard against Gerard and, seeming to sense the coming crisis, he thrust his fingers inside her sex. She was lifted on to her toes as the pleasure took her. In her mind's eye, Jean was rising from the camp bed, his sex near to bursting. He liked to spray her face as she came, then watch her lick the semen from her lips in the luxury of the after-pleasure.

It was minutes before she opened her eyes and came back to the room with the single red light bulb. When she did, the man and woman examined her curiously. They had separated and the man sat on the bed while the woman was still pressed to the wall. The woman reached out and stroked Giselle's chin.

'Is she new?' the woman asked, glancing at Gerard.

'Charles brought her.'

Giselle stiffened when she heard this. It was supposed to be anonymous but Charles had told, had set it up.

'She must be one of his models.'

'She is beautiful,' said the man on the bed.

Gerard pulled aside the dress so that they could see Giselle's breasts. The man rose and ran his fingers across the exposed flesh.

'Astonishing,' he said. 'An angel. Can I kiss her?'

'Can he?' Gerard asked. It was the first time that Giselle had been addressed since entering the room. She tried to reply but couldn't. It was all too overwhelming: the people who were pressed about her in the tiny space, the smells of sweat and sex, the images of Xavier and her brother still fresh in the imagination.

The man took her silence as a yes and pressed his lips to hers. His tongue pushed deep and his hands closed about her breasts. She was falling again. Then she was pulled away. Gerard was telling the man that she was his first, that maybe they could have her later. They were in the corridor again and she was trailing along behind the giant. He took her into the first room that was free and closed the door.

She came back to reality when he slapped her face. It wasn't hard but it was enough to remind her that she was alone with a stranger in a strange place. He slapped her again and she fell to her knees.

'What do you want?' she asked, bewildered. 'Did Charles tell you to do this?'

He began to undo his trousers. His sex was long and thick. When he raised his hand again she came quickly forward and took the sex in her mouth, looking up, to see if this was OK, if this would stop the slaps.

'I'm going to fuck your mouth and I'm going to fuck your arse,' he told her. 'Then you're going to ask me to hurt you.'

She looked at him again. He was smiling but his eyes were hard, like diamonds. She nodded, a quick movement of her head – quick to stop the slaps. He took hold of her hair and began to move back and forth. When he was close to coming he pulled out and told her to undress. She struggled with the dress, anxious to please him. Since the front was already undone it was only a matter of moments before she was naked. She fell to her knees and took his sex again. His hand slapped her away. Again she was bewildered and gazed up at him with open mouth and questioning eyes. Her reward for freezing was another slap, hard enough to sting. She finally realised what he wanted and turned around quickly, climbing on to the bed. He had said that he would fuck her mouth and then her arse. She was still on her knees but her behind was presented to him at the right height and her legs were spread. She felt him push at the opening of her anus and spat on her hand, carrying the mucus to the tight ring and anointing herself. He pushed in steadily and she sagged to the surface of the bed, back gracefully arched, breasts pressed to the cotton.

He pushed in inch by inch, allowing her to open, then, when he was fully bedded, he took her by the hair again and pulled her up against his chest. In this way the whole of her front was accessible to his hands. Her sex, neglected and rejected, flooded when he teased his finger across the smooth, hairless skin.

'Tell me what you like,' he said.

He was moving slowly, withdrawing almost completely and waiting until her anus almost closed before pushing back in.

When she didn't answer he slapped her belly and she gasped.

'Is this what you like?'

He slapped again, catching the top of her thigh.

'It's easier to answer,' he told her, slapping, this time, across her sex.

She writhed and moaned, then whispered that she liked to be told what to do – that he should choose for her.

He slipped out of her anus and told her to turn around. When she did he made her look into his eyes as he fingered her crudely.

92

'You want me to decide?'

She nodded.

'If I wanted to see you with a dog?' he asked.

'No . . . I want you to . . .' Her voice trailed away. She didn't know what she wanted. She didn't want to have to ask.

'You want me to decide what you want. But I have to guess the right things?' He was teasing her. His words were teasing her, but so were his fingers.

'Get down there while I start guessing,' he told her and pushed her head down roughly. She took his sex into her mouth without hesitation, tasting the bitterness of her anus, using the mucus from her behind to provide a smooth, easy passage across her lips.

A slap fell on the side of her face. She was doing something wrong but she didn't know what. He slapped her again when she hesitated. Tears were close as he raised his hand once more. She crouched lower and took his balls into her mouth. Again a slap. She went lower still, crawling between his legs to explore the valley beneath his balls. She was rewarded with a groan of satisfaction as her tongue swept across the tight opening of his anus. For a time she worked there. He opened his legs wider so that she could reach deeper. There was a slap and she hastily dug her tongue inside the relaxing ring. He turned around so that she could tongue-fuck him. He began to masturbate with long, easy strokes as she buried her head in the valley of his behind.

She remembered what he had said to her. He would fuck her mouth and her behind, then she would beg him to hurt her.

Nervously, expecting any moment that he would turn and slap her again, she sat up, kissing her way along his back until she reached his ear. Wrapping her arms around his waist, she put her hands over his and began to move up and down, keeping the time that his own hands had kept.

'Hurt me,' she whispered.

He let his hands fall to his sides so that she had his sex to herself.

She asked him to hurt her again and added a 'please'.

He told her to take his belt from the trousers on the bed. It was heavy in her hands as she handed it to him. She was shaking. She wanted to come.

He had her lie on her back with her legs pressed to her chest. The belt fell heavily on the backs of her thighs. After a few strokes he knelt on the bed and went into her anus again. She groaned and came. He pulled out and after she had sucked him, he beat her again. He targeted the softness of her inner thighs. Then he fucked her again. She realised that this could go on all night. With Xavier it would have gone on all night.

'Tell me what you want,' he said, fucking her again.

When she didn't reply, he pulled out and reached for the belt. There was a knock at the door, a light tapping, the hand of a woman. Gerard turned as the door opened. It was the woman from the room with the red light bulb. She was naked now, except for a sheen of sweat. Her hair was damp, as if she had been running. Gerard motioned for her to come in and the woman sat on the edge of the bed, leaning over Giselle.

'Tell her what you want,' Gerard said. 'Tell her, if you won't tell me.' The woman brushed the hair from Giselle's forehead. She had a kind smile, bright and warm.

'I want him to hurt me and make me come.'

'How?' the woman asked. 'With this?' She ran her fingers across the belt as it hung in the air, poised between heaven and Giselle's thighs.

Giselle nodded.

'I want to watch. Can I watch?'

Giselle looked into the blue eyes, the blue of summer skies. She nodded.

The belt fell again and she jerked.

'Harder?' the woman asked.

Giselle nodded.

The belt rose and fell, lazy until it exploded behind her eyes and in the pit of her belly. Giselle bit hard into her lower lip, stifling the sounds.

'Scream,' the woman told her. 'No one will come. Many will hear but no one will interfere.'

The next time the belt fell, Giselle did scream, high and long. Blood was pounding in her ears and the room seemed far away. The woman had stopped talking to her, as if she recognised that she would no longer be heeded. Small hands took her thighs, high up where they met her sex, and pulled. Giselle felt her sex opening and saw the belt falling slowly, gracefully through the air. She had time to count the hairs on the man's hand as the leather flew to her opened sex. She had time to think, this will hurt me, hurt me more than all the other blows. She smiled at the man as she saw the effort, watched the vein that pulsed at his neck. Then there was a detonation in her belly, a searing pain that brought her upright and made her scream from the place that she had been struck. In the midst of the pain, small at first, there was a seed of dissolution, growing, melting her belly, running down the inside of her thighs like cold fingers, turning and rushing back to break in her very centre, a stabbing, buckling pleasure that could hardly be borne. She fainted and as the world faded there was a sensation of joy that she hadn't felt since the quarry, as if an old scar had been opened and her insides reached.

When her eyes opened again, the woman was on her knees sucking Gerard. Giselle watched for a moment then faded back into unconsciousness. The second time that she came to, she found that the woman had been turned over and was being buggered. Again, her mind closed. It was only when the woman called insistently, relentlessly in her ear that she came back to full wakefulness. Gerard had gone. The woman was perched beside her. Her face was sticky and when Giselle ran her fingers over it she realised that it was semen.

'He came and went,' said the woman with a smile. 'Are you OK now?'

Giselle realised that her behind was very sore, more sore than the inside of her thighs. When she grimaced, the woman rested a hand on her belly.

'He used the belt again, then he fucked you hard, very hard. I thought that he would tear you, but he said that Charles had told him you were used to it.'

Giselle sat up slowly.

'Was it good when you came?' the woman continued.

Giselle nodded.

'Rest for a while, then I will lick you. I like to watch you come.'

Again, Giselle felt herself slipping back towards sleep. The woman's tongue between her legs gradually brought her mind to a full focus. She climaxed for her several times, let her watch and let her masturbate against her thigh and come herself.

It was an hour before she returned to the bar. Gerard was at the long counter, drinking. Charles was sitting at the same table but with another woman. This one was more interested than the first; her hand lay in his lap and her eyes never left his.

As soon as Gerard saw her, he gestured for her to come over.

'OK?' he asked.

She nodded.

'Do you want more?'

'No.'

He laughed.

'You will.'

She was stiff and sore. Her anus felt as if it had been burnt. She shook her head but kissed his cheek before slipping away.

'If you change your mind . . .' he called.

She took to the dance floor again. The dancing lulled her. The movement eased her stiffness. The burning feeling faded. Only the memory of the little room remained, the excitement, the sharpness of the pleasures.

An hour later she was at Gerard's side.

'I want more,' she said.

'More of what?'

'Of you. I want you to hurt me and make me come.'

At about two o'clock, Charles took her home. In the car, he asked if she had liked her present. She guessed that he had meant Gerard.

'Did you tell him to hit me?' she asked.

'I told him that you liked to be hit.'

She felt a stab of betrayal. Charles had given her secrets to a stranger. Soon she would have no secrets. They drove through the deserted streets in silence. The street-cleaning carts were already at work, spraying jets of water across the pavements. A couple were pressed against a brightly lit shop window, kissing deeply. Giselle wondered what it was like to be in love; she wanted to stop and ask them.

When they pulled up at the house, Charles turned to her.

'Will you want to go again?' he asked.

'Do you want me to?'

He laughed.

'We need to get past this. You need to know what *you* want.'

Greta was curled up on the sofa, watching a late-night film. She wore a silk kimono and was drinking tequila from a bottle. Charles kissed her and then headed to the kitchen for a beer. Greta looked at the dishevelled Giselle with amused eyes.

'So, what did you think of the Labyrinth?' she asked.

97

Giselle sat in one of the armchairs and smoothed her hair back.

'The men are like wolves,' she replied.

Greta laughed.

'Did any of them catch you?'

'One did. He kept me for the whole evening.'

Charles appeared at the door.

'I had to prise her from his jaws. Though I think she likes to be preyed on.'

'Tell us,' said Greta, sitting up and switching off the TV.

Giselle described the club, since Greta had never been. That was easy. It was more difficult to describe the labyrinth of rooms behind the bar but Charles pressed her. Sitting on the arm of her chair, he gave her a drink from his bottle from time to time. Giselle sat forward on the sofa, fully engaged as the story unfolded. They both wanted details, Charles out of cruelty perhaps – he seemed to enjoy embarrassing her. Greta seemed merely interested, fascinated even.

Between them the couple extracted every detail of what had happened and, strangely, it seemed reassuring to tell her story. In the car, it had felt that Charles had betrayed her confidences. Here, with Greta, everything was different. Even as she described the man forcing her to open her behind and the beatings, even as she knew that it was simply to satisfy the voyeurism of Charles, the telling of the story and Greta's acceptance and warmth made her feel at home. It made her feel at home in a way that she never felt in her father's house. It seemed almost cosy to describe asking for the slaps that had been delivered to her thighs and the excitement of it. Beneath Greta's benign gaze, everything seemed permissible and understandable. Any sense of wrong-doing disappeared. In fact, it was only as that sense faded that she realised it had ever existed.

* * *

A few days later, Charles took her to the club again. He didn't stay this time. He simply dropped her off on his way to a dinner with Greta and some friends. She stayed until about three. Gerard wasn't there but there was another man, an American, who took her into the labyrinth. The next day she had bruises on the backs of her thighs and Odette had to cover them with make-up before the shoot. She asked where they came from and Giselle told her.

'Is this what you want?' Odette asked. 'To be passed from man to man, to be fucked and beaten in the back rooms of a club where no one cares who you are?'

Giselle shrugged. The American had made her come many times. The belt that he had used on her thighs had made her want to come. He had known her limits and used them. If she met him on the street and he invited her to a hotel or to his home, she would go. Yet there was no emotion involved, no sense of the marvel of it all as there had been with Xavier and there sometimes was with Charles.

'You can stay with me, if you want to,' Odette told her. 'There are other photographers; it wouldn't be hard for you to find work.'

She thought about this. She remembered arriving home at three o'clock that morning and finding Greta and Charles making love in the drawing room. Greta had blushed and, after taking her dress from the floor, had covered herself like a shy schoolgirl. Giselle had apologised and was about to leave when Greta called to her, told her to sit with them and then asked about the club. Giselle had told them about the American. She showed them the bruises that were forming on her legs. Charles was annoyed because he needed her for the shoot that day and the marks would show. Greta asked if it had been good, if she had got what she wanted. There was a gleam in her eye, the sparkle of complicity. They had stayed up until morning broke. Greta had dressed and put some dance music on. They drank and danced together while Charles videoed them. It felt good – like a family. She didn't want to leave.

With those images in her mind, she thanked Odette, told her that she was happy at Charles's and then asked if she wanted to come to the club.

'Is that the place I must go if I want you from now on?'

'Maybe,' Giselle replied.

'Will I have to share you?'

Giselle laughed. 'Or fight for me.'

7

Nana

The month's passed. Giselle slipped into the life that
Charles created for her easily and completely. There
were regular visits to the Labyrinth, regular partners for
her there, as well as strangers who might take her for
two or three evenings in a row and then disappear for
ever. She became known as the beauty who would do
anything for a man.

In the studio she gradually learned the art of
modelling. Arsene showed her how to command a
catwalk. Odette showed her what make-ups looked
good when photographed. She progressed from shower
gels to the products of the smaller couturier houses.

In May, there was a change. Charles and Greta took
her to London. Charles had a house in Onslow Square,
near the Natural History Museum. It was smaller than
the house in Paris, more intimate. Giselle and Greta
were thrown together more and often spent their
evenings together. They were becoming friends but
could only achieve this by avoiding the subject of
Charles. It took a long while for Giselle to understand
how insanely loyal Greta was, how her husband was
everything. It never showed in the couple's conversa-
tions; Greta never allowed the weight of her love to
oppress her partner, but it was always there, tangible to
Giselle at least, and understandable only by reference to
her time with Xavier.

Charles worked from a studio in Islington and took Giselle with him every day, whether he needed her or not. She was still learning, still the sorcerer's apprentice, and when there was nothing else to do he taught her the techniques of the darkroom.

Without the Labyrinth, Charles took to arranging appointments for Giselle with his acquaintances. She came to know London through the desires of its men. There was a gentleman in Holland Park who enjoyed dressing her in virgin white, wining and dining her with great courtesy, then brutally sodomising her in a back alley or subway. In Camden she met two brothers who enjoyed painting her body in gold and displaying her in the window of their second-floor flat. She became practised at remaining absolutely still as men stared and children pointed at the strange, gleaming object. The encounters had the stagy feeling of Charles's sets; they were, she suspected, a continuation of his fantasies. She never knew if money was involved – it was all too discreet, too civilised. She gave the men what they wanted and took what she could for herself.

It seemed that everything was running smoothly; Giselle's bank account was filling and she had no need to think, no need to plan a moment of her days. The advice that Greta had given – to sink into the fantasy, to make money and think only of herself – was unquestioned now. Then, in July, Giselle had a frantic phone call from her sister. Nana had had enough. Their father had become impossible and she was leaving.

There were long, heated discussions. Giselle wanted Nana to wait until her school year finished, so that she could sit her final examinations. Nana was too desperate. Their father had become much worse, lashing out without provocation and refusing to give money for bills or food. Finally, Giselle gave in and wired money to Rennes so that Nana could stay in a hotel for a few days. When her current shoot was finished, Giselle would fly out and they would talk. Then one day, as she came in from work, there was another call from Nana.

'I'm in London,' said the excited voice. She was calling from Waterloo station.

Giselle was too surprised to be angry. She told her to stay where she was and they would come for her.

Half an hour later, Giselle jumped out of Greta's car and ran into the train station. The concourse was busy with rush-hour crowds and it took a while for them to find each other. The sisters embraced while the streams of commuters flowed around them. Nana cried, apologised, then cried again, making Giselle cry as well.

'We should hurry. Someone is waiting,' Giselle said through her tears.

Finally, they separated, stepping back to look at each other. Nana looked pale. Giselle knew that it wasn't easy to leave home, even when home was the last place that a person wanted to be. She kissed her sister's cheeks, then helped with the luggage at her feet.

As they emerged from the station they saw Greta talking heatedly to a traffic warden and ran. It was too late. By the time that they got to the car with the heavy bags, the traffic warden was tucking a ticket under Greta's windscreen wiper.

Giselle was apologetic and offered to pay but Greta waved her hand as if it was nothing.

'Stupid man. I told him to get a real job. He went purple. It was worth the ticket just to see that.'

As they pulled into the traffic and headed for Westminster Bridge, Giselle introduced her to Nana.

'Are all the girls from Avignon so beautiful?' Greta asked.

Nana blushed.

Something in the way that Greta looked at her sister in the rear-view mirror made Giselle wary. She would have preferred to find a hotel for Nana, but Greta insisted on taking her home.

'Charles will want to meet her,' murmured Greta.

That was what concerned Giselle.

When they reached the house in Onslow Square, Nana looked exhausted and confessed that the journey had been overwhelming. Unlike Giselle, she had never even been to Paris before leaving home. In the last twelve hours, she had passed through Paris, travelled beneath the Channel on the Eurostar and driven through London to the grandeur of Onslow Square. If Giselle was a country girl at heart, Nana was doubly so.

Greta, always so sensitive to others' needs, made an excuse that she had some work to do and left the two sisters alone. They sat together in Giselle's bedroom, drinking the coffee that Marie had brought for them.

'I still can't believe that I'm here,' Nana said.

'Neither can I.'

'Are you angry?'

'Yes.'

Giselle was angry that Nana hadn't discussed anything before coming. She was angry that she hadn't been able to make any arrangements for her. She was angry that she couldn't explain her true situation in relationship to Charles and Greta. If she did, it would mean telling everything. She would have to tell her about Xavier, and, ultimately, she would have to tell her about Jean's death. All that Nana knew of that was the story that had been told to the police; the lie that Jean and his father had been standing on the balcony of Giselle's bedroom when the balustrade had broken and they had fallen together to the concrete of the driveway below. No mention had been made of Giselle's part in any of it, not at the time anyway. What her father had said recently complicated matters, but Giselle was determined to avoid too much truth too quickly.

She hid these anxieties by lecturing her sister on what it meant to leave home so abruptly, to leave school unfinished and to have no way of making a living. Yet

104

if Giselle was angry and a little afraid of all the things that might come to the surface, she was also glad to have her sister there. Her homesickness had vanished as soon as they were together again.

'In future, talk to me. Plan things!' she said, finally concluding her gentle admonition.

'I thought you would tell me not to come,' Nana said softly, 'and I couldn't bear another day in that hotel in Rennes. I don't know anybody in Rennes. I'm not going back.'

Giselle saw the set of Nana's jaw, the determination that she remembered from her dealings with their impossible father. She knew that Nana meant what she said and sighed. There was nothing that she could do to change her sister's mind once it was made up.

Nana was perched on the edge of the bed and Giselle rose from her chair to sit beside her. They put their arms around each other's waist as they had done so many times in Briere – comforting each other, listening to each other's stories. It was this warmth and trust that Giselle was afraid of losing if Nana found out about Jean.

'We'll have a great time,' Giselle said, pushing aside her fears.

Nana smiled brilliantly.

'So I can stay?'

'We could find a place together.'

'Yes. I'll find a job. I can make a living, I'm sure.'

Nana jumped up and went to the window. A red double-decker bus was going along the street to South Kensington. The tube station was visible in the distance and, beyond that, the towers of the Natural History Museum. The girl's exhaustion had vanished. She jumped with excitement.

'I knew it would be OK once I was here.'

Later, after Nana had showered and changed, Greta took them to Langhams for dinner and afterwards they wandered through Covent Garden looking at the jugglers and the clowns.

Greta was at her most charming, but not without purpose. She managed to extract every detail of Nana's life history. Giselle, knowing her now, watched Greta carefully finding her way through her sister's mind. She seemed to realise quickly that the young girl had no real knowledge of her sister's sexual past, except perhaps for half-formed suspicions. She also managed to bring into focus Nana's hope that she could one day be a model. Giselle's protests were stifled when Greta insisted that she visit the studio with Charles and watch a shoot.

When they got home, at about eleven o'clock, Charles was back. He was sitting at the kitchen table reading a newspaper, a glass of wine in his hand.

'Hi,' he called casually, seeing his wife. His eyes came to a sharper focus when they fell on Nana.

'This is Giselle's sister, Nana,' Greta told him. Husband and wife looked at each other, exchanging understandings, and Giselle read those signals. It was almost as if Greta was saying, 'Look what I've found for you – another pretty stray.'

Charles rose from the table and walked over to the group. He smiled at Giselle, then took Nana's hand and shook it. The young girl flushed.

'You're very welcome. There's always room for another beautiful woman.'

'That is what I said,' Greta told him. 'One day we must go to Avignon and see if they are all so striking.'

Nana blushed even more deeply and Charles finally let go of her hand.

Giselle remembered the foxes that she had often seen in the moonlight at Briere. Nana was just a lamb, hardly come from her mother's womb and already out in the dangers of the world. She laid a hand on her sister's arm but Nana didn't seem to notice. She had eyes only for the man in front of her.

'I said that you would let her visit the studio. Watch a shoot,' Greta told her husband.

'Of course.'

'I'd like that,' Nana said, smiling widely.

'Meanwhile, lets have a drink.'

The bottle on the table was empty and he fetched more wine from the cellar.

When he came back, he told Giselle that it looked as if she might be chosen for some work on a launch for Takitsua, a quickly growing fashion house based in Milan.

'A lot of PVC stuff,' Charles explained. 'It will get you noticed.'

He had sent some photos of her to Milan last week and Izi Takitsua himself had seen them and was interested. A batch of clothes would come in during the next few days. If Giselle suited them, she could be featured in next month's edition of *Femmes Parisiennes*.

'I will make her a star,' Charles told Nana. 'Your sister will have one of the most famous faces in the world.'

'I knew that she would.'

'So only Giselle doubts it.'

They all looked at Giselle. She smiled.

'I don't doubt you. It's just that none of it seems real, yet. It's still a bit too much.'

'When the world follows your every step, then it will seem real. Too real, perhaps,' Charles told her.

Giselle nodded. 'I'm afraid of that.'

'Don't be,' Greta said. 'Remember what I told you. It's a wave; ride it, use it and leave it when you've had enough.'

After a few glasses of wine, Greta took Nana to a bedroom on the top floor and helped her to unpack. Giselle showered, then went upstairs to her sister's room. Nana was already in bed, sitting up and combing her hair.

'I think I'll like it here,' Nana said.

Giselle smiled, kissed her forehead and wished her goodnight in the way that she had always done in Briere. Then, looking at her sister seriously, she warned her to be careful of Charles and Greta. 'They are not everything that they seem,' she said. 'They can use girls. The fashion industry uses girls.'

'You don't have to be my mother now,' Nana said softly. 'I know that you had to be when I was little, after . . . after she left us. But I'm a big girl now.'

Giselle laughed. 'Of course you are. But I still want to kiss you goodnight. And I still want to look after you. So remember, be careful.'

Nana nodded but Giselle saw that the advice had already been dismissed. She sighed and left the lamb to sleep in the house of the foxes.

Charles came to her room that night. She had known that he would and was waiting for him in the darkness, drifting in and out of sleep. As usual, he left the door to the landing open and a rectangle of light fell across the bed. She couldn't see his face but saw that he was naked and that his sex was erect. There was the marine smell of a woman's mucus, the scent of Greta, Giselle assumed. He pulled back the bedclothes and sat beside her. She rolled on to her back and opened her legs so that he could touch her if he wanted to.

'I'm going to find a place with Nana,' she said. 'A flat somewhere.'

His hand came to rest on her belly and drew lazy circles across the perfect dome of flesh.

'Is that OK?' she asked, when he didn't reply. His hand took the mound of her sex and the thumb pressed at the opening. She was wet from waiting for him and it slipped in easily.

'As long as I have a key,' he told her. 'But I would prefer you to stay.'

She groaned as the thumb pressed hard into the front wall of the hot passage. He toyed with her for a while, then pulled out and told her to play with herself. She was used to these things now and slipped into the pleasure without hesitation, her fingers deft and quick. He switched on the bedside light so that he could watch. Soon she was close to a climax but, before she could fall into sweet dissolution, he pulled her hand away, leaving her gasping. He kissed her palm and smiled.

'Your sister was wearing the same perfume,' he said, sniffing her wrist.

'You visited her?' Giselle asked hesitantly, wondering what he meant, wondering if the perfume they shared was the scent of sex or the Givenchy that she had given to Nana.

'Only to wish her goodnight.'

Giselle looked at him carefully. 'She turned sixteen a fortnight ago. She is just a baby.'

Charles tugged at the front of Giselle's pyjama jacket and laughed.

'She fills her clothes well for a baby. Better than you do.'

His hand went back to Giselle's belly; two fingers slipped inside but Giselle couldn't respond.

'You will respect her?' she asked, feeling old-fashioned as the words came out.

'Respect? Of course. Why shouldn't I?'

Giselle remembered what Greta had said about Charles's appetite for corrupting girls, the pleasure he took from forcing them into acts they would never willingly commit. His thumb found her clitoris and her belly began to melt.

'I will have her, of course,' he told her easily and smoothly. Against her will, Giselle's arousal sharpened as she looked into his eyes and saw the mischief and the cruelty. She shook her head in protest as the first orgasm washed her away.

After she had subsided, he lay beside her and brought her head on to his chest. He wasn't usually so tender and she felt a growing unease.

'Of course, it would help if you didn't stand in the way,' he told her. 'You might even make it easy for me. Explain the kinds of things that I like from a girl.'

'I can't do that,' she replied, sitting up but avoiding his eyes. 'I don't want you to be a Xavier to her. I don't want you to ruin her.'

'Ruin? I won't ruin her. I will certainly fuck her. She needs me to fuck her. I could see that from the moment that she walked into the kitchen. And after I have her, I will let my friends fuck her. But I won't ruin her. It will make her. As you were made.'

Giselle felt a tear well in the corner of her eye. It struck her as foolish that she could shed a tear for Nana so easily, when she could shed no tears for herself.

'Don't,' she said, unable to say more, unable to explain that Nana was her baby as much as she was her sister, that she had nursed her and dressed her as any mother would.

He told her to roll on to her side. To her surprise she felt his sex nudging into the valley of her behind. Usually, he took only her mouth, but tonight something was different. It felt as if he was demonstrating his power over her, pointing out how difficult it was for her to say no.

His fingers went to her sex and carried wetness to her anus. A moment later, an erection presented itself at the opening of that narrow passage. She felt herself yielding, even though she didn't want to.

'Is she a virgin?' Charles asked, pushing into her.

The question made her tighten involuntarily, expelling his sex before it was even fully bedded.

'I don't know. I think so.'

His sex pushed again but she was tight.

'I will have her blood on this,' he said, pressing hard and gaining entry. It hurt and she groaned.

110

'Don't,' she said as he drove deep.

'In Paris, I will take her to the Labyrinth and Gerard will teach her new ways to please men.'

Tears coursed down Giselle's cheeks, softening her, making her feel both hopeless and aroused. Xavier had known how to use her tears, how tears made her so easy, so obliging.

'I could go to her now,' Charles said. 'Do you think that she would refuse me – a stranger in the night? If she is truly your sister, a sister in feelings and desires, I don't think that she would send me away.'

He began to fuck hard.

'Tell me that you won't stand in the way,' he said, the demand emphasised by the pounding of her behind. 'Tell me that she is mine, if I can catch her.'

He took her hair and pulled her face to his. Through a mist of tears, she saw his ruthlessness. She could imagine the pleasures he would want from her virgin sister, the girl that she had protected for so long.

With the last of her strength, she tried to struggle away but he pinned her to the bed, taking the lips that were resisting him and biting. She tasted blood in her mouth.

'Tell me.'

Giselle groaned and surrendered. It felt as if a wasteland had opened in her chest, but her belly burned. 'She's yours,' she whispered. The words, the giving in, unlocked the arousal. She remembered losing her virginity – at the quarry – and imagined Charles taking Nana in the same way. The dammed pleasure broke and she writhed beneath his onslaught. Afterwards, she sucked him until he came – resentfully, slavishly. Then he covered her and switched off the light.

As she watched him leave, a broad-backed animal in the half-light, she wondered if he was going to Greta or to Nana. To her shame, the idea that it might be Nana aroused her. She realised that part of her wanted to see

111

her sister corrupted. Part of her was excited by the thought that she too would be given to strangers and beaten in the Labyrinth.

With an intensity of shame that she had never felt before, she caressed herself as the images of Nana writhing beneath the belt flooded through her mind. The climax was overwhelming, disgracing her with its power.

8

Charles and Nana

The following day, Charles took Nana to the studio.
Giselle was left behind and it was the first time that she
had been left to her own devices in London. With an
effort, she put aside her anxieties about her Nana and
decided to make the most of her time in London. She
took the tube to Covent Garden and visited the British
Museum. Amongst the great relics of Egypt and Persia,
she remembered the rites and rituals of the island. She
remembered Xavier reading Simon Magus to her and
the scent of sulphur in his heresies. Before the shrouded
mummies, she felt the power of history, felt herself
bound and tied by her own, as if Xavier was preserving
her and would one day raise her from the dead.

At a little language school off the Brompton Road,
she enrolled for a course in English. The woman behind
the desk asked if she was a model and Giselle realised
that she must already be slipping into a recognisable
role. She went shopping and deliberately bought
everyday clothes. The clothes that Greta had bought for
her were too much like a label.

In the evening, Giselle showed Greta how to make
crêpes. They ate them with honey and cream and it
seemed more of a sin than sharing a man. Afterwards,
they sat at the kitchen table and drank Pernod.

Nana and Charles didn't come home until after nine.
The girl looked tired but was full of her day – the

models that she had seen and recognised, the lunch that Charles had taken her to in Mayfair, the dressing up under Odette's watchful eye.

'I took some nice shots of her,' Charles said.

He opened his case and pulled out some contact sheets, dropping them into a space on the table. They were sticky with honey and cream when Giselle picked them up.

Nana stood behind Giselle as she examined the rows of tiny images. They showed her in a variety of poses and dresses. Charles had captured her youth and the directness and clarity of her expression perfectly. She photographed well but even Giselle could see that she would never be a top model. She was pretty and she was sexy but something, whatever made a woman a star, was missing.

In the frames of the second contact sheet were a series of topless images. Nana's breasts were as elegantly shot as the dress that had been pulled aside to reveal them. She looked what she was – fresh and fine, new in the world of desire. Giselle made light of the shots, joking with her sister, but in her heart she knew that Charles was already seducing her, step by step.

For three days, Nana went to the studio with Charles while Giselle was left alone. If she had thought that Nana would ease her loneliness, she was wrong. The only consolation was the time that she spent with Greta. She met some of the men and women that Greta passed her days with. She was introduced to Greta's protégé and lover, Lyle, an artist from Dublin, who lived in a tiny flat off the Gray's Inn Road. Surrounded by his paintings, and interrupted by a stream of endless waif-like callers, Greta mothered him and Lyle abused her and then begged forgiveness in a cycle of fire and water. Giselle began to see Greta in a new light. She remembered her own days of mothering and saw how Greta needed to give but also needed the abuse, the harshness of unjustified attacks. She saw that there was power in giving to those who fear and need such gifts, those who snatch and bite at the same moment and then prostrate themselves in atonement. Giselle realised that Greta and she were more similar than either wished to acknowledge. As they grew closer, and Giselle saw the neediness in Greta's soul – the need to be fed with the trust of others – so Giselle began to trust her more and more.

Then the clothes from Takitsua arrived and Giselle was needed.

9

Takitsua

The studio was empty when Giselle arrived but she could see a light beneath the door of the dressing room and walked towards it. A set had obviously been constructed for the shoot but it was covered by dust sheets and gave no clue as to its nature.

Giselle knocked at the door of the dressing room and was grateful to hear the reassuring voice of Odette. The woman embraced Giselle warmly when she walked in.

'You aren't angry with me, are you?' she asked.

'Why should I be?' Giselle replied.

'For trying to steal you away from Charles.'

Giselle hadn't even thought of it in that light.

'Of course not.'

'I had to try.'

Giselle smiled.

'Anyway, look what they sent.'

Odette showed Giselle the racks of clothes that had arrived from Milan the previous day. Three of them were still wrapped in plastic film and covered in destination stickers. One had been opened and Odette had been sorting through this when Giselle had come in.

'Pretty kinky, but not the usual run of fetish gear,' Odette said, holding up a PVC sheath dress with a slash from hem to hip. The collar was high and rigid, designed to hold the neck very straight. With helm and shield it would have had a medieval quality.

Giselle remembered that Charles had said Takitsua would get her noticed and realised now what he meant.

'Charles is only going to shoot half a dozen or so,' Odette told her. 'When he gets out of the darkroom.'

'Is my sister with him?' Giselle asked.

'Probably. She sticks to him like glue.'

Odette unwrapped the remainder of the racks. The smell of rubber was overwhelming, toxic even.

'I'll have to oil you if you're to squeeze into these,' Odette said as she held up a series of outfits.

She had chosen a dozen or so that might suit Giselle, when Charles and Nana came in. Nana had changed in the last week, had become changeable, as if Charles was opening her in some way. Today she was sultry. Her freckled face was flushed and her eyes shone. She smelt of the darkroom, the strange alchemical substances that transformed light into enduring form.

Charles examined the outfits that Odette had set out, holding one to Giselle's neck from time to time. He accepted all of Odette's choices but picked out several more from the racks. Then he sent Nana for coffee. Giselle stripped. It was the first time that she had been naked in front of him since the day that Nana had arrived. He kissed her on the forehead in an oddly paternal way, as if, with Nana there, it was becoming a family affair.

The first outfit was cut like an evening dress. The hem was long, the back open and the bust cut low. Sewn inside were hundreds of rubber balls. As she moved, the rubber sheath flexed and the balls rolled, making the surface ripple. It seemed as if something was trying to break through from inside. The effect was sinister, too sinister for Charles even. It was discarded.

The second outfit was a pastiche of a corset. It had been constructed like an old-fashioned whalebone affair but the black rubber gave it another sense. This time the sinister blended with the sexual. Shoulderless, it lifted

117

her breasts high and was so low cut that her nipples were partially revealed. A veil of thin rubber flowed from the base of the restricting cuirass and fell in folds across her thighs. In the mirror, she looked striking. The costume cinched her already narrow waist tightly and seemed to make it even smaller. Her shoulders were pulled back and seemed squarer and wider. At the back, the elaboration of hooks, eyes and ropes beguiled the eye, but also repelled with connotations of knotted intestines and hopeless, unresolved conflicts.

'With the right hair and make-up, harsh side-lighting maybe ...' Charles said pensively. 'OK, we'll go for that.'

Nana returned as Giselle was pulling on the third costume. This was a catsuit in a clear plastic, pink-tinted but with a grey pigment that floated like smoke within it. Neither the pink nor the grey hid much of Giselle's form. The material yielded to pressure but also tightened and pulled in once the pressure was released. It held and stretched every part of the body as if a hundred hands were moulding her into the shape that they desired. It pulled her breasts apart and held them out to the viewer. At the back it did the same with her behind and it felt as if she were being opened so that she could be penetrated easily. Both sisters were embarrassed.

'I'll wait outside,' Nana said, putting Charles's coffee on one of the dressing tables.

'Don't be silly. You've spent the entire week looking at naked and near-naked girls.' Charles told her. 'Besides, Giselle doesn't mind.'

Charles looked at Giselle questioningly. For a moment, she felt a rising rebellion, but then shook her head compliantly. Odette didn't hide her irritation at this easy surrender. As she ran the costume's zip rapidly from top to bottom, she pulled the neckpiece tight so that Giselle felt as if she were being strangled.

'A sort of punk Barbarella,' Charles said, then told her to turn around.

Giselle turned slowly. She was aware that the nakedness of her sex would show between the opened cheeks as well as the pink star of her anus. 'You wouldn't wear it to meet the Queen, but it would cause a storm in the Labyrinth,' Charles said laconically.

For a moment, Giselle thought that he had told Nana about the club in Paris but a quick glance at the puzzled face reassured her.

'OK, we'll use that one.' Charles said finally.

Odette undid the zip and helped Giselle to free herself of the demanding skin. When it was unpeeled from her sex, the vacuum pulled the soft lips outwards like the petals of a flower and Odette, kneeling before her, couldn't resist a light, licking kiss. Nana looked startled and Giselle blushed.

'One of my perks,' Odette said to Nana, laughing like a naughty child. Nana glanced at Giselle and there was a trace of envy, a sense that she would pay these prices for so much attention.

Charles had been too busy hunting through the racks to notice the kiss. He handed Odette a complex tangle of tubular rubber.

'See what you can do with that.'

It took quite a while and much laughter to work out where arms and legs and head fitted. As the outfit was finally being drawn over Giselle's head, there was a shout from the studio, a man's voice. Charles opened the door and greeted the newcomer as Gustave. He was a large man with a round belly and full beard. When he stood in the door and gazed in, his frame filled the opening. Both men gazed at Giselle as the costume was fitted. It formed a tunic that encased her torso in a mesh of tubes but left her belly and legs bare. Her arms were fully enclosed in a shining black film. Her hands were encased in gloves that resembled the old-fashioned

119

silken mesh affairs that Edwardian women wore, except that, like every other part of the costume, they were made of black rubber. There was a helmet that fitted over her head with fine filigree rubberwork concealing her features but allowing her to see and breath.

It was as exposing and erotic as the catsuit. It offered her lower, sexual parts while eliminating her individuality. Charles saw the meaning immediately.

'Ideal for anonymous sex,' he said with a smile, teasing Giselle again with what they had already shared at the Labyrinth. 'It's impossible to look without wanting to touch.'

Giselle turned to the mirror. The organic, alien quality of the tubing clung to her top half while its blackness and industrial scent highlighted the whiteness and smoothness of her belly and legs. The clearly defined opening of her shaven sex drew the eye as the only symmetry to the intricate meshes and openings of her upper half. She was a chimera, made for penetration. The outfit cried out for the viewer to abuse and plunder a creature who was sexual but not entirely human.

'That I could use,' said the stranger, stepping forward and stroking the convoluted skin of rubber. 'That is filmic. Give me a dozen girls in outfits like this and I will make you a masterpiece.'

Charles introduced the girls to the stranger one by one. Odette he seemed to know already. Nana he clearly wanted to know. When he came to Giselle, his eyes wandered over her half-naked body with a mischievous pleasure. Then, bowing slightly, he took her rubber-meshed hand and kissed it with an old-world courtliness.

'Charles was right when he said that you were made for the lens,' he told her. She guessed that he was a film-maker. She guessed that the films he made were far from mainstream.

120

'What do you think of her, Nana?' Charles asked as Gustave continued to hold the outstretched hand.

Giselle turned to her sister. Safe within the rubber armour, beyond the reach of awkwardness or embarrassment, she was curious too. Nana looked her up and down, her eyes nervously avoiding the exposed sex at first but then going to it and lingering.

'Sexy,' she said and laughed nervously.

Charles reached out and stroked her chin.

'Would you wear it?'

She shrugged.

'Maybe.'

'If I asked you?'

'Maybe.'

Charles laughed.

They chose three more outfits – including a man's three-piece suit in grey latex. It was this that Charles decided to shoot first. As Giselle pulled on the shirt, Charles went into the studio to finalise the set with Nana's help. Gustave watched as Giselle struggled with the latex waistcoat and trousers. Odette had to knot the tie for her then set about the business of matching make-up to outfit as Giselle slid on the jacket. In the mirror, Giselle saw herself as a washed-out soul imprisoned in a shapeless grey suit. Yet, as the make-up was applied, the meanings were rearranged. Odette chose colours that brightened her face and made it simultaneously more feminine. The grey of the man's suit no longer drained her energy but served as a cool frame for her bright beauty. Gustave watched the process in fascination until Charles called for him from the studio.

'Do you know him?' Giselle asked, as soon as Gustave had disappeared.

'Oh yes, I've worked for him.'

'What does he do?'

'He's a pornographer – stills, movies, live shows

121

sometimes. Very arty. Very perverse. Sells direct to the high and mighty. They say that he has a clientele that rules half of the Western world.'

A sickly sensation filled the pit of Giselle's stomach. 'Why is he here?'

'Do you mean is he here for you? Or Nana? Or simply the costumes?'

Giselle didn't reply. She remembered Charles saying that Nana didn't have the look for a top model but that she could still have a career. The sudden conjugation of people, the predators who surrounded her sister, was unsettling.

Odette finally finished the make-up and led Giselle into the studio. Charles had removed the dust sheets to reveal a set composed of huge mirrors and lenses. There were also smooth, white plastic forms of varying sizes that could be arranged to suggest a variety of scenarios. The lenses were huge curved blocks of acrylic, taller than a man. As Giselle crossed to the set, she could see objects behind these blocks being magnified or reduced dramatically, as if she had fallen into the world of Alice and the White Rabbit. Some mirrors stretched or compressed while others reflected true; the most disorientating shifted the colour spectrum of reflected objects and gave ghostly auras to those who were caught in them.

Odette had given Giselle a wig of shining, obviously artificial, red hair, cut short and hanging just above her shoulders, further heightening the discrepancy of suit and flesh. As she walked, the latex clung to various parts of her body, revealing them clearly, then releasing them as she moved on. Her thighs and breasts pushed through the thin film alternately, drawing the eye across her frame, demanding that more be shown. Charles had her stand in the set while he played with the lighting at the console. She passed her hand behind one of the lenses and watched it shrink. Stepping before a mirror, she became a grey and slender spider with impossibly long limbs and a tiny head. She laughed and Nana came over and pressed her face to the surface of one of the lenses. Giselle saw her expand so that her eyes were as large as dinner plates.

'Scary?' Nana asked.

'Scary,' Giselle agreed, laughing again.

They had fun together and it reminded Giselle of once taking the tiny Nana to a fair in Avignon and how she had run off and been lost in the Hall of Mirrors, scaring herself for real.

Charles looked at them together and called Nana over. Giselle saw them talking and then Nana going to Odette. The woman took her into the dressing room while Charles hauled reflectors into place and arranged the plastic forms into the shapes that he wanted.

Gustave had taken one of the directors' chairs that fronted the set and watched patiently.

It wasn't long before Nana returned. With a shock, Giselle saw that she was wearing one of the latex outfits. It mimicked an American cheerleader's dress – blue and gold bodice and a white frilled skirt that projected from the hips – but all in latex.

There was no doubting that Nana looked good – the costume showed off her well-made thighs and calves and the apparent innocence wrapped her sweetness like a ribbon. She smiled shyly at Giselle as she stepped into the lights. There was no make-up and Giselle guessed that Charles would do with Nana what he had done with her at the beginning – use only her body.

Charles had arranged a low staging of boxes and told Nana to lie across them. Her head hung over the side and her long blonde hair fell to the ground. He had her with one leg bent and raised, the other full length on the smooth surface. She looked innocent and tempting but as surreal as Giselle in the latex. Charles made Giselle gaze pensively at the prone girl as if she had discovered

123

her sleeping. The camera clicked rapidly as Giselle slipped into her role. It was the first time that she had been obliged to look at her sister as a sexual object. The fantasies of the previous night were acquiring a fleshy, threatening reality. Giselle examined the full, curved thighs as dispassionately as she could. She noted how the gold and blue of the bodice heightened the tanning of Nana's skin. Then, something shifted in her mind, and Giselle felt as if she were looking through Charles's eyes. There was a shocking urge to run her hand beneath the dead rubber of the dress and find her sister's living membranes. Her heart stopped and blood rushed to her head. She stepped abruptly back as if she had been burnt.

'I don't want to do this,' she told Charles.

'Why not?'

She wouldn't tell him but he guessed and drew her aside.

'If you've only just noticed that Nana is a sexy girl then you've been doing her a disservice for quite a while,' he told her in a low voice. 'Handle it now, and quickly. I haven't the time and patience to see the shoot ruined.'

She saw how determined he was and knew also that he was right. Nana was no longer a child, and she must handle these new feelings towards her. No one would handle them for her.

After a moment she returned to her place. Nana was looking at her curiously and Giselle smiled self-consciously.

'It's OK,' she said, 'I'm being foolish.'

Nana lay down again and Charles picked up the camera that he'd been using. He took a few shots then had Giselle stand in front of the mirror which stretched and thinned. She realised that he must have seen her playing with the reflected image earlier. She became the man-spider that stalked the young girl's innocence. Charles took a range of shots then told Odette to work on Nana's face. The girl sat up and Odette laid out the instruments of her art beside her. Charles and Giselle sat with Gustave and watched.

'Do you have plans for her?' Gustave asked in a low voice but not so low that Giselle couldn't hear.

'Not especially. She doesn't really suit my material. I just like having her around.'

Odette was applying a dark eyeliner that gave Nana's face a new sharpness. The innocence was fading away; something else was being born.

'I might be able to use her,' Gustave told him.

'I wouldn't object. I might ask a favour in return – Katarina perhaps?'

Charles glanced at Giselle. She regarded him with a shocked expression as he bartered away her sister for an unknown woman.

'Has she any serious hang-ups?' Gustave continued.

'I don't know; she's still a virgin.'

It was Gustave's turn to look shocked.

'Really?'

'Everything but her mouth.'

'How long will she stay a virgin?'

Charles shrugged.

'I'm taking her to China with me soon. I think travel will broaden her.'

'Stretch her, you mean?'

The two men laughed. Giselle had heard enough and rose, but Charles seized her wrist and pulled her back.

'Sit,' he said. 'She's mine; you have already agreed,'

'She is still my sister and she is too young for this!' hissed Giselle.

'It's what she thinks that matters. If she says no to anything that I ask, then I will respect that. So far she hasn't refused anything.'

Seeing the ferocity in his face Giselle sat heavily.

'Her legs are shining,' Charles called to Odette, his voice calm again and entirely reasonable.

Odette dutifully began to apply powder to Nana's calves and knees.

'Is that OK?' Odette asked after a moment.

'I'll want some shots with the dress raised,' he replied.

Odette seemed to guess immediately that they had passed from business to pleasure. She, who so often tried to thwart Charles's power games, seemed more than ready to play along this time. Perhaps Nana had upset her, or maybe it was a way of revenging herself on Giselle for refusing her offer of refuge.

She told Nana to turn over, then pulled the dress up to reveal the strongly made thighs and behind. White latex, provocatively taut, hid her flanks.

'Can we see more?' Gustave asked.

'Make sure that you do the inside of her thighs,' Charles called.

Odette smiled at the two men then touched Nana's legs to indicate that she should open them. Slowly, the golden columns parted and the inner thighs glowed in the lights. The powdering of these sensitive areas took a long while. The mound of her sex was a tight, alluring dome between the wide-flung thighs and Nana wriggled when the powder puff stroked her there, lightly, as if by accident.

'More?' Gustave asked.

'Everything – in due time – if you agree to lend me Katarina.'

Gustave looked at Nana carefully then, after a few moments, agreed.

Giselle went to speak, and would have protested, but Charles rose abruptly and went over to the set, beckoning Giselle to follow. He crouched in front of Nana and she raised herself on her arms to look at him. She smiled, not realising that she had already been bartered for another. Her back arched, displaying the youthful muscles and sinews. She yawned and stretched as if she were rising from her own bed. Giselle was

126

surprised at the evident ease, as if the girl were born to this strange environment. With an effort, Giselle set aside the indignation that she felt towards Charles. She would let matters run, see how far Nana would fit herself to Charles's world.

'We need to do more with your face,' Charles said, then called Odette again. The woman came with brushes and powders, glosses and sticks of colour.

Giselle could only watch as her sister was prepared like a bird being plucked and stuffed for the table.

'Gustave is a man who can help you if you want a career in films,' Charles said to Nana quietly. 'Let me help you make an impression, OK?'

Nana nodded. Her simple trust almost broke Giselle's heart.

Charles reached down and lifted one side of the latex pants, stretched it away from her skin, then let it settle into the valley between her cheeks.

'Sexy,' he said. She giggled.

Sprawled as she was, with her legs splayed and one side of her bottom bared, she looked to Giselle like the unselfconscious child she herself had been in Avignon, once. When Odette had finished, and Nana turned around, the illusion was undermined entirely. Her face had been powdered and rouged into a caricature of a whore. The cheerleader outfit was entirely transformed, becoming decadent, degraded somehow, but also arousing. Nana glanced at herself in one of the mirrors and Giselle saw a jolt pass through her body as she saw what had been done.

Charles evidently saw the surprise too. He told her to let go, to slip into the role, to play with it. He had her strike various provocative poses and gradually the self-consciousness eased.

'How do you feel?' Charles asked.

'Cheap,' she said wickedly.

'Cheap and dirty and used?'

'Not used, not yet.'

Giselle looked at her sister in astonishment. She was leaning against the mirror, one foot raised and flat against its surface, her head to one side, eyes smouldering into Charles's. The role had enveloped her and now the virgin hooker was angling for her first John.

'OK. The scenario,' Charles told them. 'We're in a seedy dock area. You're the streetwalker, Nana, Giselle is the man on the prowl. Nana, you have to sell him on your charms. Use everything, OK?'

Nana glanced at Giselle uncertainly. Giselle shook her head, a tiny movement that escaped Charles. If anything, this signal seemed to strengthen Nana's resolve. She stood up straight and nodded.

Charles walked quickly to the lighting console. He dropped the main beams and brought up spots that lit the set at intervals, leaving deep shadows between. It was obvious that it was now night and there were only infrequent street lights.

They started with Nana in the pose that she had adopted for herself – the pose of the bored whore leaning against a wall. One of the spots lit her from directly above so that her blonde hair blazed and her costume – the only colour in the set excepting Giselle's vivid crimson hair – gleamed. Giselle was a figure glimpsed in the distance. Charles directed her from behind the array of cameras; her walk was laconic but her eyes were alert. As she walked slowly through the maze of mirrors, she underwent a series of transformations. Each step in the yielding suit heightened a different part of her body, delineated a thigh, thrust forward a breast. The lenses magnified or reduced, the mirrors repeated her image, strangely modified, and showed the narrow waist stretched and her hands as large as her head. There was the feeling of a dark dream where nothing is what it seems, where good becomes evil and evil is purified. Stage objects took new lives on to themselves. Mirrors became openings, the plastic forms became motor cars in a deserted backstreet. As Giselle approached Nana, the girl stood with legs akimbo and hands on hips. Her pelvis came forward and rotated teasingly. For a moment, Giselle forgot that this was her sister. Within the latex skin, daubed in the colours of the whore, it could have been any young girl. Simultaneously, the suit made Giselle forget that she was a woman; the drama took her and she became masculine, a predator, a creature of power. The transformation sent a thrill of desire through her body. It showed in her eyes and Nana responded, lifting one side of the dress to her waist, jutting the exposed leg forward.

The willingness of Nana to prostitute herself made Giselle want to prostitute her. She had an urge to humiliate her before the eyes of the men. She was discovering that something of Xavier had seeped into her. Elements of his cruelty had filtered into her soul and now they were surfacing. She halted for a moment when she was directly opposite the girl and looked at her carefully, examining her from head to toe. When she made to move on, Nana reached out and took her arm.

'Wrap yourself around him,' Charles said, further redefining Giselle's gender and reinforcing the metamorphosis.

Nana complied, encircling Giselle's waist with her arm, rubbing her breasts across her sister's side.

'Take his balls.'

Giselle was shocked and stirred as her sister's hand enfolded her pubis and her lips slid down her neck.

'Sink to the ground,' Charles told Nana, shooting all the time.

Nana slipped downwards, her hands drawing slowly down Giselle's legs.

'More contempt, Giselle,' Charles called.

Giselle narrowed her eyes and stared coolly at the

kneeling Nana. The girl leant back on one arm and ran her hand across her breasts. Her tongue glossed her reddened lips in the standard form of the coquette. Her pelvis raised itself, drawing attention to the domed belly and the opened thighs. Giselle saw that Charles hadn't been idle in educating her sister, that he was already transforming her as he said he would. There was a sense of Nana becoming the thing that Charles wanted before her very eyes.

'Pull open the bodice.'

Nana looked hesitant but the dynamic was already too strong. She pulled open the bodice to reveal the soft upper slopes of her breasts. Looking Giselle defiantly in the eye, she pulled further until one breast was exposed completely. There was a competitive quality in Nana's gaze, a challenge. She seemed to be saying, anything you can do, I can do better.

'OK, you're interested, Giselle. Touch her. Sample the goods,' Charles called.

Giselle leant down, a hardness in her, the rivalry of sisterhood replacing the care. Her hand took the perfect breast, weighed it and squeezed it. Her fingers pinched the nipple lightly and Nana sighed – a genuine sigh, profound and pregnant with desire. Her eyes became heavy and Giselle knew how excited she was. She remembered their brother, how he had come for her in the night. If he had lived, he would have gone to Nana as well. And now, Giselle discovered that Jean had left his imprint as much as Xavier had. She felt his desire for kindred flesh, the pleasure and cruelty of corrupting that intimate bond. She ran her hand inside the clinging bodice and exposed the other breast. She caressed it and felt the savage joy of arousing her sister for the satisfaction of voyeurs. Nana leant back on both arms, leaving herself defenceless, raising her pelvis higher, provoking and daring further outrages. Giselle let her fingers trail downwards. She had been touched between the legs and now she would touch. Her sister's sex was hot beneath the skirt; the latex slipped beneath her fingers and she knew that Nana was also wet – flooded.

'OK, Giselle, you're sold. Take her hand, let her lead you to her room.'

The room was no more than an enclosure of tall mirrors. A rectangular arrangement of boxes formed a low platform that suggested a bed. The light was a lurid red, tawdry but seductive. Nana's hair turned from blonde to pink.

Setting aside his camera for a moment, Charles took his wallet from his pocket and plucked out a bundle of thousand-franc notes. With a smile he tucked them into the breast pocket of Giselle's suit, leaving the edges exposed.

The break had left the two sister's awkward again. The roles had slipped away. Charles pushed one of the smaller plastic forms against a mirror.

'That's a sink,' he told Nana. 'You need to wash.'

Nana walked over to the box and began to go through the motions of washing her face.

'No. Not like that. You're a whore: this is your client. He wants to see you wash between your legs. He wants to be sure that you are clean for him.'

Nana flushed.

'Do I take off my pants?'

Giselle prayed that Charles would say no. Embarrassment for her sister's sake was making her burn from head to toe.

'OK.'

Nana looked awkward for a moment but then reached under her skirt and hooked her fingers around the waistband of her pants. Watching the slow unrobing, sensing the vulnerability of Nana as the white pants edged past her knees, Giselle found herself slipping back into role. There was an irresistible urge to go to the girl, seize her, drag her to the bed by her hair

131

and sink sharp teeth into her shoulders – to lay waste that marvellous flesh.

The feelings only intensified as Nana opened her legs and squatted a little, to feign the washing of her sex. She kept her head down as she did this but Charles made her look into the camera. In the mirrors, Giselle could see her flushed face in profile. A wash of shame passed through Giselle as she witnessed her sister's distress. Now, the urge was to comfort and protect, but she held steady, reminding herself that Nana had chosen this and could refuse it if she wished.

All protective feelings faded when Charles set aside the camera and kissed Nana. Giselle saw the look on her face as he touched her – the desire, the intensity and focus of her eyes. Giselle remembered how Charles had kissed her in front of Mimi and now experienced the sharpness of that betrayal from the other side. That it was Nana who had taken Charles only made the insult sharper. Nana was no longer the innocent; she was the seductress.

As Charles returned to his camera, Nana glanced at Giselle. The vulnerability was still there but there was also triumph. She had her prize and wanted Giselle to know it. The sisters were children again, fighting over a toy.

The toy told Nana to go to the bed. The girl perched on the edge as Giselle came to stand before her.

'Reach up, Nana. Take the money from her pocket with your teeth. Look her in the eye.'

Giselle allowed her sister to pull the notes from her breast pocket like a dog. Charles shot from behind the girl, catching her naked behind beneath the short dress as she half rose from the make-believe bed. It was unbearably provocative for Giselle – the pouting lips of her sister, the warm, sweet breath, the eyes, lustrous and taunting. Unable to help herself, Giselle took control. She pulled her sister into an embrace and taking the

132

hem of the skirt pulled it high, exposing her behind fully to Charles and the man who watched from the chairs.

'If you like these games so much, little sister, let's play them for real,' she whispered fiercely. Her hand cupped Nana's behind and squeezed. She had expected Nana to struggle but the girl melted into the embrace and allowed these liberties as if they were natural. It was only when Nana glanced over her shoulder at Charles that Giselle understood the easy consent. She was still angling for the man who had bartered her away. Giselle was helping as she exposed and mauled the alluring flesh.

'Did you do these things with Jean?' Nana whispered when she turned back to her sister.

A rage that Nana could ask such a thing seized Giselle, but she controlled it and directed the fierceness into her voice and eyes.

'He did them with me. To me. Shall I show you?'

Nana's eyes smouldered. For the first time, Giselle realised that Nana was jealous and aroused rather than shocked by the revelation that she had had sex with their brother.

She turned Nana around and wrapped an arm about her waist. Giselle's lips and teeth were quick as they nipped a path down the fair skin of her sister's neck. Her free hand raised the skirt again and this time cupped the hot sex. Charles stopped shooting for a moment, frozen where he stood. Giselle's sudden aggression was obviously unexpected and she enjoyed seeing his eyes widen and jaw drop. After a moment he started shooting again, more quickly than before, hungrily taking everything that she gave him.

Giselle pushed Nana to the bed. The girl sprawled there like a lazy cat waiting to be petted.

'He liked me to excite myself first,' Giselle said, her voice challenging. 'He was too lazy to make me wet himself.'

133

Nana reached under the dress and began to caress herself. Giselle saw her sister's sex for the first time since she was a girl. The pubic hair had been carefully shaven, rendering the lips naked but leaving a splash of blonde above. This would have been a request or order from Charles, Giselle guessed, part of the lovers' game. As Giselle stared, Nana opened her legs wider and pulled the dress higher. The two sisters glared at each other as each dared the other on.

'He liked me to get both openings ready.'

Nana hesitated. Perhaps in her innocence she had never thought that a boy might want to take a girl's anus. It was a moment before her fingers slipped downwards and circled the tighter opening.

Giselle watched with a mounting madness of desire. She remembered the many times she had done the same things for Jean, remembered the fear of discovery and the overwhelming excitement of it all in the dark, quiet house. With an effort, she put those images aside and took her sister's hand, raising it to her lips. She bestowed a series of fleeting kisses, licked the sweet, clear mucus and became intoxicated again. She pushed the girl flat to the make-believe bed and knelt astride her. Looking down, she began to undo the rubber belt that held the grey latex trousers in place. She felt for all the world like a man and expected to find an erect sex between her legs. The delusion was so complete that she already saw Nana writhing beneath her thrusts.

Then, suddenly, a sound from off set caught her attention. Gustave had risen from his chair and was moving closer, stealthily. The illusion of the role play collapsed. She was not a man; the girl beneath her was not a whore. It was Nana, her sister, and she deserved protection not these outrages. Giselle felt her rage swing to the men who preyed on Nana's innocence.

'That's it,' she said to Charles. 'You've had enough.'

Charles looked at her in surprise.

134

'I need a few shots with the Hasselblad,' he told her, swinging the large black camera on its tripod.

'If you want this shoot, then shoot me. If you want to shoot Nana, then you can shoot her on her own!'

Charles stood up slowly and walked over to the defiant Giselle.

His hand reached for her face. She expected to be slapped. She had seen him slap girls often enough before. But there was only a soft caress from cheek to chin.

'If anyone went too far, you did,' he said quietly. 'Remember that. If anything happens that shouldn't happen, it was because you have paved the way.'

Her heart sank. He was right; she couldn't escape her complicity. Even so, her defiance didn't fade. For now it was over, she had pulled back from the brink. They gazed at each other for a moment, then Charles turned to Nana.

'I think you have a career, if you want it.' he said with a smile. 'But humour your sister for now. Get dressed and fetch us another coffee.'

Nana was gazing at them from the bed, obviously bewildered. After a moment, she shook herself as if trying to wake from a dream, the dream that Charles and Giselle had constructed for her. With an effort, she pulled herself upright and looked long and hard at Giselle.

'I'm more than just your baby sister,' she said carefully. 'And you aren't in charge here, Charles is. I'll go because he wants it.'

Giselle watched in astonishment as Nana rose and walked with careful dignity to the dressing room.

It was well into evening by the time all the costumes had been photographed. As soon as Charles declared an end to the shoot, Giselle headed for the shower. The hot water eased away the tension of so many straining poses. The soap cleansed the make-up, if not the guilt of what she had done with Nana.

135

When she came out of the shower, she saw Nana standing in a fur coat, talking intently with Gustave. The coat was unfamiliar and must have been a gift from Charles. The long, light fur floated about Nana like the coat of a husky, giving her an old-fashioned Hollywood glamour. Giselle watched as Gustave touched Nana's sleeve from time to time and moved closer to press whatever case he was making. Giselle was tempted to intervene but forced herself to leave it and hurried into the dressing room. She wanted to get home. She wanted to get Nana home so that they could talk. She wanted to make sure that what had happened earlier would never happen again.

Charles drove them in silence. Lyle, Greta's young lover, was just leaving as they turned into the driveway and Greta was at the door seeing him off. She waved as Charles drew up at the steps and let the two girls out before parking at the side of the house. Lyle hurried away in embarrassment as Greta gave each of the girls a hug.

'Is that real fur?' Greta asked, stroking the coat that still enveloped Nana. 'I don't approve of real fur, you know.'

Nana shook her head. 'Odette lent it me, she said it was . . . I can't remember, but it wasn't an animal.'

A moment later, Charles bounded up the steps and, kissing his wife on the cheek, swept them all inside.

Nana looked awkward as Giselle took off her coat. Greta offered Nana help with hers but Nana shook her head. Charles was smiling.

'Is there something that I don't understand?' Greta asked.

'You have to take it off sometime,' Charles told the girl.

Greta could contain her curiosity no longer and pulled the coat from Nana's shoulders. As she did,

Nana blushed more deeply than Giselle had ever seen. Beneath the fur was the corset that Giselle had tried on in the dressing room. As the coat parted and was pulled away it revealed the complete nakedness of Nana below the waist.

'Mie, mie,' said Greta softly. 'Now *that* is a show-stopper.'

The mesh of tubular rubber was as striking on Nana as it had been on Giselle. Greta ran her fingers across the complex networks of rubber as she walked around the blushing girl.

'Takitsua must be a very disturbed individual,' she said softly.

Charles laughed.

'Let me show you something.'

He stepped forward and told Nana to put her arms behind her back. When she did, he pressed her forearms together and secured them by a series of hooks and eyes that Giselle hadn't noticed in the labyrinthine construction. When the last hook had been slipped home, Nana was unable to move her arms at all. She looked at Giselle pitifully but Giselle felt only the eroticism of the creation before her. That creation became even less her sister as Charles slipped the helmet over her head and attached it to the neckpiece of the tunic.

In the elegant, palatial hall, no other clothing could have been so arresting. The girl, bared below the waist, bound, defenceless, her black rubber prison gleaming in the light of the candelabras, stood as still as a statue except for the rapid rise and fall of her chest.

Charles slapped her behind, a sharp rap that ricocheted across the hard marble surfaces.

'Go to your room. Wait for me,' he told the creature.

It was a moment before there was any movement. Then they watched as Nana slowly moved to the stairs and ascended with the graceful gravity of a marquessa.

As she reached the top, she turned and looked back,

affording them a view of her long thighs and the blonde smudge of her pubic hair.

Giselle, seeing all that beauty, all that willingness, wondered how Charles could wait, how he could watch Nana disappear to her bedroom and then lead her and Greta into the drawing room.

She watched in even greater astonishment as he poured drinks for them all and proposed a toast.

'To virginity.'

Greta laughed and seconded the toast. Giselle remained stony-faced, the glass motionless in her hands.

Setting down his drink, Charles rang for Marie and, when the girl arrived, he asked when dinner would be.

'An hour, Monsieur.'

'Mademoiselle Nana is in her room. Will you take a plate for her when it's ready?'

'Of course, Monsieur.'

'She will need to be fed.'

The girl looked puzzled.

'Is that a problem?' he asked.

'No, Monsieur.'

The girl turned and left.

'So the Takitsua was a success?' Greta asked.

'Very striking pieces – as you saw. Giselle was excellent. She has a side that I didn't realise existed, something predatory, exciting.'

'My sister –' Giselle began.

'Is waiting of her own volition,' Charles said sharply, interrupting her.

'It is inhuman.'

'Have you never waited for a man?'

Giselle had waited for men and boys. Many times. She had waited for Xavier on the island and often she had been tied. She had waited for Jean to come to her bed in the night and take her while her father slept in the next room.

'I don't want her to get used to waiting. I don't want her to have a life of waiting.'

138

'She is losing her virginity tonight. Her wait is a vigil. Let her savour it. And let me make it something that she will never forget.'

Giselle collapsed into silence.

'But this side of Giselle that you had never seen before . . .' said Greta curiously, returning to the earlier conversation.

Giselle felt awkward. It was something that she didn't want to discuss.

'I think that she is as interested in her sister as I am,' Charles said slowly.

'No, that's not it!'

Giselle rose from her seat and would have fled the room if Charles hadn't seized her by the wrist and pulled her on to one of the sofas.

'Then tell us,' he demanded.

Giselle looked from Charles to Greta with the air of a trapped animal. Greta showed the same interest and compassion that she always showed. Charles looped his arm around her waist and squeezed reassuringly. Looking at him, she recognised the manager of human feelings, the part of him that could make a girl do anything in front of a camera.

'I want to tell you . . .' she began, but then gave up. To tell anything of what she had felt with Nana on the set, meant to tell all. It was the same dilemma that she had with Nana, the dilemma that she had with everyone. The past held her prisoner; her young self was its hostage. She was blackmailed by history with crimes she had only committed for the sake of love.

'Is it something very difficult?' Greta asked. 'Something to do with your family?'

Giselle looked at her suspiciously. To be understood, to be known – this tempted but also frightened her.

'Tell us a little,' Greta suggested. 'An easy part.'

Giselle sighed.

'My brother . . .' she began, then stopped. Even in her

139

own mind, the memories would begin, then stop abruptly. To speak them aloud seemed impossible.

'Your brother?' asked Greta.

'He . . .'

'You had sex?'

Greta had spoken the shocking for her. To hear the fact, stated in a voice that neither trembled nor condemned, strengthened her. But even Greta's steady, all-forgiving gaze didn't exonerate her.

'Is that so very bad?' Greta asked after a moment.

'Yes,' said Giselle simply, shame colouring her face.

Greta rose from her seat and knelt before Giselle.

'Why is it so bad? Did he hurt you?'

Giselle shook her head.

'Then you liked what he did?'

That was it. She had liked what he did. Every touch beneath the bedclothes, every kiss, every erection that her mouth devoured, every drop of his seed that she had swallowed, she had wanted. The power of that wanting, remembered now, made her dizzy. The irredeemable wrongness of wanting her sex filled by her brother clouded her mind and paralysed all thought.

'And now, when you see your sister, it all comes back?' Greta asked softly.

Giselle burst into tears. 'Yes. Everything. All at once.'

Greta sighed, took Giselle's head and pulled it to her breast.

'You must tell us what happened. It will help you.'

'She did more than remember,' Charles said. 'She acted it out.'

Giselle turned to him. Through the mist of tears she saw his smile. It was as reassuring as Greta's in its way but it said something quite different. There would be no condemnation from him either. But, unlike Greta, he would use what he knew. Everything that she said would be used to fuel his pleasure both with Nana and with her. This knowledge ran like fire down her spine

140

and exploded in her belly. She had opened everything to him now. It wasn't just her sex and anus and mouth that he would want to plunder in future. It was that nexus of nerves and memories that ran to her very core, to innocence lost and deeper still, to the most primal desires. She was lost and the eroticism of being lost, the excitement of being so completely naked before him, made every tissue of body and mind burn.

Greta seemed to sense this. She clearly saw Charles's cruelty in the same instant.

'If Charles ever hurts you, I will leave him,' she said icily.

'I take my pleasure as I like,' he replied quickly. 'But I will not hurt her any more than she wants to be hurt.'

Giselle looked from one to the other in bewilderment. She wanted Greta's softness as she had never wanted another's softness. She wanted her protection and love as much as she wanted Charles's ruthlessness. She wanted to be torn by him while Greta held her in warm enfolding arms. It was too much. Too confusing. She ripped herself from their embrace and curled into a ball. They left her to sob. Charles fetched another drink while Greta sat on the sofa with a hand on Giselle's hip. Nothing was said until the tears had subsided.

When she felt a little better, Giselle sat up slowly.

'I will tell you,' she said. 'Everything. I want to. But give me time. I need time.'

'There is all the time in the world,' said Greta softly.

As the two women sealed this compact with their eyes, there was a knock at the door. It was Marie. Dinner was ready.

'But let me take Nana her dinner. I don't want a stranger to see her.'

Charles shrugged.

'As you wish.'

* * *

Five minutes later, Giselle pushed open the door to Nana's room. The creature on the bed turned quickly. If the mask was mute and expressionless, the hands that twisted in an effort to escape the bonds were not. Giselle took a step back in sudden panic. She was not welcome. It hadn't occurred to her that she wouldn't be welcome.

'I brought your dinner,' she said after a moment, holding up the tray that she carried. 'Can I come in?'

The mask turned away from her. The hands became still. There was at least an acquiescence and Giselle crossed to the bed. After setting the tray on the bedside table, she sat beside her sister.

'Charles said that I could remove the mask but that I must leave your arms bound. Is that OK?'

The mask nodded. Giselle knelt on the mattress and told Nana to sit up. It wasn't easy to locate the series of tiny press studs that secured the neckpiece but once she had, Giselle quickly undid them and pulled the helmet clear. Nana wouldn't look at her but sat with head bowed.

'You look marvellous,' Giselle said in an effort to reassure the girl.

'Why did he send you?' she asked.

'He was going to send Marie but I didn't want a stranger to come. I . . .' she halted, wondering why it had seemed so important for her to do this. 'I wanted it to be someone who loved you,' she said after a moment.

'A stranger would have been easier. I wouldn't have to explain anything. I don't want to explain anything.'

'Then pretend that I am a stranger. Say nothing. Just let me feed you.'

Nana turned and looked into Giselle's eyes. The gaze was intent, as if she needed to read every thought, every feeling.

'I want him so much,' she said. 'Do you understand that?'

'Of course.'

'I will do anything that he wants. I will wait like this for ever if he wants me to.'

Giselle nodded. She understood that feeling. She had wanted to give Xavier everything and, the more he took, the more imperative it was to give.

'We aren't rivals,' Giselle told her.

'But you want him too.'

'Maybe. But not as you do.'

'Then how?'

'He reminds me of somebody. A boy – a man that I knew.'

'Jean?'

'Someone else.'

'Tell me.'

Giselle shook her head.

'Another time. Your dinner is getting cold.'

'I'm not hungry.'

Giselle laughed. 'If you are to wait for ever, you must eat. And I have been ordered to feed you.'

She reached for the tray and set it in Nana's lap. The edge pressed into the soft flesh of her belly, indenting a neat, straight line. The coolness of the metal against her naked thighs made her jump.

'Careful. That outfit probably cost more than we have earned today.'

Lifting aside the silver cover, Giselle revealed a plate of pasta and mushrooms in a cream sauce. The scent of it made her hungry and she took a fork and sampled the mushrooms.

'It's very good. We could share it.'

Nana nodded. 'If we can share Charles.'

Giselle sighed. Any thoughts of warning Nana away from Charles finally evaporated. The strength of Nana's desire, the relentlessness of it, made all thoughts of interfering impossible. But that didn't mean that she couldn't send her to him with eyes open.

143

'You will have him. Or, more accurately, he will have you.'

'That is what I want.'

'Do you know what it means to be a man's property? To always be ready to give him exactly what he wants? That is what Charles will want. You do understand that?'

'I think so. This week – it was something so different. With our father there was only endless struggle. I don't want to struggle. I want to give in. I want . . .' Nana shrugged. 'I want to let go. I want to slide. I want to be carried . . .'

Giselle laughed.

'You have it bad. Love is a demon.'

Giselle realised that she was quoting from what Xavier had said. Love is the incubus that comes into your bed, he had told her. She sucks the heart from your chest and the seed from your sex. She is the enemy of peace, the destroyer of order. If she is not satisfied that you have given everything, she becomes an angel of despair. And, while she is the only reason for living, she is crueller than hatred, more destructive than war.

Giselle glanced at the smooth skin of her sister's belly and knew that Charles would soon enter there. He would be a storm inside the softness of the girl. She would break and he would leave her unmended, so that she would always need him. The more that she tried to heal herself in his arms, the more he would render her incurable. It had already happened to Giselle. Now she would be a party to her sister's destruction and to the birth of a new, endless hunger.

They ate in silence for a while. Giselle apportioned the food with the greatest fairness, as if the meal was the man that they both wanted. From time to time, she took the napkin and wiped the corners of her sister's mouth. Twice she kissed her forehead because she couldn't help it. Love for a sister was quite different to love for a man.

If it couldn't protect it could at least understand, forgive and redeem.

Giselle didn't sleep that night. The image of her sister climbing the stairs, her lovely behind bared, her waist and torso cinched tight in the embrace of the corset, preyed on her mind. She had fed Nana, then left her for Charles, her sexual parts exposed and offered. She imagined the tenderness within the hard rubber, the oyster softness within the black carapace. She knew too well the cruelty that such clothing would provoke in Charles. She tried to resist both the panic and the desire that these images produced. She tried to convince herself that she had been right to decide that Nana was old enough to take care of herself and no longer needed protection. She reminded herself of Nana's determination to belong to Charles.

At a little after three o'clock, the door to her bedroom opened as Giselle knew that it would. She sat up on her elbows as the figure moved through the darkness. There was a click and then a flood of light from the bedside lamp. Giselle closed her eyes abruptly against the shock. When she opened them again, she saw Charles towering above her. There was something wild in his eyes and in the disarrangement of his hair. Looking down his naked body, she saw the blood on his half-erect sex. It was Nana's blood, a flower of dark red-brown that matted his pubic hair, that brought her to full wakefulness. She sat up abruptly and wanted to touch, as if she could hardly believe what he had done.

He sat on the edge of the bed and looked at her intently.

'I've discovered her special talent,' he said, reaching for her chin and drawing her to his lap. His sex grew to full erection as he pressed her lips towards it.

'Taste her,' he said.

She saw the wildness in his eyes again. Knowing that

145

it was inevitable, she knelt up so that she could suck him. The blood tasted of iron. She used her tongue to search through the folds of his balls. She reached beneath and laved the bulging root.

'Is she okay?' Giselle asked thickly, her mouth still full of him.

He ignored the question, took her head and began to fuck her mouth with a steady motion.

'She's mine now,' he told her after a while. 'In a way that you could never be.'

His sex nudged at the back of her throat and, with an effort, she opened to him. His pubic bone came to rest against her lips. He moved only slightly, the head of his sex deep in the tightness of her throat.

'She tries very hard but her mouth doesn't compete with yours,' he told her, pushing harder.

He groaned as she opened her mouth wide to allow her tongue to delve between his balls. She swallowed quickly, three times in succession, so that he could feel the muscular waves caressing him. 'Tighter than her virgin cunt,' he murmured.

The final contraction triggered his orgasm and she began to swallow rythmically as the semen flowed, a series of contractions that milked him without any effort on his part. When she was sure that every drop of seed had issued forth, she withdrew and looked up. He looked drained, exhausted.

'Greta said that I should send you to Nana. Will you go?'

'If she wants me.'

'I was rough with her. She needs someone to wipe away the tears.'

Giselle, suddenly anxious, sat up quickly and began to pull on her pyjama bottoms. Charles took them from her. He collapsed into the soft mattress and used the silk to wipe himself. It was a gesture of contempt, not just for her but for all things feminine. A flaring anger

146

stirred Giselle and made her hurry. She went as she was, naked below the jacket, her wet sex making the inside of her thighs gleam.

The door to Nana's room was open and Giselle was shocked at what she saw. Nana was lying belly down on the bed. The cushion below her hips raised her behind and displayed a series of bright red stripes. She still wore the heavy corset and her arms were still tied. The helmet was gone though, and beneath the brilliance of Nana's blonde hair Giselle could see the tear-streaked face and quivering lips.

In a state of mind close to shock, Giselle approached the bed as if approaching the scene of a murder. Her instinct told her to flee. The violence of what had happened seemed to linger in the room like a dark cloud.

With a heavy heart she sank to the bed. Close now, she could see that it wasn't just Nana's lips that quivered. Her entire body shivered – a constant vibration as if she were running a high fever. It was only when Giselle touched Nana's behind – a tentative exploration of the ridges and furrows – that Nana seemed to realise she wasn't alone.

'I didn't think that he would do this,' Giselle said in a guilt-stricken voice. 'I didn't know . . .'

Her voice trailed away as she saw the expression on Nana's face. In the tear-filled eyes, Giselle saw a joy and exultation that astonished her.

'He asked,' Nana told her weakly. 'Before each stroke, he asked.'

'And you said yes?'

'Until I couldn't speak any more. Then he took me. It was so good. I haven't stopped shaking.'

Nana lay beside her sister and held her. The shivers grew to tremors and the tears became great gulping sobs. 'So good,' she kept murmuring. She was feverish, exalted and shocked, it seemed, by the depth of what she

147

had felt. Giselle remembered the night that she had lost her own virginity, but then there hadn't been just one man – there had been many, and they had all wanted her again and again. She too had been laid waste. She too had suffered and revelled in that deflowering.

She kissed her sister's tear-stained cheeks over and over again, holding her for a long time, until the shaking subsided and she heard a series of long sighs as if something had been completed, as if the great upwelling of feelings had come to its natural end. It was only then that Giselle sat up and looked carefully at the length of her sister's body. She was covered in sweat. Between her legs there was blood and semen. The front of her thighs carried the same stripes as her behind.

'Let me wash you,' she said.

Nana didn't reply. Her eyes were closed and she seemed on the verge of sleep. Giselle knelt up and undid the clasps that held the girl's arms. Nana groaned as they were released and the knotted muscles of her shoulders relaxed.

There was an old-fashioned bowl and ewer on the dresser, which would serve for what Giselle needed. She set the bowl on the bed and took the ewer into the bathroom to fill. When she came back, Nana had turned on to her side and lay curled around the pillow.

Giselle poured hot water into the bowl and opened the flannel that she had found. The touch of the water on Nana's flanks roused her and she rolled on to her back. When she opened her eyes, she smiled brilliantly. Giselle rubbed the flannel across her belly in a slow, circular motion.

'Do you remember me washing you when you were little?' Giselle asked.

Nana nodded shyly. 'Yes, but I didn't think that you would ever do it again.'

Giselle laughed and told her to open her legs. Nana seemed hardly able to move but slowly complied.

'Am I a mess?'

Giselle nodded. 'That is what happens when you let men into your bedroom.'

'He was very kind.'

Giselle picked up the cane that lay on the bedside table.

'Kind?'

Nana smiled shyly.

'I told you, he asked if he could. He said that it turned him on like nothing else.'

They looked at each other with the sympathy of those who are damned and know it. Then Nana's expression changed, became nervous.

'He said that he wanted to watch you use it on me,' she said quietly.

Giselle shook her head. 'Never.'

'He said that during the shoot he saw something in you. A part of you that would enjoy it.'

Giselle shook her head even more emphatically. She was aware of those impulses but she would never surrender to them. Those practices were the province of men. She would never betray herself with such cruelties.

When Giselle worked the flannel around her sister's sex, the girl flinched.

'Are you sore?'

'He was so fierce – like a wild animal. I didn't think that I could do that to a man. He wanted me so much.'

Giselle remembered the look in Charles's eyes when he had come to her room. Wild was the only word that could have described him. Like a wolf. Yet who or what he wanted, she wasn't sure. There was a feeling with Charles that sex was an idea, that he constructed his sexual pleasure in the way that he constructed a photograph. The woman was just a cipher, an element of the design. On the set and in bed, he demanded complete control but never a complete person. His capacity to abstract scared Giselle sometimes, as if she

149

would be drained of herself and left only as an imprint in a magazine or a ghost in one of his erotic fantasies.

With a sigh, she put these thoughts aside. To Nana he was a god. He had wanted her and he had taken her. What else could any young girl want from a powerful and attractive man?

She finished washing the tender and inflamed sex and tossed the flannel on the table. Taking the edge of the corset between finger and thumb she peeled it back a few inches. The revealed skin was slick with sweat.

'I'll take this off.'

'He might want me again,' said Nana abruptly.

'Then he can have you naked. If you leave it on you might get a rash.'

Nana was too weak to protest. She allowed Giselle to pull her into a sitting position and roll the mesh of rubber tubing up and over her head. Sweat ran in rivulets from the exposed skin.

Giselle took the flannel again and, after rinsing it in the bowl, carefully washed her sister's torso. The perfection of the girl's skin, the sweetness of the softly quivering breasts, moved Giselle in a way that she had been moved when she had washed Nana as a child. The warmth of her breath and smile as Giselle worked beneath the girl's arms stirred other thoughts – carnal, libidinous thoughts. This time, Giselle allowed herself to enjoy them. In such an intimate, caring setting, they seemed as natural as breathing. Her body, where it brushed her sister's, became alive and tingled with the pleasure. They both knew it; it was something between them that couldn't be denied.

Once all had been cleaned, Giselle let her sister sink to the bed. Lying full length with her trusting, loving smile framed by golden hair, it was impossible not to bestow kisses. Giselle kissed her forehead and her cheeks and used pet names that only they knew.

Finally, tearing herself away, Giselle went into the

bathroom to fetch talcum powder. She shook some on to her hands as she returned to sit on the bed. Nana was almost asleep again. Her eyes flickered for a moment but then closed with an air of luxurious finality. Glancing at the window, Giselle realised that light was already filtering in through the edges of the curtains and she hadn't slept for a moment. She shook some powder on to Nana's belly. The coolness made the girl quiver but her eyes remained closed. Giselle worked her hand in slow, reassuring circles across the whole of her sister's front. She avoided the raw, abused sex but made sure that all the folds between thigh and pelvis were thoroughly dried with the powder. At her breasts, Giselle was nervous. She had an impulse to caress as much as to soothe the skin that had been so cruelly confined. In the end, she surrendered to the impulse, running her hands over the yielding mounds with a rush of delight. Nana opened her eyes for a moment and Giselle saw that the pleasure was shared. Leaning down, Giselle gave a long lingering kiss to each strawberry nipple. When Nana did no more than smile with her eyes still closed, Giselle repeated the kisses, spending longer this time and using her tongue.

'No . . .' Nana groaned. But it was not the no of a rejection, it was the no of having already had so much pleasure.

Giselle sat up and looked down on all that available beauty. There was a sense of wonder; a joy that she should be permitted to gaze on that which she loved; an astonishment that she should be permitted such access.

Her hand returned to the domed belly. For a moment it simply followed the gentle rise and fall, attuning itself, feeling the interior, the trust and the warmth. Then, because she might never have another chance, she began to do what she had wanted to do in the studio. Her hand slipped down to rest on Nana's thigh and the thumb teased a line around the splayed lips of her sex.

151

Giselle avoided the tender opening but brushed repeatedly across the hood that protected the sensitive bud.

Again, Nana murmured a no, but this time there was a note of surrender and arousal. Giselle leant down and ran her tongue under the hood of skin, wetting and caressing the nub of sensitive nerves. Nana's hands fluttered but remained at her sides. Giselle sat up and returned to using her thumb. She watched as the girl's breathing quickened, as her belly filled and rose with greater and greater urgency. There was the sense of being on a roller coaster: the car was pulling to the top of the ride; in a moment there would be a pause and then the long descent, the rush of excitement that comes from letting go and allowing elemental forces to take control.

Nana began to groan and her head started to move from side to side. The tendons on her neck tensed and jerked. Her tongue flicked across her lips as if some delicious substance had been smeared there. The gold of her hair flickered in the light of the lamp. Giselle felt the same delirium. She too wanted to cry out as Nana did when she could bear the excitement in silence no longer.

It must have been those sounds – so compelling, so driven – that brought Charles to the door. Giselle saw him as he stood in the frame but nothing could have deflected her from giving her sister the final satisfaction. This came as a series of waves that ran through her body like peristaltic contractions. As each wave swept upwards, Nana bucked and opened her mouth in a scream.

The final scream was beyond all bearing for either of them. Giselle took her hand away as Nana buried her head in the pillow and tore at it with savage teeth.

Charles walked slowly to the bed as Nana subsided.

'You've made me want her again,' he said to Giselle thickly.

He was still naked and monstrously erect. Giselle watched as he sat and took hold of Nana's hair, then kissed her deeply. The girl's arms came up and enfolded him but fell heavily to her side again when he released her lips.

He told her to lie on her belly and she rolled slowly over. Charles stood and picked up the cane, making Giselle gasp.

'Not more . . .' she began.

'It's the way that I want her. She will be caned every time I fuck her.'

Giselle sank to her knees in front of the man.

'Not now. Let her rest. Take me.'

He looked down at her.

'If I wanted to cane you?'

Giselle hesitated. She had been caned many times on the island but it was never easy. If anything, it was worse each time because the memories built one on another. The very sight of the smooth wood in Charles's hand made her break out in a cold sweat.

'Let her sleep and I won't refuse anything.'

Charles ran his hand through her hair.

'I need you for a shoot on the day after tomorrow. I can't afford to have you marked.'

He started to push her away but Giselle seized him with her mouth, impaling herself immediately, taking his sex deep into her throat as she had done earlier. He groaned and let her move rapidly back and forth. She had never wanted to make a man come so much, and cared nothing for the pain in her throat each time she jammed him deep.

'The belt,' she said, pausing in her efforts for a moment. 'Use the belt. There will be no bruises.'

He reached for her breasts, squeezing hard enough to make her wince. 'Have you ever been whipped here?' he asked.

Tears filled her eyes as she nodded.

'OK,' he told her.

She jumped to her feet quickly and took his hand. She wanted to get him away from Nana.

'I have belts in my room,' she said.

He laughed and allowed her to lead him downstairs. Before she had even crossed the hallway, she was shaking. In her room, as she opened the door to her wardrobe, the shaking became almost uncontrollable. She knew that he would hurt her badly. He would make her pay for deflecting him from what he truly wanted. She had to pause and take several deep breaths before reaching to the shelf where she kept her belts neatly coiled like snakes. They weighed like iron in her hand as she turned and walked to where he stood at the window.

'I like to see a woman shake,' he told her. 'Let me look at you in the light.'

He pulled the curtains open and a wash of pinkish light entered the room.

She stood close to the glass as he examined her. The shaking became worse as he caressed those parts that would soon feel the belt.

'Paler than lilies,' he said.

'I need to have this over with,' she gasped, as his hand went to her sex and penetrated her. But he was in no hurry. He caressed her in a leisurely way. For the first time in a long while, he seemed to want to make her come. Recently, he had only ever wanted to satisfy himself. She leant against the cool glass when her legs would no longer support her. The green of the garden seemed a million miles away. She gasped repeatedly and came, once, twice, three times. Xavier hadn't entered her mind. She had never come without thinking of him before. This time, there was only the belt and the certainty that her breasts would be beaten. The thought filled her mind as the hand worked her relentlessly and the orgasms came and went in a long, slow caravan.

'I think it is more exciting to beat your sister,' Charles

154

told her. 'She allows it to please me. You find it arousing.'

Giselle was hardly listening to what he said. It was only when his hand withdrew and he told her to kneel on the bed that she could focus her attention.

She knelt shakily and pulled up the silk pyjama jacket until the material was gathered about her neck. He plucked the belts from the floor where she had let them fall as the orgasms took her. He shook each one out in turn and lay them on the bed.

'Do you have any preferences? Thick or thin? Light or heavy?'

When she didn't reply, he knelt beside her and sucked each breast for several minutes, as if drawing pleasure to them, so that the belt would be sharper when it fell. Finally, he knelt up and chose the thinnest of the belts. She collapsed after the third blow. He tied her down and gagged her, then took his time, alternately beating and sucking on the swollen nipples. Her tears stained the pillows. It was Greta who found her the next morning, still tied, her breasts reddened and her sex still sticky with the excitement of what he had done.

'Such a bad man,' she said as she undid the belt that held Giselle's hands. There was something darkly comic in the way that she said this and both of them laughed.

10

Telling

A week after Nana had lost her virginity, she and
Charles flew off for the shoot in China.

With Charles away, there was no work for Giselle. It
would have been easy to approach an agency and find
work that way but she didn't want to. She knew that
Charles wanted exclusive access to her – she was his
discovery after all – and for a while, at least, she was
happy to go along with that.

The only time that they heard from him was when the
crew was arrested. A local official doubted that they had
a permit to shoot in Tibet. Greta showed Giselle the
email: 'Chinese jails no fun. Luckily they had a chink in
their armour, but it took many dollars to exploit. Send
more as soon as you can.' Giselle didn't see the joke and
renewed her English studies with greater zeal.

Greta spent a lot of time with her various men but
still had time for Giselle. As they grew closer, Greta
encouraged Giselle to tell her story. At first Giselle shied
away, despite her promises. The quarry still lit her life
like a blinding sun. Its brightness blotted out the present
as much as the darker side of her memories obscured it.
Finally, Giselle had no choice but to open up. Greta's
offers brought too many things to the surface that
Giselle had forgotten or half-forgotten. Her past was
demanding to be heard and she was obliged to
surrender.

156

Storytelling became a late-night ritual. Greta would sit curled on the sofa in the drawing room, a drink in her hand. Giselle would speak low and soft, in the beginning at least, as if she were back in the priest's confessional in Avignon. Sometimes, she would tell the more difficult or embarrassing parts of her story as if it had happened to another girl, carefully substituting 'she' for 'I'. It couldn't have been easy for Greta to listen and follow what was said. The stories didn't necessarily follow any chronological pattern and Giselle could tell the same story many times, as if trying to work it out of her system. Often, there were differences in the various renderings. Yet, if Greta ever doubted the truth of what was said, she never showed it.

Giselle could never sit while she talked. Usually, she would wander from one end of the room to another in a dream, tidying items that didn't need tidying, checking and correcting her make-up in the mirror, avoiding the eyes of her listener and seeing her home town instead, and all that had happened.

Parts of the story she told in English, parts in French. The English seemed to help her achieve a distance from, and a control of, the events. When the memories were especially overwhelming, even her native language would fail utterly and she would sit suddenly – in silence. Greta would wait for her and she would eventually begin again, as if there had been no interruption.

In the fortnight that Charles and Nana were away, Giselle managed to describe most of what had happened with Xavier. The telling and retelling helped her to make the story coherent for the first time. Instead of gaps and breaks, where her mind had feared to wander, there was one seamless flow. She might not have mastered the past but she had made a framework to contain it.

She loved Greta like a mother for her patience. Often, Giselle would end the evenings curled in her arms. The smell of perfume and tequila became as soothing as the smell of a mother's milk. It was these experiences – sprawled forgetfully in a woman's arms – that made Giselle realise for the first time how good it was to be held by somebody who didn't want her sexually. There was a peace that she hadn't known since she was a child. But later, when she was in her bed, she thought of Charles and the visits in the night. In the silence of that great room, her belly ached to be opened by a man. The memories, which still frightened her, also made her wet. She wanted to be found like that: wet and dizzied by the ghosts of desire. She wanted to be punished for her sins and then made to commit more.

11

The Quarry

Jean had been one of those boys who liked to torment
girls. When he was eight, he had taken Giselle to the bus
stop and put her on a bus to Nice. 'You want to go to
the seaside don't you?' he had asked. The six-year-old
Giselle always wanted to go to the seaside. On this trip
though, she was met at the bus station in Nice, not by
her grandparents as Jean had promised, but by
gendarmes with guns. The guns were tucked into black
leather holsters and had never been drawn, but they had
impressed the tiny Giselle.

In the end it was Giselle who got the best of the
prank. The bus driver had let her sit in the front seat on
the way and the gendarmes made a great fuss of her as
they took her to her grandparents.

After confessing to their mother, Jean had been
locked in his room for a week. It was only when Giselle
pleaded to have her brother back that the family forgave
him.

At seventeen, Jean was still full of cruel schemes and,
as much as she loved him, Giselle was wary. His best
friend then was Giscard, a tall, dreamy, good-looking
boy with long blond hair. Jean used Giscard as a fool
and as a butt for his jokes but Giselle had a crush on
him. If Giscard didn't notice, and he seemed not to,
Jean did. He teased her cruelly; told her that she was too
young, too plain, too silly. Yet, beneath the teasing,

Giselle sensed something else, the feeling that her big brother did not want to lose her. Then Jean changed. Suddenly he seemed to be pushing her into Giscard's arms. She was old enough and wise enough at fifteen to suspect plots and stratagems.

In that last summer, after school finished, Jean and Giscard spent most of their days at the quarry. In the evenings, they would cruise into town with the rest of the gang in an old Land Rover. Xavier would be at the wheel, cool and commanding.

Giselle saw them sometimes when she was out with her girlfriends. Jean would ignore her but one or other of the boys would always make some comment about 'Jean's skinny sister'.

Then, one day, Giscard asked her if she wanted to go to a party with him. They were in the garden at her father's house. Jean was looking at them with a strange expression from the kitchen window, as if he knew what was being said. Giselle was astonished and flustered. As she said yes her mind was spinning, and immediately afterwards she had run away.

The party was at a favourite picnicking spot in the woods beside the river. One of Giscard's cousins, Amelie, had just turned sixteen and her mother had driven out the equipment for a barbecue, then disappeared, leaving adolescence and the night to each other. Jean had stayed away – deliberately leaving them alone together, Giselle suspected.

She and Giscard had walked along the river bank where fires had been lit and boys and girls milled around. There was music and, in places, people were dancing. Giscard seemed awkward at first. She wondered for a while if he really wanted her to be there. Then he sat on a fallen tree and held out his hand. Nervously, she took it and he pulled her on to his lap. She giggled and wriggled. He kissed her quickly as if she might try to escape. It was her first kiss and the evening dissolved into soft caresses and whispers.

Later, as they walked home, she asked if Jean had anything to do with inviting her to the party. He blushed. 'I would have asked you out sometime,' he said, 'but he pushed me.'

Giselle was grateful for that push.

The next day, Giscard rang and asked her out again. They went to see *American Gigolo* at the Gaumont in the centre of Avignon. They had to pretend she was eighteen. He bought popcorn and they sat at the back, where he could kiss her. It was an early showing of the film but, by the time they had walked back to her home, it was late and her father was furious. In the old stone-floored kitchen he had the appearance of a demon with his eyes flashing and his hand slamming into the ancient oak table to emphasise his points. He had already forbade her to go out after dark. Now he forbade her to go out in the evenings as well. When she made a protest he slapped her and left her speechless.

Jean came in and father and son shouted at each other until Giselle fled upstairs and locked herself in her bedroom. Jean came up later and told her it was OK to go out as long she was back by nine o'clock. He was already bigger than his father and just as ruthless. One day she knew that they would fight and one of them would be hurt badly. She didn't want to be the cause of it. Even so, she was glad that she could still see Giscard and kissed her brother on the cheek for taking her side. When he returned the kiss, it was to her lips, a light brush only but it shocked her and she pulled back. It was the first time that she realised he might see her as anything other than a sister. He left before she could say anything.

Thinking back, Giselle saw the girl she had been with a sort of pity. She had been so easy. So easy to impress. So easy to get excited. Xavier must have seen it straight away. Jean loved her but he was at that age when sex is

161

more important than love. She was passed around. Giscard was just the bait. However, realising that he was interested in her had meant so much. She would have done anything for him. She often suspected that Jean had put him up to it, but she also believed Giscard when he said that he cared. Even if the seduction had been planned by Xavier and Jean, Giscard had given her something she had never had before.

All that ended when he took her to the island. That had also been arranged by Jean and Xavier. Giscard admitted that afterwards, when it was too late, when there was no going back to innocence.

When he first asked her, she didn't know much about the island except that it had a bad reputation, or at least Xavier did, and it was Xavier's island.

Everyone knew about Xavier. He was the son of a renegade priest who had been drummed out of the Church for breaking his vows of celibacy and impregnating a young girl. Xavier's mother was an uneducated woman who grew fat and unattractive as soon as the priest had married her to save his soul. The priest took solace in unsanctified wine and taught the boy from the pulpit of a bitter self-pity. Perhaps it was his mother's cassoulets running in goose fat that had made him so tall and strong. Perhaps it was the ancient Church of Rome running in his veins. Certainly, Xavier had both parents in his nature; he could be crude or cultured, eloquent or dumbly insolent. Added to this was a scent of evil, which some said was a personal gift of the devil to such an unholy union. It was whispered that his gang was really a cult and that he was the arch priest, a new antipope. They said that the island was a place of pagan rituals, of blood sacrifice and the conjuring of demons. Most saw him as just another misfit, and his gang as a band of clowns.

One thing that Giselle knew for sure was that he had been expelled from school the previous year. A teacher had caught him smoking and, when she tried to take away the cigarette, Xavier had slapped her. This didn't deter the girls. The teacher was universally hated. Besides, Xavier was tall, tough looking, but romantic in a piratical way. There were bluebirds tattooed on his wrists and he wore silver earrings.

At school, while he was still there, Giselle had avoided him. She was only a child then, and he was scary.

Once, she had seen him at the drive-in McDonald's near her house — everybody went there; it was such a new thing. She had been with Claudette, her best friend, and they had bought Pepsis and were sitting on the wall of the car park drinking them when Xavier drove in with his gang in the old Land Rover. It had a left-hand drive and English number plates — cool, somehow, cool in a way that even the young Giselle could understand.

Xavier swung into a space not far from where the two friends sat. Jean was in the back with some other boys and a blonde girl. When they got out, Jean ignored Giselle and Claudette. Xavier looked though, and it was exciting to be noticed. Giselle remembered how Claudette's legs had swung faster as he looked them up and down. They could hear him asking Jean about his sister, saying she was cute, saying he should introduce them. Jean pulled him away, and they disappeared into the restaurant.

Claudette wanted to go. She was easily embarrassed and didn't want to be teased. Giselle was too curious. They agreed that if the boys came over, they'd run.

When the gang came back, they had hamburgers and milk shakes. The blonde was all over Xavier. The other boys were touching her. She didn't seem to mind. There was milk shake running down her chin and the boys were making jokes about it, trying to lick it from her chin.

Xavier jumped up and sat on the bonnet of the car.

163

It was high, so he seemed like a king surrounded by his subjects. He told the blonde to come over to him, calling her Claire. She leant against the radiator between his open legs. He took her hamburger and kissed her. It was a full, deep kiss – too sexual, too intimate, for such a public place. Jean looked at his sister and made a 'go away' face but Giselle wouldn't have moved for anything.

When the kiss stopped, the blonde girl reached for her hamburger but Xavier held it high in the air. Claire jumped to snatch it back and her short dress showed off her legs. Giselle was envious of those legs; they were the kind of legs you needed to play netball – strong, slender and long. Then Xavier asked how much she wanted it and the girl said that she was really hungry. The boys laughed but Xavier was serious. He told her to kiss Thierry if she wanted a bite. Thierry was a lanky boy with long unruly hair and an unpleasant smile. Claire glanced at him, and Giselle could see her flushing with embarrassment. Thierry leant back against the side of the car with a big annoying grin, waiting like a spider for a fly.

Finally, the girl surrendered, and started to go over to him. Xavier called her back. He undid the top buttons on her blouse while she pouted, sulkily.

'You've got to interest him,' Xavier told her. 'He might not want to kiss you.'

Claire snorted, and Giselle guessed that Thierry was always interested. Xavier let her go, and she walked over to the boy reluctantly, dragging her feet at each step. She tried to get away with a kiss on the cheek, but Thierry grabbed her. He gave her a long, deep kiss and his hand snaked inside her blouse, making her struggle. When he let her go, she looked angry and flushed.

Xavier held out the hamburger and she returned with a defiant look in her eye as if this was a game that she had played before and was determined to win. When she

164

reached for the prize, he wouldn't let her take it. She was only allowed a bite. Strangely, her anger cooled as she ate. Her body visibly relaxed and the defiance ebbed away. It was incomprehensible to Giselle. The girl seemed to be in a trance, like the people Giselle had seen on TV shows where a hypnotist makes them do strange things against their will.

When Claire had finished eating, Xavier asked if she wanted more. She nodded.

'So who are you going to kiss this time?' he asked. She shot a quick, shy glance at Jean.

'Jean. You are the chosen. Kiss our Mary Magdelen. Make it good. She's hungry for the flesh of the beast,' Xavier told him.

It was a slow kiss and, this time, the blonde girl made a thing of it. Everyone could see that she meant that kiss. It was getting dark and one of the boys went into the car and switched on the headlights. The light splashed across her thighs and lit her face. It didn't stop the kiss. Jean took hold of the girl's behind and she pushed into his groin, hard.

'She needs more,' Xavier said. 'Give her something that you know she wants.' Jean glanced over to the wall again. Giselle realised that her mouth was gaping foolishly and closed it.

Jean shrugged, then leant back against the bonnet and told Claire to undo the blouse completely.

This seemed to be going too far and the girl seemed suddenly nervous. She looked at Xavier as if hoping to win a reprieve. There was no comfort in his stern expression and she slowly reached for the buttons of her blouse. Her hands weren't working properly and she fumbled. Thierry stepped forward and undid the buttons for her, then pushed the fabric down her arms to her elbows. Her bra was pink – a soft, baby pink, striking against the tanned skin. Her breasts were large. It would be a while before either of the girls on the wall had breasts so large. Claire glanced at the road, and the traffic that was passing in the half-light. She seemed worried that someone who knew her would pass by. Jean told her to look at him, and, reaching out, ran his fingers around the margins of the bra. It was a very light touch and the girl shivered. Then his hand slipped inside and cupped first one breast, then the other. The girl turned to Xavier again. This time she seemed ready to cry, but Xavier looked away. Jean's hand slid down her belly and brushed over her sex. She pressed her legs together abruptly and pulled her pelvis back. She looked like a little girl who needed to pee. Her face was burning and she was biting her lip to stop herself from crying. Giselle's heart pounded. She was sure that the girl would turn and run. The tension was almost unbearable. The boys were frozen and seemed to have stopped breathing. Jean crouched down and ran his hands up the outside of her legs. As they disappeared under her skirt, Claire gave a little gasp. Giselle could see that he was touching her behind, squeezing the cheeks. Then the hands came slowly downwards. A tear rolled from the corner of the girl's eye. She looked at Xavier again, a mute pleading in the raised eyes. When Jean's hands emerged from beneath her dress they were drawing her panties down.

Claudette suddenly took Giselle's arm. 'This is wrong,' she said, 'we should go.' Giselle didn't want to. It was the wrongness that made it exciting. When the panties reached the girl's knees, Jean left them there, and stood up. He glanced at Giselle and she saw a fire in his eyes.

Claire was shaking. Her eyes gleamed with the moisture of self-pity.

The headlamps made her the sole focus in the gathering gloom, as if she were an actress on a stage. A second tear ran down her cheek but she made no effort to close her blouse or pull up her underwear.

'OK, that's enough,' Xavier said.

She was too shaky to do up the buttons on her blouse, so Jean did them for her. When it came to her panties though, he pulled them down rather than up and, after a miserable protest too weak even to draw a rebuke, she was obliged to step out of them.

Xavier held out the hamburger but she shook her head. He told her to eat. It would stop her shaking. Dutifully, she took a bite and chewed. He was right. The tears stopped and colour returned to her cheeks.

For the final bite, Xavier made her dance. They turned on the car radio and she danced in the headlights. They told her to make it sexy. She looked uncomfortable at first but gyrated her hips slowly and showed her legs, even the paleness of her behind when she span around. The mood changed and the boys began to whistle appreciatively. The girl was smiling now, enjoying the attention. Then Xavier pulled her up on to his lap. He gave her the rest of the hamburger and his hand went under her dress. She seemed to be eating in a dream. Thierry came up close and undid her shoes. He pulled them off then stroked her bare legs. Xavier whispered something in her ear and she kissed the boy. This time, the kiss was unreserved; she kissed him as she had kissed Jean. After a while, she began to wriggle. The hand under her dress moved more quickly and she began to gasp.

Suddenly, Claudette had had enough and jumped from the wall.

'Come on,' she said. Giselle still wanted to watch but Claudette was too frightened. She took Giselle's hand and pulled her down. As they ran away, Giselle could hear the half-stifled groans of the girl on Xavier's lap. It was a sound that she would never forget – half despair, half longing, but also full and rich as if nothing could have felt better.

Giselle remembered all this when Giscard asked her

to go to the island. She refused and, when he asked why, she told him about that time when Xavier had made a girl beg.

'Xavier's OK,' he told her. 'I'll be there anyway. You won't have to do anything that you don't want to.'

When he saw that she was still reluctant, he made her promise to think about it. She promised, but didn't expect to change her mind.

It was only later – in bed that night – that she realised that it was wanting to do things for Xavier that frightened her. Giscard was so safe and so sweet. Yet, in her daydreams, Xavier was there and he was something else: not safe, not sweet and never willing to take no for an answer. Unable to help it, she caressed herself as she remembered the car park at McDonald's. She imagined that it was her, not the blonde girl, doing those things for Xavier and came noisily, forgetting herself. There was a banging on the wall. Her father had heard, and Giselle curled up with the humiliation. As she lay in a tight, burning knot, another feeling surfaced; a rage that her father should have made her feel such shame.

It was anger towards her father as much as anything else that made her agree to go to the island. For the first time she would truly defy him. And, if Xavier and Jean behaved badly, so would she.

The first visit to the island was on a hot afternoon in late June. The air had been still, suffocating, all day and Avignon slept. People and dogs fought for shade in the streets. The only comforts were the fountains and those few shops that had air conditioning.

Giscard had come for her at four o'clock, wearing blue cotton shorts and a tie-dyed T-shirt. They sat under the sweet chestnuts in the front garden waiting for the Land Rover. Jean came out and climbed into the stained canvas hammock that hung between two of the trees.

168

Giscard seemed nervous and asked several times if she was sure that she wanted to go. Jean darted angry glances at him each time he asked. She could see that Jean was excited, though she didn't know why.

Finally, they heard the roar of an engine in the distance and Giselle had a moment of panic. Her stomach turned a somersault and she had to be pulled out of the old deck chair by her brother. The Land Rover drew up in a cloud of dust.

Giscard took her hand as they walked out of the shade of the trees and up the sandy driveway. He wouldn't meet her eye, and kept his head down as they walked to the car. He reminded her of a condemned man walking to the scaffold. She squeezed his hand but it had no effect.

Xavier smiled easily at Giselle through the open window of the Land Rover.

'The new girl,' he said. 'New girls always sit by me.'

He leant over and threw open the passenger door. Giselle hesitated for a moment, then let go of Giscard's hand and swung in. The old, cracked leather of the seat was hot against her back. As she slid over to the driver's side, her miniskirt slid high on her thighs and Xavier cast a leisurely eye over the expanse of tanned skin.

'Long enough?' asked Jean through the window, examining her legs in the same way.

Xavier laughed and told him to get in the back. Thierry was there with another boy who she didn't know, and a girl she knew only by sight. Xavier introduced the boy as Billy and the girl as Paige. Giselle turned to say hello as Giscard squeezed into the front beside her. She felt the dampness of his sweat-soaked shirt against her arm. It was hot, and would get hotter. Paige smiled from beneath a fringe of auburn hair, cut short like a boy's. Billy seemed shy, meeting her eyes only briefly.

'OK!' cried Xavier and they roared away. The rutted

169

road tossed them about like peas in a can but the cries of 'slow down' from the back only made Xavier push the old Land Rover harder.

Giselle glanced at him from time to time. She examined the tattoos on his wrists – miniature blue swallows and dragonflies. There was a feeling of great strength in his body, a wiriness. As he wrestled with the steering wheel, she could see the sinews of his forearm breaking the surface of the smooth, tanned skin. She could feel the power of the broad hands with their long, elegant fingers. When he glanced at her, she was aware of the candour of his eyes and an unusual self-possession. He seemed to know exactly who he was and what he wanted.

They were climbing all the time, heading into the hills to the east of Avignon. There was the occasional farmhouse and yards full of chickens and broken machinery.

A tinder-dry pine forest shrouded them in velvet gloom once the farmland was left behind. Then, for the first time, Giselle saw her new world, the world that she would carry with her for the rest of her life. The Land Rover emerged abruptly from the shade of the high, dark fir trees on to a beach of white sand. The water that lapped at the shore was an intense ultramarine blue that could have come, unmixed, from an artist's palette.

They piled out of the car and Xavier watched her as she took it all in.

He pointed to the island in the middle of the lake, a pyramid of green trees and grey rock amongst the blue. When she squeezed her eyes against the sun, it lost its sharpness and looked like an enchanted castle.

'Wow?' he asked.

She nodded slowly.

'It's a special place. And nobody comes here but us.'

Thierry kicked off his trainers and waded out amongst the reeds that lined the shore. Water soaked into the bottom of his jeans and rose steadily as he hunted amongst the tall green spears. There was a flurry of feathers and a pair of swans reared up and spat at him. He waved his arms and the birds broke cover and paddled away with hostile backward glances. After a few moments he found what he was looking for, and started to haul out a boat. The dented, aluminium hull shone in the sun. For Giselle, everything shone. The smiles of the boys – white teeth in tanned faces – dazzled her. The eyes that examined her were alive with a wild energy. Light seemed to burst from the blue waters like discharges of static electricity. Everything, it seemed, shone with its own light and, in the sky, the sun burnt like a great fire.

'Trips around the island free today,' Xavier said.

They took off their shoes and waded out to the boat. Thierry held it steady while Giselle climbed in, then jumped in and sat beside her. He flicked the water from his fingers so that it fell on her bare legs. She laughed. The others piled in, and Jean picked up the old wooden oars.

Soon they were in open water. Giselle watched the dragonflies as they hummed above the surface of the water and the swallows as they made their great sweeping runs from one bank to the other. She glanced at the tattoos on Xavier's wrists, reflections of what surrounded her. If he was the antipope, this was his new Rome.

Jean asked her if she wanted to row, but she shook her head. She wanted to be carried like a child in the lap of the boat.

Giscard and Xavier sat together at the front of the boat. Giscard still looked uncomfortable as the two of them talked together quietly. From time to time, they glanced at Giselle. She smiled in return, not caring what they were saying. To be away from her father, to be in this magical place, was enough.

171

A fish jumped, not ten metres away, its broad back silver in the sun.

'Carp,' said Thierry. 'I'll teach you how to catch one. There are rods on the island.'

She looked at him in surprise. He was still the gangly boy that she remembered from the car park at McDonald's, and his smile was still unattractive, but she realised that he was also a simple country boy, friendly enough when he wasn't being cruel.

'OK,' she said.

'You can eat them. We have barbecues.'

They were interrupted by water splashing across them from one of the oars. Giselle saw from Jean's face that it was deliberate, and realised that he was jealous of Thierry. She enjoyed that. Not only was this a place of magic, it was also a place where she had power – even the power to make her big, tough brother jealous. She scooped up a handful of water and threw it at him. He grinned and splashed her with the oar again. Soon, everyone in the boat was throwing water. Giselle could hardly see. When it stopped, they were all soaked and laughing. Jean had dropped one of the oars and they had to go back for it, paddling with their hands.

The island was close now. On one side there were steep cliffs of greyish stone surrounding a small sandy bay; on the other, trees, mainly firs, clothed a slope that ran to the water's edge. A fringe of willows draped graceful branches across the reed-beds that protected the shores.

Jean swung the boat into the sandy bay and a large hut, painted a bright blue, came into view. The ground around the hut was flat and open, as if it had been deliberately cleared. Geese, with black-and-white banded necks, strutted and pecked at the dry, bleached grass. As the boat drew closer, the geese hissed and flapped their wings before slipping into the water and swimming away, heads high, disdainful.

Once the boat had grounded on the gently sloping shore, Xavier jumped into the water and waded to where Giselle sat. He offered his hand and she stood up unsteadily, making the boat rock. The others watched in silence as he took her in his arms and carried her ashore. There was a sense of ritual, like a man carrying his bride across a threshold. He set her down on dry ground and let his hand trail down her back and across her behind. He laughed when she jumped away from him. Her eyes narrowed. The island might be his, but she wasn't, not yet at least. She turned to watch the others coming ashore, Thierry pulling the boat behind him.

Giscard took her arm. 'I'll show you around,' he said, then led her past the hut at the far end of the open ground and up a path into the woods.

It was beautiful. Giscard had told her about the cliffs and the fir trees. He had told her about the reeds and the willows. But he hadn't described the light and shade – how the air was thin and bright over the lake and thickly mysterious in the woods. How the water coated the grey rocks making them shine like marble. How, beneath the branches of the trees, there were beds of soft pine needles and plants with pale flowers like trumpets that seemed to watch visitors as they passed.

Giscard stooped to pick one of the flowers for her but she stopped him. It seemed wrong, a violation of the serene indifference of that shady place. He took her to the highest point on the island, a pinnacle of rock topped with a small, flat area. As they climbed the last twenty metres or so, they emerged from the trees and could see the lake in its entirety. She gazed at the blueness of the water and at the cliffs that surrounded it, until he pulled her to the ground and kissed her. It seemed as if he was checking that she was still his after the attention of Xavier and Thierry. She kissed him back, passionately, in an effort to show that she was. He slipped his hand under her blouse and touched her breasts. She had allowed this before only in the darkness of the cinema, and was now uncomfortable.

'No one will come,' he told her. 'If they do, we will hear them.'

She let him touch her and tried to relax as he undid her blouse. When his eyes fell on her breasts, encased in white cotton, they expanded to fill his face, and she laughed gently.

'Am I pretty?' she asked.

'Oh, yes.'

'Tell me.'

'Prettier than the flowers that you wouldn't let me pick.'

'Do you want me to undo it?' she asked, as he stroked the edges of the cotton.

He nodded.

Sitting up, she reached back and undid the clip. It was time for him to see her. It was the place to be seen. The bra opened, and she felt suddenly shy as her breasts slipped forward under his hungry gaze.

He kissed her lips, then each of her nipples, lightly, making her giggle.

'It tickles,' she said.

He took one of the nipples more firmly and sucked deeply. She let her head fall back as a slow pleasure ran through her system.

Strangely, as he sucked, she realised that he was shaking, that he was more nervous than she. She gently rested her hand on his head, like a mother with an infant. Xavier had carried her ashore like a pirate's prize; Giscard sucked at her breasts like a baby, and shook.

When he released her, she sat up and re-clipped her bra. He reached for her hand and took it to his groin. She let him press it to the hard cylinder of flesh there, but only for a moment. He was showing her that he was a man and she let him, but that was all. Jumping to her feet, she pulled him up.

They were about to head back down the path when he said that he wanted to show her something. He helped her the last few metres to the very pinnacle of the island. Here, the grey rock bore a thick vein of pure quartz that gleamed in the sun. She reached out to touch the sharp crystals but Giscard stopped her.

'It lets the sun into the island,' he told her.

She looked at him curiously but saw that he was entirely serious. Then, as if he had said too much, he pulled her back to the path.

They walked down the slope slowly, each lost in their own thoughts. A bittern was calling across the lake, a hollow, empty, booming sound. The dark shade had a melancholy quality and Giselle began to feel the other side of the island. They were far from home, creatures in a world not made for them.

As soon as they were in sight of the hut, Giscard let go of her hand and seemed shy of being seen with her. The letting go surprised her. It seemed somehow final, as if he no longer had confidence that she was entirely his. His weakness was more apparent than ever in contrast to Xavier's strength. Giselle had already realised that, on that island, the strong prospered, and Giscard wasn't strong. She wondered if he really wanted to keep her. If he had truly wanted to, would he have brought her here amongst these other, fiercer boys? As that thought swirled through her mind, another equally sad thought followed in its wake: if she had wanted to remain Giscard's she wouldn't have come. It wasn't for Giscard that she had made this pilgrimage – it was for the possibilities offered by Xavier. They were both accomplices in this. Giscard was sacrificing her, and she was letting him.

As they came out into the open and felt the sun once more, Giselle's mood lightened. There was a lot of activity on the sands. Someone had lit a small fire and an old steel bucket sat on a griddle above it. There was the smell of mussels cooking in wine. Music played on a radio and Paige, who had changed into a yellow bikini, danced lazily in the sun. Xavier watched her from the trunk of a great fallen tree, slowly rocking his leg from side to side. There was a book open beside him, a book that she had seen in the car – the writings of Simon Magus. Further away, at the edge of the bay, Thierry was skidding stones across the water.

When Xavier saw Giselle, he called her over. Giscard trailed after her.

'There is a little ritual. Something for all initiates,' he told her.

Thierry came over, smiling, as if he had been waiting for this.

Giselle glanced at Giscard, but he avoided her eye.

'It doesn't hurt,' Paige called. She was stirring the mussels in the bucket and smiling from amongst the steam like an apprentice witch.

Xavier jumped to his feet. 'There will be a solemn procession.' He went over to the fire and picked out a burnt branch that was still smouldering. He reached into his pocket and pulled out a length of string. He tied one end around the branch and handed it to Thierry.

'Lead on,' he commanded.

Thierry set off, swinging the branch in circles as if it were a censer. Xavier took Giselle's arm and they followed, wood smoke enfolding them. Giscard, Billy and Paige trailed behind in single file.

This time they took a different path out of the clearing, steeper and more rocky. It led them, eventually, to the side of the island with the grey-stone cliffs and overhanging firs. There was an especially large and ancient fir that projected its branches far over the water below. From one of its branches hung a thick nylon rope.

'Paige. Demonstrate the ritual of the rope,' Xavier said.

The rope was too far over the edge of the cliff to reach. The girl picked up a stick and hooked it.

'I'm not letting go,' she said, as she walked back up the slope. Xavier nodded. 'Just show her what to do.'

After setting herself, Paige ran down the slope to the cliff edge and launched herself into the air. She looped through the air gracefully and at the end of the arc, when she was well over the water, she looked back at Giselle excitedly.

'Let go here,' she said, then began to swing back as gravity dictated, landing gracefully on the cliff top.

'Do I really have to do that?' Giselle asked.

'Of course. And you have to let go,' Xavier told her.

She looked at the water ten metres below.

'Is it deep?'

'Deep enough.'

She thought about it for a moment, then sighed. 'OK.'

'But no clothes,' Xavier told her. 'It has to done naked. In honour of the gods of earth, air, fire and water.'

Giselle looked at him incredulously.

'Everybody else has done it,' Jean told her.

'There are certain words that must be said. If you get them wrong, it has to be done again.'

Giselle crossed her arms and checked the faces around her. She suspected that she was being teased, that they were making it up as they went along. The faces looked serious, intent.

'You must say: "For the gods of the earth" as you run down the slope, "For the gods of the air" as you swing out, and, "For the gods of the water" as you fall. Then, when you have swum into the bay, you must go to the fire, kneel and touch your forehead to the ground before saying, "For the gods of fire."'

'I won't,' she said flatly.

'Then you can swim ashore and walk home,' Xavier told her, unemotionally.

'Let me talk to her,' Paige said, taking Giselle by the arm. The others were silent as she took Giselle aside.

'I know how you feel,' Paige said sympathetically. 'But everybody has done it. Honestly. If you don't do as they say, Xavier really will make you swim back.'

Giselle believed her but still didn't want to expose herself before the others.

'If you strip in the trees, I'll bring you the rope and then you just have to run as quickly down the slope as you can and swing.'

Finally, Giselle agreed.

The boys were solemn as they watched Giselle disappear into the undergrowth at the top of the slope. As she unbuttoned her blouse, she wondered if she should ever have come to the island. But, after the cotton had slipped down her arms and she undid her bra for the second time in an hour, she realised that she was excited. The thought of the boys seeing her naked stirred her – even the thought of Jean seeing her. She remembered the kiss to her lips and the smile afterwards. She remembered the times that he had seen her hurrying from the bathroom in only a towel. There was something beneath the teasing – a thought, an intention that made her realise that no boy was trustworthy. The fluttering in her belly as she pulled down her skirt made her realise that she didn't want them to be. She had liked Jean to look, even as she frowned from the door of her bedroom before slamming it in his face. Now, he would see more. The other boys would see too.

Paige stood with the rope, a few yards from where she had undressed, and smiled encouragingly through the curtain of bushes. Giselle kicked off her shoes. Only her pants remained. She felt vulnerable as that last protection fell to join the pile of clothes on the ground.

'What shall I do with my clothes?' she asked. 'How will I get them back?'

'Give them to me,' Paige replied. 'I'll throw them down to you once you've swum to the bay.'

'Everybody has to do this?' Giselle asked again.

'Everybody,' Paige confirmed.

Giselle sighed and passed her the bundle of clothes, still warm with her body heat. In return, Paige handed her the rope. The nylon felt slippery in her sweating hands.

'Don't forget the words,' Paige told her. She repeated them and made Giselle say them back. 'And don't freeze or forget to let go of the rope. I saw a girl have to swing out three times before she got the courage to let go. That *was* embarrassing – although the boys liked it.'

Paige disappeared and Giselle was alone, naked in the undergrowth. The boys began to call for her. Someone started clapping, another whistled. The blood was pounding in her ears but, as soon as she began to run, the excitement came back. She burst out of the undergrowth like a hunted animal breaking cover. It was twenty metres to the edge of the cliff. She ran as fast as she could, shouting out the ritual words to drown the catcalls of the boys. At the last moment, she almost lost her footing but her momentum was enough to take her on a long arc through the air. In a ringing, exultant voice, she shouted out her praise to the gods of the air.

As the rope slowed at the peak of its swing, she looked at the boys gathered on the edge of the cliff. It was one of those moments when time slows. She had time to read the desire and the excitement in those young faces. Her hands released their grip without her telling them to. For a moment, she was frozen in midair, naked, exhilarated. She saw Jean looking at her breasts then her belly. She felt the thrill of being seen, before gravity took her and she was plunging. She just managed to acknowledge the gods of the water before

179

they swallowed her. Her feet touched a soft, sandy bottom before she stopped plunging.

When she surfaced, everyone cheered. Aware of her nakedness and the clarity of the water, she started to swim for the bay. Somebody shouted for her to do the backstroke. She swam faster and soon she was round the shoulder of rock and in the bay. She looked up at the cliffs again and saw that the boys had followed and she was still visible to them. A dark shape flew through the air and landed on the sand near the fire. As she scrambled up the slope to more catcalls, she realised that the dark shape was her clothing. She ran for the fire, water flying from her legs and arms. The bucket with the mussels was still bubbling on the rusted griddle. It felt absurd to worship such a thing but she dutifully fell to her knees and pressed her forehead to the ground in obeisance, then recited the words to the gods of fire.

A moment later she was on her feet and, snatching up the bundle of clothes, scampered away into the lee of the hut where she could dress without being seen. The boys were still cheering. She opened the bundle and looked for her underwear. There was none. For a moment, she was going to shout at the boys and demand her underwear, but she realised that it would be easier to dress in what she had and argue later. Her skin was still wet as she pulled on the blouse and her breasts showed pink through the thin fabric. She heard the boys coming down the slope as she started to pull up the short skirt. In her rush, she didn't notice that the zip at the waist had been done up and wouldn't pass her thighs. She fumbled and struggled and just managed to pull it to her waist as Xavier rounded the corner. The boys behind him stopped and watched as she self-consciously tucked in her blouse and tidied back her hair. Xavier gestured for her to approach.

He looked solemn again, though there was a glint in his eye.

'Kneel,' he told her.

Still out of breath, she was beyond arguing and sank to the sand in front of him.

He raised his hand and made a sign, similar to the ones made by priests but more elaborate, taking in not just her forehead and heart but her breasts and lips as well. Then he leant down and kissed each of her cheeks.

'I declare you a bride of the island,' he intoned, before stepping aside. Thierry stepped up and kissed her cheeks too. One by one, they all filed past her and kissed her. The boys' solemnity was strangely touching.

When the last person – Paige – had kissed her, Xavier stepped forward and told her to repeat the oath that he would give her, word for word. She nodded.

'Give your full name,' he told her.

'Giselle Geiret,' she said.

'I, Giselle Geiret, being of sound enough mind to make an oath on this day –'

'I, Giselle Geiret, being of sound enough mind to make an oath on this day –'

'Do swear on this ground that I shall henceforth worship, to honour all customs, practices and rituals.'

'Do swear on this ground that I shall henceforth worship, to honour all customs, practices and rituals.'

'I offer all that I have to be shared for the common good.'

She hesitated, but Xavier looked at her sternly, forcing the words from her lips.

'I offer all that I have to be shared for the common good.'

'Without restraint, let or hindrance.'

Again she hesitated.

'Without restraint, let or hindrance,' he repeated and she dutifully voiced the words.

'For as long as I remain here.'

'For as long as I remain here.'

He smiled. 'That's it, you're one of us.'

He held out his hand and pulled her to her feet. They all touched her, or kissed her, then Xavier led her to the fire to eat. Paige brought bowls from the hut and Thierry dished out mussels and steaming juice. Cold beer was passed around. There was an awkwardness in the conversation after the mock solemnity of the ceremony. Giselle felt that it was her. She only half belonged. She wanted to belong completely but could do nothing to ease the transition.

After they had eaten, Paige took her into the hut. It smelt of fish and stale bedding. A collection of smoke-blackened cooking pots hung from nails embedded in the wooden walls. In one corner there was an old chest and Paige threw open the lid to reveal a tangle of clothes – strange garments that she rummaged through while Giselle watched.

'We dress up sometimes,' Paige explained, holding up a long white gown. 'My virgin bride outfit,' she said with a self-conscious smile. She dropped it back into the chest and plucked out a circlet of fake gold, chipped and battered. 'For the Queen of the Island – when Xavier decides that we need a queen.'

There were sashes of vividly coloured silk, and Paige tied one around her waist. 'Sometimes this is all that I wear,' she said, adjusting the silk and pulling it between her legs. When she wrapped it around her behind, it looked like a psychedelic loincloth.

'What happened to my underwear?' Giselle asked. She had been wanting to ask ever since the swim, but something told her that if she had, she would have been teased. Paige laughed.

'Do you need it?'

'Well . . .' Giselle's words trailed away as the other girl smiled mischievously.

'The only reason that I'm wearing this bikini is because this is your first day and they didn't want me to scare you.'

'You mean that normally . . .'

'Normally nobody wears anything at all, unless they want to. I like to wear a sash like this.' She span and the silk floated out from her waist, revealing her bikini clad mound. 'I think it's sexier than being naked.'

When she saw that Giselle was looking apprehensive she dropped the subject.

'Do you like body paint?' she asked, pulling a box out of the corner.

'I don't know.'

'It's fun. I'll show you.'

They sat side by side on one of the trio of camp beds. The smell of fish, which Giselle had noticed when they entered the hut, was stronger here. She looked beneath the stained canvas and found a box of fishing tackle.

Paige saw Giselle's pained expression as she was setting out bottles and brushes.

She stood up. 'Come on, I'll show you the paints outside. The smell is getting to me too.'

They sat in the shade of the hut, leaning back against the painted walls. Paige drew a flower in pink and white on her thigh and then a stalk in green that looped down to her knee.

'It's pretty,' Giselle told her.

'Let me do a flower on your forehead.'

Giselle looked doubtful.

'They wash off easily. Come on, it will get you into the spirit of it.'

Giselle laughed. 'OK.'

Paige knelt and brushed Giselle's hair back. 'Hold still.'

The brush was itchy. Giselle was aware of the girl's breasts, and the scent of wood smoke and wine, as she leant forward and concentrated on her task. After a few minutes, the girl sat back and looked critically at her work. She applied a few final touches, then jumped up and disappeared into the hut.

183

'Don't touch it till it's dry,' she said as she brought out an old mirror.

She held up the glass for Giselle.

It was one of the flowers that she had seen under the pine trees, when Giscard had taken her to the top of the island. The slender, trumpet-shaped bloom filled her forehead. The stem curled down and around her nose.

'It's beautiful,' Giselle said.

She took the mirror and examined herself. It seemed that she was already becoming part of the island; allowing it to grow over and into her. She remembered some climbing plants amongst the bushes where she had undressed and described them to Paige.

'Columbine,' said the girl.

'Can you do those?'

'I can draw all the plants on the island. Do you want me to?'

'I'd like that.'

Paige looked at Giselle's legs and arms.

'Legs would be best. You'll have to stand up.'

Giselle stood.

'Pull the dress up.'

Giselle pulled it as high as she dared while Paige sorted through the paints. She seemed to take the painting very seriously, mixing the colours carefully and trying little spots on Giselle's legs before beginning in earnest.

Thierry drifted in their direction but Paige told him to go away.

'You can send them away during the day,' she told Giselle. 'It's more difficult at night.'

When Giselle asked what she meant, Paige looked at her with a wry smile.

'If you stay, you'll find out.'

The flowers gradually extended themselves across Giselle's thighs; the stems coiled down to her ankles.

'Very pagan,' Paige said, looking at her work. 'Xavier will like that.'

184

'Is he serious about the –' Giselle didn't know how to describe it, 'about the gods of the air, that sort of thing?'

'Who knows? He's serious about the island, about the magic here. We all are. You will feel it too, if you stay long enough. It comes over you and stays with you afterwards, even in the city.'

Giselle had already felt the island entering her blood. She held up her leg and looked at the columbine.

'It's certainly growing on me,' she said, and they laughed.

Later, as evening drew in, it grew cooler. The waters of the lake turned from blue to black, like a bruise. The shadows of the woods became sinister.

Thierry piled wood on the fire so that the flames leapt high. Soon there was only the moon and the shifting light of the flames.

Xavier told Billy to get the torches. The boy fetched bundles of bulrushes, soaked them in paraffin then staked them out around the perimeter of the clearing. When they were lit, they burnt blue and cast an ethereal light over the cliffs. It would have been easy to see the forms of sprites and goblins in the restless shadows. It would have been easy to be afraid of the night.

Giselle drew closer to Giscard. He kissed her neck lightly and she turned to him and offered her lips. It was intoxicating to be kissed in that place – as if she had been plucked from the earth and carried to a dreamland. When Giscard broke the kiss, she realised that Xavier and Thierry were looking at her intently.

'Remember that we share everything here,' Xavier told her.

An image of the girl in the car park fired in Giselle's mind. The hairs on the back of her neck began to rise.

'It's her first visit,' Giscard said.

'She took the oath.'

There was a long silence; Giscard hung his head. Xavier gazed at Giselle expectantly.

185

'What am I to do?' Giselle asked finally, surprised by her courage.

'As much as you give to Giscard, you give to us,' Xavier told her.

'Then I must kiss you?'

Xavier nodded.

'You don't have to –' Giscard began, but Giselle was already rising – it was only a kiss.

As she walked by the fire, she felt the heat on her thighs and saw the looks on the faces of the boys. They wanted her – all of them – even Jean. Paige smiled in encouragement as Giselle knelt gracefully in front of Xavier.

'The meek shall inherit the earth,' he said, then leant forward and brushed his lips with hers. It was a tantalising touch. Just enough to leave her feeling cheated.

'Is that how he kisses you?' Xavier asked.

She shook her head.

'Show me then.'

She sat up and leant forward, looking into his eyes. He was patient, seemed almost indifferent, as her lips approached. When she opened her mouth though, he took it fiercely, and she was kissed as she had never been kissed before. She fell back as soon as he released her. Whatever drug he had left in her mouth moved swiftly, and her belly liquefied.

'There are others,' he reminded her.

With an effort, she tore her eyes from his, and looked around the expectant circle of faces. In the shifting light, they seemed changed. They waited like a pack that knows it will soon be fed – nervous, excited, expectant.

Xavier offered his hand, and she rose uneasily. Billy, the quiet one, was closest. She went to him first and he stood to kiss her. His mouth was softer than Xavier's, more seductive, but less exciting. Thierry pulled her into his lap when it was his turn. He took his time, but the

186

kiss was harsh and she felt some of the magic leaving her. Then it was Jean, her bold, beautiful, cruel brother. She looked at Xavier, wondering if she must really do this.

'We are all brothers and sisters in the eyes of the Lord,' he told her. The voice was at once serious and mocking.

Jean reached for her, forcing the issue. It felt very wrong as she sank into his lap. It felt even more wrong as she felt the hardness of his erection beneath her behind.

'Hi, sis,' he said.

He took her hand first, and kissed that.

'So?'

She looked at him, then glanced around the ring of faces. The expectation was palpable, the collective will inescapable. She kissed him. The sense of wrongness doubled as his tongue went into her mouth and doubled again as his hardness pulsed and slid into the valley of her behind. It was too much and she jumped to her feet. Jean laughed, but not harshly.

'Don't forget Paige,' Xavier told her.

She was already reeling with the wrongness of kissing Jean, and shook her head.

Paige rose and came over slowly, as if approaching a nervous cat. She was still wearing the bikini and the flowers still snaked around her legs.

She took Giselle's hand and smiled.

'It's for the boys really, they like to watch,' she said softly, so that only Giselle could hear, 'but you may enjoy it. Girls kiss differently.'

Giselle allowed the girl to run her lips across her own. She was expecting to feel nothing but when Paige's tongue pushed aside the shielding lips, there was a little frisson of excitement in her belly. She yielded to a full-blooded kiss and lost herself for a moment. When the two girls pulled apart, they glowed. Then, as if it had

187

been rehearsed, they linked arms and bowed to the boys.

'Is there anything else?' Xavier asked.

Giselle turned to see that he was looking at Giscard and that the boy obviously didn't want to reply. Xavier turned to Giselle.

'Is there anything else that we are entitled to?' he asked.

Giselle didn't understand. She glanced at Paige for help.

'Has he touched you?' the girl asked quietly.

It was only then that she fully realised what her oath had meant. She thought of that afternoon when she and Giscard had climbed to the top of the island. She remembered undoing her bra. She remembered Giscard sucking on her breasts. The thought that Xavier would do the same made her knees buckle. She rested her hand on Paige's arm to steady herself.

Xavier gestured for her to approach. He seemed like a medieval king as she went to him, her legs weak with fear and excitement. Without being asked, she sank to the ground.

She couldn't speak. Instead she undid her blouse. The two halves still hid her breasts as she let her hands fall away. He gestured for her to open them. After a moment, she did, and the light of the fire caressed the soft mounds.

'How does he touch you?' he asked.

'With his hands and his lips,' she replied after a breathless silence.

'Gently?'

She looked at him in surprise. 'Of course.' How else would a boy touch a girl?

'He says that you are still a virgin. Is that true?'

She nodded, wanting him to know that.

He reached out and his fingers trailed around the circumference of her breasts. She wanted to ask if he liked them, if she was good enough. She remembered the greed in Giscard's eyes on the little rocky plateau. She saw only curiosity in Xavier, that and the pleasure of acquisition.

He told her to kneel up. When she did, his lips encircled a taut nipple and his tongue span until she groaned and let her head fall back. It felt as if he was sucking out her soul, taking it for safe keeping.

The release was painful, a loss. Her chest was heaving.

'Now you look like a bride of the island,' he told her. 'Now you are beginning to belong.'

She smiled.

'Go to the others.'

It seemed easier this time. Billy was shy but became intense when his lips took her. Thierry mauled her like a bear. With Jean, she felt as if she were doing something with her body that she had always done with her mind. He took suck and there was the peace of something resolved. When he finished, she wanted him to take more and offered her breast again, lifting it in her hand. He leant forward and nipped her with his teeth. He had had enough and she laughed as she backed away.

Finally, there was only Paige. The girl dipped her head and sucked one breast then the other, quickly. Her smile was as sweet as any infant as she went down for a fuller feed. Afterwards, they stood together, shyly aware of their beauty.

'Next time, I want to taste you between the legs,' the girl whispered, making Giselle blush hotly, and giggle.

'Time for a baptism!' Xavier cried. He jumped to his feet and caught Giselle around the waist before she could react. He hauled her on to his shoulder and trotted towards the beach as she screamed her protests. He waded out into the dark water until he was waist deep. She was kicking her legs, and screaming. The

189

others gathered on the shore, shouting and laughing. Suddenly his arms were around her waist and she was lifted high in the air.

'I baptise you in the name of the Moon, and the Rocks, and the Wind,' he cried, and let her fall. The water was warm but it was still a shock and she rose to the surface, spluttering. He pushed her under again but she grabbed his legs and pulled him down with her. They wrestled but he was strong. Finally, she succumbed and let herself be held to his body and kissed.

When he'd had enough of her mouth, they waded ashore and Paige took her into the hut. In the light of an old storm lamp, Giselle peeled off her wet clothes. The flower that Paige had carefully painted on her legs and face were hopelessly smudged and Paige helped her to clean off the running pigment with a cloth. Once this was done, Paige opened the chest with the clothes.

'Will you wear this?' Paige asked, holding up one of the long silken sashes.

Giselle shrugged.

'Will it cover me?'

'It will cover you down there,' the girl replied, glancing at Giselle's naked belly and sex. 'Everything else they've seen anyway.'

'How do I wear it?' Giselle asked.

Paige carefully wrapped the sash around Giselle's hips and pulled it between her legs. The vivid violets and blues glowed in the light of the lamp. Paige left it loose so that Giselle felt almost naked. It was enough though – as much as she wanted to wear.

'And you?'

Paige smiled and slipped off her bikini, first the top and then the bottom. Giselle couldn't help but examine the flat belly and smooth breasts that were revealed. Neither could she ignore the carefully trimmed pubis or the sweet, pink-fringed opening. Paige threw her arms out wide so that Giselle could look, but Giselle was suddenly embarrassed.

'Sorry, I didn't mean to stare,' she said.

'You will see plenty of me in future, there's no need to blush.'

Giselle looked at the girl's breasts again, and at her sex.

'Do you shave the hair?'

'Billy likes it.'

'Is Billy special?'

'He's my boyfriend away from the island. Like Giscard is for you.'

Giselle nodded and Paige hunted through the clothes again.

'I could wear nothing, of course,' she said, turning over and rejecting a series of skirts and dresses. 'They will want me now. I saw how much you excited them. Whatever I wear will be taken from me.'

Giselle looked at the girl. She wondered if she would be allowed to watch, if Xavier would take her in the light of the fire.

'Wear something,' she said. 'I don't want to be upstaged.'

Paige laughed and chose a man's shirt that came down to the top of her thighs. She did up only one button, at waist level, so that, as she moved, it was obvious she was naked beneath.

They stepped outside bravely and walked to the fire, holding hands.

The boys stared. Giselle was aware of the eyes that brushed her skin and burrowed beneath the silk between her legs. She straightened her back and neck to emphasise her natural grace. Her long legs and slender waist moved in fluid harmony. She would be more than breast and hips. She would be a princess.

Paige let go of Giselle's hand when they reached the fire and went over to Billy and sat in his lap. The shirt fell open so that everyone could see her nakedness. She kissed Billy but gazed at Xavier. It was obvious who she wanted. Her legs opened and her sex glistened in the firelight, beckoning him. Following Paige's example, Giselle went to Giscard. He stared in awe as she approached, making her feel the princess that she wanted to be. She was about to sit in his lap when Xavier motioned to Paige. The girl rose immediately. From the fire in her eyes, Giselle knew that something would happen, and felt a rush of excitement. Before it could, Giscard rose and, taking her hand, led her into the darkness. She didn't want to go. Glancing back, she saw Paige sink to her knees and reach between Xavier's legs. Giscard tugged harder and Giselle almost stumbled in the sand. Only when they reached the water's edge did he pause. When she looked back this time, she saw Paige dancing around the fire. The shirt was gone and she was naked.

Giscard pulled her around so that he faced her.

'Kiss me,' he said.

She kissed him but her mind was filled with the vision of the naked girl dancing in the firelight. Giscard pressed her back steadily until her shoulders were against the wall of the cliff. The stone was rough and cold against her skin; Giscard's lips were hot and soft on her breasts. She heard a girl cry out, then a peal of laughter, and tried to see what was happening. Giscard took her face in his hands and held her.

'Let me see,' she said.

'He doesn't want you to,' Giscard told her. 'He doesn't want you to see what you aren't part of yet.'

Giselle realised that there were stages of belonging, that she would have to do more than kiss the boys and offer her breasts.

'If you were there would you –' She didn't know how to ask.

'With Paige?' he asked.

'Yes.'

'Maybe.'

She smiled. There was no jealousy, only a curiosity – that and a little fear. She was with somebody who had used his sex to pierce a girl. He would use it to pierce her if she asked him. There was another cry, sexual this time, and without the reassuring frame of laughter. One day, Giselle would dream of those sounds. She would dream of rooms full of strange groans, rooms that she couldn't enter until a man carried her, naked and ready.

Giscard took suck again. Her breasts filled with warmth and her belly tingled.

The cry came again, higher, fuller. Giselle's sense of exclusion was acute. Giscard at her breasts was no longer enough. She wanted to belong fully, completely. Yet, when his hand slid down her belly and threatened to enfold her sex, she wriggled away. She wanted to belong but wasn't ready. Realising this, knowing that Giscard was her protector and that Giscard would always take no for an answer, she kissed him again. This time she poured herself into the boy. When the cries from the camp became too much – too sharp, too high, too full of feelings that still frightened her – Giselle made him take her further away.

They rounded the shoulder of rock that protected that side of the bay. They passed beneath the cliff that she had jumped from, treading the narrow fringe of sand as if walking a tightrope between earth and sky. Two pale faces watched them, the moon of the heavens and her sister in the reflecting waters. Once past the cliffs, they climbed into the interior of the island. The trees twisted around them like the limbs of dancers frozen by darkness. To be naked, near naked in such a place! Giselle felt her body hum with life. The pine needles beneath her feet tested her trust of this new kingdom. She walked without fear and no sharp stones cut her, no briars tore at her exposed skin. The wonder of it was beyond human words. Instead, the sighs of the trees, the soughs and gasps as the wind touched the heavy branches – these spoke for her. The island's music played itself into her fabric. She was its bride now; Xavier had said so. She wanted to cry out with joy but it would have been wrong, wrong to fracture that perfect calm, a crime against paradise.

They sat by a stream and looked between the columns of trees to the sparkling waters of the lake.

'Will your father give you a hard time for staying out?' he asked, bringing her back to unwelcome reality.

'Probably.'

They were silent for a moment.

'How do you leave?' she asked suddenly. 'How do you go back to Avignon?' The treadmill of life in her father's house, the aridity of school, seemed unbearable after this brief taste of freedom.

'Once it has you, there is no going back,' he replied.

But there is always a going back. Giselle knew that the body returns to places that the mind has long quit. She would sleep that night in her father's house and dream of a lake the colour of a bruise. With a sigh, she banished such thoughts, banished all but the trees and the lake and the boy beside her. He wanted to touch her breasts again. She lay down on the bed of pine needles and stretched her hands above her head. The pleasure of watching him in the moonlight was intense. His features were even softer, even dreamier as he kissed her. The moon, single now, watched as her fingers coiled and uncoiled and her head rolled slowly from side to side.

There were new feelings in her belly. Twice she took his hand and carried it to the place between her thighs; twice she lost courage, pushing it away at the last moment. Even so, her arousal kept mounting. It felt as if she were bleeding into the island. Tenderness and desire poured from her sex. Her breasts, the altars of such worship, became constellations of pleasure, the feelings more wonderful than the stars that hung over them.

Finally, he had had enough. This was new, too. She had to adjust to the knowledge that he could be sated, that she was no longer wanted. The power of saying no to him was also the power of making him want her continually. To be left with her breasts exposed, unkissed and undesired, hurt. She was glad that she had refused to yield her sex. He would come back to her still. He would come back for that moist opening.

'It's late,' he said.

It seemed early to her, only the beginning, but she allowed him to pull her to her feet.

They walked back through the woods hand in hand. He didn't touch her again. She wanted him to. At every step she was aware of her inflamed sex. She wanted to be pushed against a tree and penetrated without asking. She wanted her protests ignored.

When they reached the camp, the boys were busying themselves clearing up. They were purposeful and silent, bent on their tasks.

Giselle helped Paige to wash the bowls. Squatting together at the edge of the lake, Giselle kept glancing at the girl, wondering how it had felt to dance in front of everyone, wondering what she had done afterwards, who had taken her and how. Even in the light of the moon, Giselle could see the change in her. Paige's face was as fluid as the surface of the water; she had been through something powerful and somehow it had cleansed her. The cleansing power of sex had never occurred to Giselle before. Her father had taught her that it was dirty; the priests taught that it was the sin of all sins. Yet Paige seemed to have been bathed in something that had left her as fresh as the night air.

'Did you have a good walk?' the girl asked, smiling shyly, as if she were aware of the examination and of all the unasked questions.

Giselle nodded.

'Stay next time,' Paige told her. 'You'll see things that you won't see anywhere else.' Her eyes sparkled like the waters and Giselle could see the moons in them.

'Will you do what you said you would?' Giselle blushed as soon as she'd spoken, shocked at her own forwardness.

'If you want me to.'

Paige kissed her. It was a kiss for the girls alone. There were no boys to see them.

After that first visit to the island, Giselle was changed. Her father no longer frightened her. Her school no longer seemed so large. Avignon was no longer the centre of her world. The centre had shifted east, out into the rocky hills.

Jean was more familiar with her, too. She realised that the island had been a secret that had come between them. Now it was a shared secret, and there was a new understanding. He called her 'sis' and was more affectionate. Sometimes she saw his desire for her, and saw that it was an effort for him to control it.

Giscard still called in the evenings and in some ways nothing had changed. They still walked down to the river or went to McDonald's to drink milk shakes and eat French fries. There was a sense of waiting, though, of anticipation of her next invitation to the island. They didn't discuss it much. Xavier would decide when she should go.

Jean still disappeared every evening and often told her that he had been to the island, but he never gave details. She burnt with curiosity. When he came back late and tired she wanted to ask who had been there, why she hadn't been invited. She longed to see Xavier again. Her fantasies were filled with tattooed hands touching her naked body.

* * *

196

A week after her first visit, another Saturday, Giscard told her to be ready for Xavier that evening. The day passed slowly. She tried and retried her clothes and experimented with make-up. In the end she dressed as she always dressed, but used some make-up to appear older. Giscard smiled when he saw the lipstick, but made her take it off: Xavier wouldn't approve. It was a mark of the other world, the world they escaped from on the island.

As soon as Giselle was inside the old Land Rover, Thierry slipped his hand inside her shirt. She was in the back this time – another girl sat next to Xavier. Giscard watched from the corner of his eye as Giselle let Thierry explore her breasts. Any thought of protest was snuffed out by Xavier's eyes in the driver's mirror. It felt as if Thierry was the agent of his desires and, before they had travelled a kilometre, she was wet beneath her skirt.

The girl in the front seat turned to watch as they entered the pine woods. Her jet-black eyes sparkled.

'I'm Joan,' she said, holding out her hand. Giselle shook it self-consciously. The girl laughed when Thierry refused to let go of Giselle's breasts.

'Are you his?' she asked.

'No,' replied Giselle quickly. The word was half strangled as Thierry ran his fingers in quick circles around her nipples.

'He likes you, though,' said the girl with a giggle, watching the hand beneath the shirt. With that, she turned in her seat again and whispered something in Xavier's ear.

'What is she saying?' demanded Thierry.

'She thinks that Giselle can't be a virgin. She gets turned on too easily.'

Giselle blushed, partly because they must have been talking about her earlier, and partly because it embarrassed her how quickly Thierry – a boy that she

197

hardly knew – could arouse her so. She glanced guiltily at Giscard. He shook his head in disapproval, but smiled.

'Kiss me,' she said, wanting still to be his.

He leant across and she closed her eyes as his lips opened and pressed about hers.

When she opened her eyes, the Land Rover was slowing as it slid down the white beach to the lake. There was already a car parked on the sloping sand and the boat was half-full of people. Thierry undid the buttons of the shirt completely as Xavier parked. Her breasts were free as Thierry pulled her out of the door and led her down to the water's edge. Billy and Paige waved from the boat. There were two other boys, boys that Giselle had never seen before. They looked at her with unconcealed interest.

Xavier and Giscard hauled some provisions out of the car in large cardboard boxes and carried them to the boat. It sank lower and lower as boxes and people filled it.

'We'll have to throw you out if we start to sink,' Jean told her.

The others thought that he was joking but Giselle wasn't so sure.

As soon as they reached the Island, Paige slipped off her clothes. The boys whistled and she waved her naked behind at them. Giselle envied her naturalness. She left her shirt undone but didn't have the courage to remove the little skirt of shiny silk. A boy would have to do that – if any boy wanted to when Paige was so beautiful and so easy.

They spent the afternoon swimming and sunbathing. Giscard fished from the rocks at the edge of the bay and caught a carp. He refused to gut it and Jean was forced to, calling him a baby and throwing the intestines at him once it had been done.

Giselle helped Paige to prepare a barbecue. Fires were lit as the sun began to sink.

Night was the great transformer; night and fire. Thierry took Joan into the shadows and they heard her groaning. They heard his grunts as he came. Giselle was handing out plates of charcoal-grilled chicken when the girl came back on her own, naked but carrying her clothes. Giselle saw the languor in the girl's tread and the brightness of her eyes.

Xavier had spent the afternoon reading, talking to no one. Now he was drinking from a bottle of cheap wine with Paige on his lap. He took the food from Giselle without even looking at her. It stung. She wanted to be noticed.

It was only later, after they had all eaten, that he called for her. Paige smiled from his lap as Giselle came to stand in front of them.

'So, what do we have to enjoy from Giselle tonight?' he asked.

Giscard looked up as if the question had been directed at him, but Xavier's eyes were locked into Giselle's. She shrugged self-consciously. Thierry appeared behind her, entering the light of the fire for the first time since he had taken Joan into the shadows. She caught the scent of girl mucus as his hand slipped inside her open shirt. His fingers twisted one of her nipples sharply and she jumped, but didn't struggle. The feeling was too good to escape, the sharpness like cold water on a hot night.

'Let's see her,' said Joan from her place by the fire.

Thierry slipped the shirt from Giselle's shoulders. He licked the side of her neck obscenely, and she giggled. Now all that she wore was the short silk skirt – hardly a scrap about her waist. If Thierry had undone the little zip at the side it would have fallen to her feet.

'Still a virgin?' Xavier asked.

She nodded. Joan laughed, but Xavier silenced her with a quick glance.

'Don't you want Giscard?'

199

She couldn't reply. She couldn't say, 'It's you that I want,' not with so many eyes on her. Perhaps he would read it in her face. She wanted him to see her desire. She wished that Thierry would undo the little zip and let the dress fall. It would make her seem less childish. It would make Xavier want her more.

Xavier pushed Paige from his lap. The girl rose with good grace as Thierry delivered Giselle into Xavier's hands. Paige didn't go far. As Giselle sank into Xavier's lap, Paige sank down beside him on the fallen tree.

Xavier's closeness, and Paige's eyes, pinned her firmly to the fabric of the night. She was a butterfly laid out on a black field. They could do as they liked with her. She wanted to say that; she tried to show it in the meekness of her gaze. Her belly was already on fire. She wanted them to lead her into temptation and to deliver her unto evil. Still a virgin – it embarrassed her. Giscard's cowardice, his respect for her protestations of innocence, was costing her too much. No flesh was innocent. This was her education. Xavier was her priest, and she wanted him to take confession with the hard penis that she felt pressed into her behind. Her penance would be the other boys, satisfying them – even her brother, who watched her every move.

Xavier's hand was on her breast. He had already sucked out her soul, now he explored the void. Soon he would feel the wetness that was seeping from between her legs, down to the sex that it desired.

'Giscard,' he called, and he motioned to the boy. She watched from her dream as a figure came out of the shadows and stood before her.

'She will whore for you if you want it,' Xavier said. 'Can't you see that, can't you read it in her face?'

Giselle looked up and saw Giscard's troubled eyes.

'Don't you want a whore of your own?'

Giscard seemed upset by the words. Giselle knew that she should be upset as well. But she wasn't. She knew that Xavier was right. Her unused belly needed to be filled.

'Undo his shorts,' Xavier said.

She was being addressed but it took a moment for the fact to register. It took even longer to understand what had been said.

Xavier picked up her hand and rested it against Giscard's belly. With thick, heavy fingers, as if she were drugged, she began to pick at the buckle of his belt. Amazingly it opened. The buttons too. Each opened, one by one.

'Pull them down,' Xavier told her.

She had never seen a boy's sex before. Not close to. Not a grown boy's sex. With both hands, she eased the shorts and the underpants beneath them down. The tube of flesh sprang free, bounding upwards, frightening her for a moment, then fascinating her. The head was rounded and smooth, the eye, a moist slit. It was so close that she felt the heat of it on her cheek.

'What do you want to do?' Xavier asked.

'Touch it?' asked Giselle, not really knowing. Looking would have been enough, familiarising herself with the strange, ugly, beautiful thing that pulsed so close to her lips.

Her fingers were tentative, her expression reverent, as she ran the tips of her fingers slowly from head to base. Further down was a tight sac of skin covered with curls of blond hair. She wondered if she could touch these too, but was too shy to ask.

'How else could you touch it?' Xavier asked.

She glanced from Giscard to Xavier and back again. Giscard's face seemed to shiver as she stroked his sex. Her fingers made a loop around the girth of the tube and drew slowly downwards. His eyes widened. There was sweat on his forehead, a film that made him shine in the firelight.

'Kiss it,' Paige told her. She was leaning forward, close enough for her knees to touch Giselle's thighs.

201

When Giselle did nothing, Paige darted her head to the exposed flesh and her tongue emerged wet and pink. The tip was pointed and flew like an arrow to the head of Giscard's sex. It swept quickly across the moist eye and circled beneath the bulging head. The boy groaned as Paige enveloped him with her lips and Giselle felt him stiffen beneath her enfolding fingers. Looking up, she saw from his face that he liked her lips. He had never asked for this from her. It would have been a pleasure; she wanted that pleasure. When Paige removed her mouth, Giselle gave hers. The flesh was hot. Her tongue was nervous as it teased its way across the tight skin.

Giscard pulled away suddenly. She didn't understand. He had wanted Paige. She looked at him, the hurt showing. He had wanted Paige's mouth – she had seen that in his eyes. Why didn't he want hers? If he thought that he was sparing her in some way, he was wrong. Didn't he realise that to be spared this was to be deprived of Xavier? If she took his sex, Xavier's would follow. And her mouth was made for Xavier – every instinct and nerve told her that.

Xavier moved abruptly, his hand as quick as a snake. He seized Giscard's balls and pulled him back to where he had been. Giscard's fists clenched and Giselle sensed that he would fight. Rapidly, she took his sex again and moved her head in quick circles, wanting, in her unskilled way, to make it as good as she could. She felt his relaxation and knew that he had accepted her gift. Her eyes closed and she lost herself in the pleasure of sucking. It was awkward leaning forward – her dress was restricting her. She pulled the hem upwards until her legs could move freely and so that Giscard could see her sex and know that she was showing it to everyone. Now she was like the other girls and she would belong. They wouldn't send her out into the night so that Paige could dance for them. Giscard groaned as she opened her legs wide and crouched closer to him, driving his sex deeper, to the frontier of her throat and the promise of the tightness beyond.

She gave herself as fully as she was able. Fingers came to caress her lips. She felt them work over Giscard's shaft too. Paige's, she thought as they began to masturbate Giscard in long, easy strokes. When she opened her eyes though, she saw blue tattoos on the wrist that owned the fingers and sat back in surprise. There was something demonic in Xavier's eyes. Giscard looked beaten, humiliated. But his erection didn't fade. There seemed to be a guilty pleasure in being caressed by a boy.

The hand moved more quickly. Paige ran her fingers up the back of Giscard's legs. She grinned as the fingers made a spear and jabbed upwards. Giselle couldn't see what was happening but Giscard suddenly sighed and groaned.

'Be ready for him,' Xavier whispered.

She watched as Giscard swayed and his belly filled with deep, successively quicker breaths. He was panting and she knew that soon he would come. She had heard how it happened, how a white fluid spurted from the tip of a boy's penis. Some of the girls in her class regularly performed this service for their boyfriends, used hands and mouth, and were drenched in the fluid that would have made a child in their wombs.

Xavier took her chin with his free hand and tipped her head back.

'Open,' he told her.

Feeling foolish, but also unbearably aroused, she waited with open mouth while Xavier pumped harder and harder.

'Look at her, Giscard. Look at the virgin at your feet.'

Giscard looked and came. Thick ropes of milky liquid sprayed across Giselle's face and fell into her mouth. Xavier pulled them together, mated sex and mouth, so that she felt the final pulses coating her tongue.

As soon as the last drop had issued and Xavier had released him, Giscard tore himself away. She tried to smile but all she saw in his face was hurt and a sense of betrayal. He stumbled away, pulling up his shorts. At the edge of the firelight, he paused to look at her in a sort of horror, then he ran into the night. Bewildered, she turned to Xavier, hoping that he would understand, hoping that he would explain what had happened.

'Find him,' he said. 'Make it all right.'

She rose, picked up her shirt and hurried in the direction that Giscard had taken. In the pitch darkness, outside the circle of firelight, she stumbled as she called out his name. She passed the fishing hut and climbed the slope to the cliffs, buttoning her shirt as she went. Some instinct told her that he wouldn't want to see her unclothed.

Gradually, her eyes adjusted to the night and the moon lit her way. She called again as she passed under the trees but there was no reply. Then, as she reached the place where the rope hung, she saw a figure slouched on one of the rocks looking out over the lake. She went to him tentatively.

'Giscard,' she said softly.

His face was pale in the moonlight when he turned to her.

'Go away.'

She hesitated. 'Please, I don't understand. Don't send me away.'

He looked at her again. She saw the evidence of tears in his eyes.

'He shouldn't have done that,' he stated flatly. 'I'm not ... I don't ... He shouldn't have touched me like that.'

She understood. It was the excitement of being touched by Xavier. Another boy had made him climax. Her mouth was secondary, just a receptacle.

'Is it so very bad?' she asked, remembering the pleasure of being kissed by Paige.

'I know what people will think.'

'Xavier has a power,' Giselle began. 'I think that the other boys will understand that. Perhaps they would want the same thing.'

He shook his head, but seemed calmed by these words.

'Now they will all want you to suck them.'

She was silent as he looked at her. She couldn't say that she wanted that. She didn't know if she did. The thought that Xavier would enter her mouth was overwhelming; that she did want. But the other boys, her brother amongst them? She didn't know.

'Is that why you never tried to make me do it before?'

'Everything that you do for me you have to do for them!' he said in a burst of anger. 'I want you for myself.'

'Then we should leave the island and never come back,' she said without conviction.

He looked at her derisively. 'Neither of us want that.'

She drew nearer to him. 'When we are away from here, I will be yours alone.'

'A whore of my own!' he said, spitting out the words as if they were poison.

'Someone who won't say no.'

She saw his eyes flare.

'If that is what you want, I'll take you back naked and open your mouth for each and every boy. I'll come for you every night and bring my friends!'

His rage shocked her and she stepped back.

'Will you say no to that?' he asked.

A tear eased from the corner of her eye.

'If you hate me so much, I'll go, and you can forget me.'

'I don't hate you. Don't you understand? I love you. That is why I don't want to see you on your knees in front of anyone who wants you!'

She sighed.

'It's all gone too far.'

'Tell me that you don't want Xavier and we'll leave.'

She looked at him steadily, unable to lie.

'Tell me!' he said again.

'You wanted him,' she said softly. She saw shock in his eyes, then rage. He jumped to his feet and she backed away, but not quickly enough to avoid a slap across the face. It was her turn to be shocked. Seizing her, he pulled the shirt from her shoulders and tore the skirt downwards, tearing the waistband. When he stepped back, her naked body was quaking and the tears were coursing down her face.

'Then it will be me who gives you to him.'

He took her hand and pulled her roughly down the slope. Twice she fell. Branches struck at her nakedness, the pine needles stung and made her cry out. Giscard was beyond pity; all sweetness was gone. He seemed mad to her and she was frightened. As they drew closer there was the sound of raised voices and laughter. She saw Joan chasing Thierry around the fire. She saw him dodging and laughing as the girl tried to hit him. They froze as Giscard dragged Giselle into the light of the fire. All eyes were on her as she was thrown at Xavier's feet.

'Tell him what you want.'

Giselle looked from Giscard to Xavier. She was gasping for breath and half-blinded by tears.

'Tell him!'

She shook her head, and began to curl into a ball.

Giscard fell to his knees and took hold of her ankles, pulling them wide. When she struggled, he slapped her across the face. It was harder than the first slap, even more shocking because it was calculated, cold-blooded. She lost the will to defend herself and became rigid. He spat on his hand and smeared the wetness between her legs, then began to undo his shorts. It felt as if she had fallen into a nightmare. The boy who pulled his erect sex

206

into the light of the fire had the appearance of Giscard, but Giscard was never like this, never so cruel, never so full of hatred. He took her wrists and pinned her hands above her head. His mouth took her breasts and bit as his sex nudged between her legs. She struggled, and he bit harder.

'You want this. It can be easy or hard,' he hissed in her ear.

His sex lodged in the wet slit, the head nudged forward and found the beginning of the virgin passageway. This quietened her, like a knife at the throat. Fear and disbelief staked her out like a blood sacrifice.

'Now say it!' he shouted. 'Say that you want them all.'

His sex was pressing hard at the membrane which had sealed her innocence since birth. His eyes blazed. It shouldn't be like this. It had always been soft in her imagination. The boy would be tender. There would be intimacy and trust. But then she turned her head and looked at Xavier. He watched like a statue from the vantage of the fallen tree. She had his attention now. She had everyone's attention.

'I want it,' she said with a sudden surge of strength and, before Giscard could move, she jammed her pelvis upwards, hard, impaling herself. The membrane tore and she screamed but her eyes never left Xavier. She heard Giscard call her a bitch and then felt him pull out. He struggled to his feet and she looked up in fear as he towered over her with clenched fists. The hatred in his eyes had become contempt. She knew that he would never forgive her. She had robbed him of the chance of taking her virginity. She had given it instead to Xavier. She had given it with her eyes – Giscard's rapidly shrinking sex had merely been the tool, his rage the mechanism.

'She's your whore,' Giscard told Xavier savagely. 'Take her.'

She lay open-legged in the light of the fire. Her hands were still and quiet behind her head. Her newly opened sex gaped wide. There was absolute silence. For a terrible moment she thought that Xavier would refuse her. A sudden movement from the other side of the fire caught her attention. It was Jean, standing up, undoing the buckle of his belt.

'If you don't want her, I do,' he said, through clenched teeth.

She wanted to say no, tried to say it in her face when she turned back to Xavier.

'Oh, I want her,' Xavier replied, 'but you will be next.'

He pulled his shirt over his head, revealing the tight, tanned muscles of chest and abdomen. There was a tattoo that she had never seen before, a pair of crossed torches in the centre of his chest, blazing as if they were the fire of his heart. He stood and pulled his trousers down. His sex was hard, curving upwards like a scimitar. A golden snake had been engraved on the tall column and seemed to dance in the light of the fire. When he knelt between her legs she was aware that every part of him was hard. The beauty of taut muscles and stretched sinews made her feel weak. His hands, as they ran along the insides of her thighs, were like polished steel. They dug beneath her behind and lifted her easily so that only her shoulders were pressed to the sand and her sex was an open wound for him to explore.

She groaned as his tongue entered and arousal flared in her belly like the torches on his chest. Savage words formed in her throat. The night had her now; she was its creature, dark and lost, willing and easy. She was aware of faces around her, coming closer, of expressions of envy and desire. The soil of the island abraded her shoulders as Xavier's tongue explored her wounded belly. There were murmurs from the watchers, a joke and low laughter as she strained upwards to open herself more fully. Xavier was crouched over her like a wolf gorging itself at a kill. When he released her, his mouth was covered in virgin blood. The faces moved back a little as he stood, respectfully giving him room. Giselle, looking up through half-closed eyes, was aware only of his hardness. He loomed over her like an executioner's sword, ready to slice away all remaining innocence.

The murmurs rose in pitch, became more excited. This wasn't just Xavier and her. It was all of them, and the island too. If the cliffs had shouldered their way forward, parted the group around the fire and stood waiting for her with erections of jagged rock, she would have felt it as right. She was the island's bride, sworn to honour and obey the desires of sky and earth. More than that – she was a receptacle for all desires, and for all those who needed her.

There was a flush of pleasure as Paige knelt by her side. The softness of the girl seduced her and Giselle's mood changed. Now she was on the other shore of that vast lake of desire. Here were all things feminine; petal-soft kisses, moist heats, enveloping mists of care. Paige kissed her with a tenderness that made Giselle want to weep, made her want to be an infant in her mother's arms again. The rapacity of men, the hardness of rock, which had seemed so desirable a moment before, was suddenly a sharp threat. Xavier, as he took his sex and worked it around the entrance to her belly was rapist and assassin. Giselle reached out and took Paige's face. She had never felt such a desire to belong. She would be a votaress of the goddess's order, a worshipper of the goodness in Paige's smile.

Then Xavier brushed the head of his sex over her clitoris. There was a spasm in her belly, sharper than the stones that desired her, more compelling than the soft kisses of Paige. The conflicting desires bisected her. She was suspended over the dark lake, torn between the desire for a woman's tenderness and a lust for the penetration that would break her to pleasure.

Xavier let her down to the ground slowly. Her body fell open as she settled to the soil. Paige fastened soft lips on her breasts. Jean knelt on the other side and ran his fingers down her cheek. He was naked and erect. Paige whispered for her to look, to see her brother's desire. Giselle looked, and wanted him – wanted them all. She wanted to be enough for any who came to her. Her hand went to Jean's lap and lightly brushed the hard flesh – the caress of waterweed across smooth stone. She saw him tense, saw the involuntary tightening of his abdomen and the upwards thrust of his sex. She smiled, letting him know that she would welcome him as more than a brother. Xavier slipped his sex home, but lodged only the head. She turned to him with the same smile, letting him know that she was also his. He asked her if she wanted it, and she nodded. He buried himself with a quick thrust and she twisted like a fish as the pleasure stabbed through her. Her groan was the groan of someone who has waited too long, the groan of the believer when their god finally answers them. She wrapped her legs around his behind and held him strongly, so that he would never quit her. Jean pressed his lips to hers. Her mouth was penetrated as swiftly as her sex. Her brother's tongue writhed and stabbed. Paige bit into her breasts making her doubt the kindness of women.

Xavier began a slow rhythmic movement and her groans became a steady, unbroken keening. Jean released her mouth and the sounds spilled out into the night. He knelt up and, touching Paige's cheek, brought her mouth to his sex. Giselle watched enviously as the girl sucked her brother. Her neglected breasts, imprinted with Paige's teeth marks languished and Giselle was obliged to caress herself, to squeeze hard and pinch cruelly at her own nipples. Then Jean swung a leg across her chest and his sex came to her mouth. Paige lifted Giselle's head so that Jean could fuck her more easily. He fucked her as she wanted Xavier to fuck her, hard and fast, jamming into her throat. Then, abruptly, he withdrew and Paige used her fingers to milk him. Gelatinous semen rained on to Giselle's face as he arched his back and cried out. The stream seemed endless and Paige – pumping the brother with one hand, cradling the sister with the other – directed the flow to cover Giselle's face completely.

'The perfect baptism,' she murmured as Jean gave one final cry and slumped to the ground. He watched with sleepy, hooded eyes as Paige husbanded the semen into Giselle's mouth, using tongue and fingers. There were soft words and girlish giggles as they shared in the liquid feast.

Then Xavier began to move more quickly, torturing Giselle with the pleasure that he refused to bring to completion. As Jean rested his hand on Giselle's chest, she fought for air to fuel her gasps and sobs.

'You will kill her,' Paige told Xavier. It was Paige's pity, her fingers at Giselle's sex, that brought the relief of orgasm. The lightest of grazes across Giselle's clitoris was enough. She screamed and Xavier fucked her hard, pounding her behind into the soil as if he would first kill her, then bury her.

He didn't come. He fucked her until she was too exhausted to respond, then pulled out and took his place on the tree. Sweat glistened on his body but his expression was the same as ever. He had changed her for ever but had been untouched himself.

Giselle closed her eyes as Jean lay his head on her chest. She felt Paige curl around her and the girl's cheek settling on her belly. For a moment there was absolute peace and Giselle felt that at last she belonged. She could have stayed as she was for ever, but others wanted her. Paige's head was pushed aside and a boy's sex was hurriedly buried within her belly. The first was Billy. He was quick from the beginning, almost frantic. She lay her hand on his back and stroked him with the patience of a mother as he pistoned his desire. He came in a rapid series of spasms and she rained kisses on his neck and cheeks as he yelped out the pleasure.

Before Billy had completely finished, Thierry appeared, lifting the smaller boy by the shoulders and pushing him aside. Thierry's sex was long and thin. He was clumsy but strong, and she came again. He laughed crazily as she writhed with pleasure but it wasn't cruel or mocking. There was exhilaration and joy in his voice. His rough energy pushed her to further madnesses. She took Jean's hand and sucked his fingers as she came, revelling in letting them see her greed. Thierry came in a disjointed cataclysm of thrusting pelvis and shouted obscenities.

'I'll take her now,' Xavier said as Thierry finally rolled aside. They had all had her but, from Xavier's tone, Giselle guessed that it was only the beginning. There were other places to go, new rites to perform.

Xavier stood and fetched one of the torches that always lay ready in the shadows. He thrust it into the flames and the sudden flare of ignition highlighted the muscles of his chest and abdomen. He took Giselle's hand gravely and, pulling her to unsteady feet, led her out of the circle and into the night. She was shaking from head to toe and her thoughts swam as if her head had filled with treacle.

They followed a path that she hadn't noticed before; one that led them into the centre of the island. The flickering light of the torch on their naked bodies made them seem like spirits, as ephemeral as fireflies. The path became tortuous; they had to squeeze between rocks and scramble up steep inclines using the roots of trees as hand- and footholds. Xavier helped her, but said nothing. Finally, they reached a clearing and paused to recover themselves. As her breathing eased, Giselle became aware of a profound silence and absolute stillness. The water of the lake was gone; its perpetual movement was lost. This was the island's sanctuary, a respite from things fluid and changing. Xavier allowed her to experience this for a few moments, then drove the torch through the covering of pine needles, deep into the soil. Once it stood safely, he led her to a place beneath a tall, broad fir tree. Symbols had been carved into the rough bark, indistinct in the half-light. She could make out birds and fishes, signs of the zodiac and men and women crudely sexualised. Tatters of fabric hung from the overarching branches. Attached to them were dolls roughly made of straw. At the base of the tree, the carpet of pine needles had been cleared and there was compacted soil, as if the place was used regularly.

It felt as if they had slipped somehow, passed into another world. The dolls, as they turned in the light breeze, chilled her. The images of men with erect phalli and the women with inflated breasts and bellies were shocking – not because they were sexual but because they were keys and signposts to something archaic. He was leading her somewhere, taking her further from her known world. She wondered if these were the gates to a place that the priests called hell. Xavier would qualify as guide and demifiend to that place. The torches on his chest lit passageways that sense and fear occluded. There was also moonlight, pushing its fingers into the clearing and turning their naked flesh a silver blue. He told her to squat and then knelt between her opened thighs. He kissed her and told her to pee.

It wasn't easy. She was self-conscious. Her belly hung between her open legs like a hard, unripe fruit refusing to yield its juice. He stroked her face reassuringly. So many fluids had issued from her that evening, but this was the hardest. Finally, with a great sigh, she relaxed and the sphincter eased.

The fluid issued in a steady stream, hot and strong. He mixed it into the soil with his fingers where it fell. Once the self-consciousness had gone, it was strangely erotic to urinate with a stranger watching her. It was even more erotic when he slipped the fingers of his left hand inside her belly so that the stream played over his hand and ran back along the inside of her thighs. The liquid caressed her like a tongue, found her most sensitive places, seethed in hot swirls across the pouting lips of her anus.

The fingers of his left hand were still inside her as the fingers of his right made the sign of benediction. He took in lips, breasts and forehead as before, but this time her sex as well. At the extremity of each sweeping pass, his fingers pressed into her flesh, leaving a dark mark, an amalgam of the island's soil and her own fluids.

Anointed thus, he led her to the other end of the clearing, plucking up the torch as they went. Half-hidden behind a bush was a dark, narrow opening. Xavier squeezed through first. When Giselle followed she found herself in a low passageway. They had to crouch and edge forward like crabs. Narrow spaces had always made her nervous. When the torch brushed the roof, stones fell, bringing a feeling close to panic. There was a sharp turn to the right.

Suddenly they were in a large, high-ceilinged chamber, lit not just by the torch but by a column of light in the centre. As Xavier moved forward the column became brighter and she realised that it was pure rock crystal sparkling in the light of the lamp. The crystals were large and well formed, their geometry striking amongst the rough-hewn walls of the chamber. Xavier walked around the column slowly and Giselle followed. She remembered the rock crystal at the summit of the island and wondered if the mineral vein ran clear through the island, from base to summit. Peering within the transparent pillar she could see refracted images of Xavier and reflections of her own awed eyes.

They walked twice around the pillar, then Xavier knelt and gestured for Giselle to do the same. The feelings that she had had as a girl in the Church of Saint Saviour filled her breast. Then, she had knelt and gazed in awe at the statue of the Virgin Mary. The pillar had the same power and was a greater mystery – a natural column that pierced mother earth like a phallus.

Xavier reached out and touched the column, his fingertips tracing the edges of the crystals, testing the sharp edges, encompassing the octagonal sections. There was reverence, and surprise, in his eyes though he must have seen them many times before. This unselfconscious absorption was so different to his usual coolness.

'In daytime there is a snake that dances in this column,' he told her. 'The energy of the sun is drawn downwards, concentrated, metamorphosed. Sometimes, too, on nights such as this, when the moon is full . . .'

He snatched up the torch and buried the head in the soft soil. Abruptly, they were in darkness. Giselle's feeling of claustrophobia returned. She had to wrestle with the feelings of panic, push them into the corners of her mind.

They remained silent as their eyes adjusted. Then, Xavier grasped her hand suddenly, making her jump.

'Look! There.'

He ran her hand across the column but, at first, she saw nothing. All was blackness. Then, as she looked more closely, she was aware of movement. In the midst of the column there was a faint blue light, a snake that coiled and uncoiled before her astonished eyes. It was one of the most beautiful things that she had ever seen, as mesmerising and seductive as the gaze of a lover.

'It is the moon,' Xavier breathed.

'How?'

Even as she spoke, she remembered the crystal at the tip of the island and realised that the column really must be continuous. Somehow, the light of the moon had been captured and transmitted through the column, down through the island itself, passing beyond them to depths that she could only imagine. She remembered the tattoo on Xavier's sex, the gold and blue snake that writhed as he came to erection. It was a symbol of power, but not corporeal, not the power of flesh. The essence before her was spirit, a natural magic whose power was wonder.

The memory of his sex fired baser feelings; there was a jolt in her belly as if she had been touched deep inside. The knowledge of their nakedness, an awareness of the hard body beside her, produced a need to be filled. In the darkness and isolation she felt weak, and that weakness amplified her desires.

Perhaps it was her hand squeezing his that transmitted those feelings, perhaps he heard her breathing snag, then quicken. It seemed that something prompted him to push her to the ground and enter her. His hardness in her belly was a revelation, as if the darkness had parted to reveal the gardens of Elysium. The arousal she had felt when he had taken her beside the fire was a mere taste, a foreshadowing of the arousal that swept through her body there in the bowels of the earth.

All sense of who she was disappeared. His flesh was an envelope. He was her air and earth; the feelings in her belly were fire and water. The thing inside her moved slowly. The teeth at her neck bit deep. There were words and groans as if overheard. Perhaps it was her cries that filled her ears, perhaps it was the creatures of the island. In the darkness, her eyes made their own images. Snakes of blue and gold danced. Crossed torches blazed. Beautiful boys touched and tore at her.

216

In the centre of all this was the pleasure – high and fine like a stretched piano wire. He struck chord after chord from her womb and the chamber reverberated to a mighty symphony. His sex was a hardness that burnt and her belly was consumed in its flames. When he withdrew, her screams were suddenly real. She lay in the darkness, alone, not knowing who or what she was, and the sense of loss was complete. It was as if she had woken from sleep in deep space, without even the comfort of the stars.

Then there was a flare of light and she saw Xavier holding a match to the torch. It blazed with a sudden golden light. The pillar gleamed and she quietened herself.

When he knelt and looked down at her heaving chest and disarranged limbs she had the sense of being read. Without the strength to resist, she let him thumb through her as if she were a text written in blood and sweat. It felt good to be so known. She was grateful that an inventory was being taken. If she ever forgot herself completely, he could reinstate her, make her who she was again.

'You will be mistreated,' he told her softly. His expression was regretful, as if the decision was beyond his power, as if external agencies had made the decision. 'You will not be Paige to be doted on, or Joan to be tolerated and indulged.'

She looked at him in surprise. He talked for a long time and it felt as if she was being instructed in inescapable facts, as if he were helping her to accept a fate that couldn't be altered.

'Your innocence and beauty fit you perfectly to the path of suffering,' he said at the end, after he had spoken for what seemed hours, but could only have been minutes.

Reality returned with a sudden chill feeling in her stomach. She remembered Giscard as he had dragged her into the circle of the fire and thrown her at Xavier's feet. She remembered the slaps – how they had shocked her, but also quietened her. Would there be more of that? Worse? She wanted to ask him exactly what would be expected. Instead, she responded like an automaton as his hand pushed her head to his groin. She sucked him as he described what would be done. His language was blunt and crude. Each obscenity was like a stab to her sex, cruel and arousing. A tingling began in her stomach as he said that she would be tied. A wetness bred in her sex when he said that she would be beaten.

She was lost again.

He turned her over and slapped the inside of her thighs. She looked up at him, mildly. The pain was a long way away; only the echoes of it touched her. Afterwards, he might have penetrated her. Or he might have licked the tears from her eyes. She seemed to remember both things. The pleasure of being treated softly after she had been hurt was intense. She didn't protest when he told her they would use more than their hands.

She would be a toy for the boys who came to the island. She would be a sink for their most perverse desires. She would bring all evils to the surface, she would cleanse them with her suffering. She would never condemn. Her lips would bless their cruelties. She would seek out the secrets of their hearts – their darkness would be her light. She would ask if they wanted more. She would win their trust.

The great storehouses of sin would be opened and she would enter in. Her innocence would survive. She would transform all things, be the philosophers' stone transmuting base metals to gold, remaining pure and unchanged in herself. Silver would be her colour, the moon her planet. Lacking light in herself she would be like rock crystal, lit by the lights of others. She would hold all of their images. The souls of the boys would refract through her. The impurity of the ages would flow through her and issue as golden light. The Bacchae would collect her tears in adamantine jars. Her pain would be a healing unguent, her excitement the elixir of the ancients.

His voice changed as he spoke. There seemed to be many voices in the small chamber; as many voices as there were lights. She gazed up at him, meekly accepting the metamorphoses. She saw her priest and her teacher. Her father glowered from dark eyes. He was Paige and Joan, soft but demanding. The shifting light of the torch on the rough walls allowed her to see all creatures: foxes and bats, swans and magpies. Many of the apparitions were too transitory to be named. Wild boars frightened her but her fears were contained. The chamber around her was warm like a womb. An antelope drank from a silver pool. The man touched her forehead and smiled – Xavier again. The shades that she had seen now vanished. The walls were blood red and warm.

He enunciated his words with gravity and passion, as a priest speaks. It was a voice that used a mortal frame but had no earthly origin. It seemed that the crystal spoke through him, and the island through the crystal.

She was drunk with his sex. The places that he had anointed burned. She wanted to feast on his seed, to consume his essence. She seemed to be only a mouth – formed to swallow, bred to need, blessed with the grace of giving and taking. Her throat opened as she drove down on his sex. It was effortless to take him all. A relief for the void to be filled.

The thought that she would be beaten seized her and she groaned, rubbing her sex into the beaten soil. Her legs opened to their fullest and her belly pressed down of its own accord. When she asked, he told her how she would be beaten – those parts of her body that would be spared, those that would not. At each word she grovelled more deeply, impaled her throat more fully on his sex. There was a lust for the rivers of impurity that he promised. She wanted to be used, to transform all that is bad into the goodness of pure light. Her spirit would be crystal, her body the island. The boys would climb her, tear at her roots, bury their treasures in her, take her fruits, cast their seed and empty their wastes into her uncomplaining soil. She would be a Mary to them and a Magdelen; a whore, a sweetheart and a mother. As this madness washed through her, Xavier sat back on his heels, raising his pelvis and arching his back. The semen began to flow. She was greedy for it but he seized her hair and pulled her head away. The first pulses of white coated her lips and cheeks.

'Agree!' he told her. 'Agree now and never renounce me!'

She nodded, gazing into his eyes with the devotion of a pilgrim. He released her hair and she immediately buried his sex deep in her mouth, catching the last pulses of semen on a worshipful tongue. There was a gratitude that came from beneath conscious feeling – from her muscles and bones; deeper still, from cell and membrane, enzyme and protoplasm.

It was a long time before he ceased shuddering.

He filled her mouth many times but seemed always to remain hard. Perhaps there were quiet times. She had a memory afterwards of being held, but it was indistinct, like a dream. Only his hardness as he filled her mouth and the taste of him was clear – and the words that outlined her fate: his insistence, though she made no argument, and his hardness when she was as soft as love.

12

The New Nana

With Greta's patient help, Giselle reconstructed her past. Not all of it. Not those parts which revolved around the horror of Jean's death. The rest though: the slide into the luxury of shamelessness; the pleasure, and the pain, of giving.

She could think clearly of the times that Jean had come into her bedroom at night; his use of her mouth; the times he had taken her on to the balcony of her bedroom and pressed her belly to the warm wall. She could remember without regret how he had lifted her nightdress and pushed inside her while she bit her hand to stop the cries that would have fetched her father. Those things that came later – her father's discovery of them, the fall – she still chose not to think of.

By the time that Charles and Nana returned from China, many things had changed. Nana was no longer a child. She was a young woman. Her eyes were steady, her tread more languid. She occupied space as if she owned it. In truth, Giselle was a little scared of this new incarnation. It was as if she had been overtaken by her younger sister.

Nana was so full of stories of the shoot in the Himalayas and their stay in Hong Kong that Giselle's own story was temporarily forgotten. They spent their first day together at Onslow Square, looking through the hundreds of photographs that Nana and Charles had taken. Giselle noticed that in many of the photographs Nana wore a bikini top and sarong but that none showed her legs. She wanted to ask if Charles had made good his threat to beat her every time that they had sex. She noticed a certain stiffness whenever her sister sat or stood and suspected that he had.

It wasn't until they were alone together one evening, a few days after their reunion, that the sisters talked about such things. Nana was cool as she described the times that Charles had taken her. She recounted an incident on a mountain road in Tibet, when he had pulled her into one of the terraced paddy fields and stripped her bare. The mountains and the sky had gazed down impassively as he used his belt on her thighs and then sodomised her where she knelt in the clinging mud, water washing above her knees. She was equally cool as she showed photographs of herself tied and gagged in a hotel room in Shanghai. Through the open window of the bedroom a grey city bustled with life while Nana was held motionless by rope and nails. The bruises on the front of Nana's thighs shocked Giselle. The look in the girl's eye as she gazed at the camera, the debauchery evident in the fluids that smeared her breast and lips, shocked her even more. Nana had the eyes of a succubus – demonic and lost. As usual, Charles had made the images beautiful and that beauty had a distancing quality. But as much as Charles had transformed Nana into an object of art, a thing for the gaze, she was still Giselle's sister and what Giselle saw scared her.

There was a whole series of similar images: Nana impaled on the statue of a dragon, its curved stone tail lost in the opening of her anus; Nana in the midst of orgasm on the back seat of a jeep; Nana with an elderly Chinese businessman, his hooded eyes fixed on the hand that Nana used in her sex. The matter of fact way that Nana showed her these things made Giselle question the girl's motives.

'Did Charles ask you to show me these?'

Nana shook her head. They were perched on the edge of the sofa in the drawing room. The table in front of them was covered in jumbled images of Nana in the most obscene situations.

'Then why are you doing it?'

Nana handed Giselle a new set of images. These were more extreme, more shocking than the others. In a dingy hotel room in Hong Kong, Nana was being fucked by a gang of street boys. She was tied in some of the images. In one, a boy urinated in her mouth while another laughed and pinched her cheek. There was a look of weary concupiscence as she looked at the camera and offered this image to Charles, invisible behind the camera.

Giselle dropped the photographs abruptly.

'Did you enjoy it?' There was a note of anger in her voice that she knew she had no right to. She was angry that Nana had succumbed so easily after all her attempts to protect her.

Nana smiled. 'Of course. You would have too.'

She rifled through the pile of photos of the hotel room. She pointed out the one where she had made herself come by masturbating against the rail of the bedroom balcony.

Giselle looked at the image of the girl rubbing herself on the rounded hand rail. The bruises on her behind were black and fresh red slashes marked her thighs. The tiny hands of the boys were saffron on her breasts. Her face was a howl of pleasure. Giselle sighed. Had she looked like that when Jean had lifted her nightdress? Had the boys on the island laughed at her arousal with such cruelty?

'It reminded me of the balcony of your room in Avignon.'

Nana's jaw set and Giselle suddenly understood why she had been shown these things. It was time to share secrets. Time to tell.

'I can tell you some of it,' Giselle said finally. 'I can tell you about the island. For the rest, you will have to wait. I need to think about it. I need to understand what happened before I can tell you.'

It was a long evening. Giselle tried to explain about Xavier without equivocation. She tried not to leave out details that embarrassed her. Nana was rapt as the story unfolded, envious of her sister's experience. It was clear that the priests had touched Nana's mind less than they had touched her sister's. Giselle still struggled with guilt; the beatings she could tell of easily, but the pleasure of them – that was more difficult. That was wrong, would always be wrong. Her courting of that pleasure was unforgivable.

By twelve o'clock she had told most of what had happened on the island, including Jean's role. She described how he took her into the field at the bottom of the playing fields during school time. How she had knelt for him there and bared herself while his friends watched. She told a great deal but said nothing of what had happened in the house while Nana slept. That was too close to the final horror.

When she begged to be allowed to rest, Nana gave her a reprieve. There had clearly been enough revelations for her to digest. Yet, when Giselle rose and said that she would sleep, Nana clasped her hand.

'Tomorrow, tell me how Jean died.'

Giselle felt her heart contract. 'Maybe,' she said softly.

The next day, Charles surprised them both. He swept into the kitchen at ten o'clock as they breakfasted on toast and honey. The day after tomorrow, they were going to Paris. The Takitsua project had finally been given the go-ahead. Giselle would work again and she was grateful. She had spent too much time alone with her thoughts – besides, she liked the idea of being in

Paris with Nana. It would be almost like going home. Nana jumped up from the table and went to Charles's side. He kissed her cheek and put his arm around her waist.

The pleasure that Giselle had felt while imagining Paris evaporated. There was something about Nana's gaze that unsettled Giselle. Together, Nana and Charles were the couple, and she was the outsider. Charles seemed very certain of Nana since their return from China. He no longer made allowances for her, no longer equivocated his desires. Nana could expect to be touched or compelled to kneel and satisfy his desires in any situation. Giselle had watched many times in the past few days as her sister took Charles's sex into her mouth or lifted her skirt to bare her behind.

Giselle also saw Nana regularly take the initiative. She teased him constantly with her provocations – a skirt lifted to expose her sex, a flash of brightly painted nipples or a tongue that swept invitingly across inflamed lips. As they drove through the London streets, Nana would inevitably have her hand on Charles's sex. She would brush against him in the street and whisper impossible, outrageous suggestions in his ear. She was endlessly inventive and persisted until Charles was obliged to penetrate her, or compelled to allow her to caress herself until she came. In all of this, there was a sense that Nana was seeking for herself, and in a way that Giselle never could. Giselle was too often just a blind servant of a man's desire.

As Nana and Charles stood side by side and arm in arm in the kitchen, Giselle knew that soon she must leave. Soon there would be no room for her, except as an accessory to her sister's passions. Charles seemed to notice none of Giselle's alienation.

'I have a little treat for you both,' he declared with a broad smile. 'I think that you both need pampering more.'

Nana agreed readily. Giselle shrugged carelessly.

'Today I must work, and Nana must come with me, but tonight we will go out. The three of us.'

Nana walked over to her sister and ran her fingers through her hair.

'Giselle needs to be pampered. She's a worrier.'

'Well, from now on, we will look after her together.'

Giselle watched in amazement as Nana went back to Charles and they left together arm in arm. The changes had been more profound than she had imagined: not only did she no longer have to look after Nana, but Nana now seemed determined to look after her.

13

The Sauna

Giselle spent the day as she had spent so many others in London – alone and palely loitering. Greta had disappeared to the country for a few days, making the emptiness and homesickness even more profound.

Giselle was reading in her bedroom when Charles and Nana came back. She listened to the sound of their conversation as it drifted up the narrow stairs. Their easy intimacy was painful and Giselle tried to block out the laughter and the warm tones by burying her head in the book.

There were footsteps in the hall. Her door opened a few moments later and Nana's excited face appeared.

'Hi,' she said.

'Hi.'

'We bought something for you.'

Giselle put her book down and yawned.

'It'll wake you up,' the girl promised, laughing.

'I need waking up,' Giselle told her, yawning again.

'I'm going to shower. See you for dinner.'

Giselle nodded as the door closed. She picked up her book again but her interest was fitful. After a few false starts she put it down and hauled herself off the bed.

In the kitchen, Charles was leaning against the fridge, eating yoghurt from a plastic pot. Paul Weller was playing on the radio – 'The Changing Man'. Charles had changed Nana, of that Giselle was sure. He nodded

to her as she walked over to the window and looked out
into the tiny garden.

'You'll need something cheap and tarty for tonight,'
he told her. 'Did I see a leather mini-skirt in your
cupboard once?'

There was a short leather skirt that Greta had bought
for her but Giselle had never thought of it as either
cheap or tarty. It was all in the eye of the beholder.

'Where are we going?' she asked.

'It's a surprise.'

'Pleasant?'

He shrugged, then laughed. 'I'll enjoy it.'

She didn't see the whip on the kitchen table until he
pointed it out. Perhaps she hadn't wanted to see it.

'It is only partly yours of course,' he told her, picking
it up and handing it to her. 'You will have to share it
with Nana.'

The short leather handle was rigid, as if reinforced
with wood. The leather blade – the length of her
forearm – hung stiffly. It would become flexible with
use, she knew that. She remembered the angry blazes on
Nana's thighs in the photographs and shook her head.
It wasn't refusal. It was bemusement that she could
accept it so easily.

'The marks?' she asked. 'Will Odette be able to hide
them?'

'There will be no need. Not for the Takitsua shoot.
They will add to the costumes.'

Her body had been so virginal for so long now, the
skin unmarred by anything but cosmetics. The idea that
she would carry the secrets of her desire for all to see
was suddenly exciting. He would take them to the
Labyrinth in Paris. That had already been promised.
Gregory would like the marks, if he was there. If not,
they would provoke outrages from a stranger.

An hour later, the three of them ate a microwaved
chicken *moglai*. This was as complex a meal as Charles

was prepared to attempt in the over-equipped kitchen. The huge Viking gas cooker, obviously designed for a restaurant, watched them reproachfully, its stainless steel spits and griddles and grills gleaming with disuse.

Afterwards, as they drank coffee, Charles toyed with the whip. Giselle could sense the fear in her sister, a fear that made her eyes shine and speech quicken. The whip had an opposite effect on Giselle. It slowed her, took her back to Avignon. There, she had cultivated patience for the boys who liked to beat her. She had nursed them and stroked their hair as they gathered their courage. When they told her to kneel and offer her wrists to be tied, her warmth never faded, her movements never betrayed the fear of what would be done. She had kept in her mind the tenderness that she would be shown afterwards – the attention that she would receive from Paige or Giscard that would soothe and transform.

An hour later, Charles was pulling up outside the zoo in Regents Park. There was the sound of elephants trumpeting and the chatter of monkeys. The aviary spread its steel web across the canal as if cast by a giant spider. None of these things interested Charles though. He was looking for somewhere quiet in the park, somewhere they wouldn't be disturbed. It was getting dark as they walked down the tarmacked pathway towards the sports enclosures. They paused for a moment to watch the golfers in a wire cage practising their driving. The sound of the balls being struck was like gun shots. Behind the tennis courts was an area that claimed to be a conservation area. The grasses were waist high and bristled with dry seed heads. A sign asked them to keep to the footpaths. Charles ignored this and struck out into the wilderness. Nana and Giselle followed dutifully, the ochre and green plants brushing their bared legs. Trees screened them on two sides, the empty tennis courts on the other. Nana was

229

excited. In her bag was the whip, coiled like a spring. Giselle was more aware of its latent presence than she was of Charles's voice as he chatted with Nana.

Only when he told her to kneel did the sound of his words come into focus. She had known from the moment that they had stopped that it would be her who was beaten.

'Pull up her skirt,' Charles told Nana.

Nana sank to her knees in the soft grass beside her sister. The girl that she had bathed so often, the girl that Giselle had stripped before bedtime, now stripped her.

Charles was trampling down the grass, making an arena for the drama. As the tight skirt rose, Giselle felt the evening coolness on her behind. Stray spears of grass tickled her legs.

'It won't stay up,' Nana said, laughing as the skirt slid down over Giselle's perfect behind.

'Hold it, Giselle.'

Giselle complied, with trembling hands.

'Roll down her stockings.'

Nana carefully folded the nylons down, then rose and stood away. Kneeling in the long grass she could have been in any wilderness. Only the sounds betrayed the city. There was the occasional muted roar of a car in the distance and the sound of golf balls being struck. She looked up and saw the fire in Charles's gaze. He had waited a long time for this.

Nana undid her bag, not waiting to be told. Charles took the whip and let gravity uncoil the long blade. With the first blow she gasped and fell forward on her hands. Her skirt was of the softest, most supple leather and it slipped down again, covering the stripe that burnt like acid into her behind.

Nana helped her to kneel up again. This time she didn't move away. She took Giselle's arms and wrapped them around her waist. Then, leaning over, she unzipped the skirt so that it slipped down completely. It settled over the back of Giselle's calves, leaving her bare from waist to knee.

As the blows rained down, Giselle clung to her sister's waist and buried her head in the softness of her sister's belly. Finally, Charles stopped, but not before Giselle could hardly breath and her eyes were blinded by hot tears. When Nana released her, Giselle sank to the ground and curled into a ball. She was aware of nothing but the searing pain until a hand traced a path along the inside of her thigh. Fingers prised open her sex.

'She's wet,' Charles said.

There was a note of triumph in his voice, as if a long-held theory had been vindicated. 'Now we need someone to fuck her.'

Giselle felt a wave of rebellion. She hated them. His fingers in her sex were cold, like dead fish. The arousal in her belly shamed her. Suddenly, she had a desire to be home. Not in Onslow Square, not in Briere, but really home – home in Avignon.

They let her lie for a while, then Charles said that he wanted to mark the front of her thighs as well. Nana helped her sister up and held her from behind. Giselle was shaking before she was struck. There were three quick blows to each thigh. She was obliged to open her legs so that the tip of the whip could find the inside of her thighs. Each time the leather rapped across the curved muscle, and the tip struck home, she screamed, and Nana pressed a hand to her mouth to muffle the sounds. When he had finished, Charles kissed Nana deeply. Giselle, sandwiched between them, felt his erection hard against her face. Through the pain she realised that Nana and Charles were shaking as much as she was. For them it was excitement. For her it was the shock of violation, and the shock of being ignored. Xavier had hurt her many times, but afterwards he would hold her and rock her in his arms. Then there would be the attention of the boys. For such attention,

231

such devotion, she was willing to pay the price demanded. Kneeling on the damp grass of Regents Park, the transaction had been unilateral. She had given and Charles had taken. Her only reward was the hardness of his sex, the knowledge that she had aroused him.

Half an hour later, they were cruising along Kilburn High Road. It was a place that Giselle had never heard of before. If Charles had opened the door and left her there she would have had no idea of how to get back to South Kensington.

The long row of featureless shops seemed to go on for ever. Finally, he found the place that he was looking for and pulled up. Nana and Giselle looked about them in shared bewilderment. There was nothing – only the blank, closed shopfronts and a few people waiting at a bus stop a hundred metres away.

'There,' he said, pointing. The sisters' eyes followed his finger to a massage parlour.

'What –' Giselle began, but he was already getting out of the car.

Nana giggled as she opened her door and glanced at Giselle in the back.

'Come on. He said that he was going to pamper us.'

Giselle looked at the parlour with its garish neon sign and unwashed windows. Since he had touched her in the park, a feeling of revulsion had settled into her soul. Her heart sank a few more fathoms as she imagined the evening that he had planned for them. The sight of Nana and Charles together, and the kiss they exchanged as they waited on the pavement, irritated her.

'You can't be serious,' she said to Charles as she clambered out of the car.

'It'll be fun,' he told her. 'I wouldn't have brought you if I didn't think you would like it.'

'A massage parlour! If it is anything like the ones in Paris! It's so . . .'

232

'Cheap?'

'Yes.'

'Don't be a snob. Anyway, look at yourself.'

She looked at her reflection in the window of a laundrette. He had dressed her in the leather skirt, black stockings, high heels and a tight white blouse, open enough to show most of her breasts. Her make-up was thick, visible even in the poorly reflected image. She looked fit meat for where they were going. He put his arm around her shoulder and, reaching around, his hand squeezed her breast crudely.

'All right, darlin'?' The accent was that of a drunk on the Walworth Road.

She elbowed him away, but he grabbed her hand and pulled her along the pavement. Nana was already peering in through the window of the massage parlour, or trying to. Crooked venetian blinds shielded the interior from the eyes of passers-by.

As they drew nearer to the garish frontage, Giselle's heart started to race. This wasn't the Labyrinth with its exclusive clientele and its unwritten rules and conventions. This was sordid, like sex with a drunk in an alleyway. But there was more than that, something beneath the surface that was frightening. Something that she couldn't grasp. She made one last effort to stop him, digging in her heels and protesting loudly. He halted and stood in front of her, smiling. He listened to her protests until she became silent. Then, when she had given up, in the face of his coolness, his certainty, he reached a finger to her lips and drew it slowly sideways, smearing a line of bright red lipstick on to her cheek.

'Perfect,' he said. 'The kind of woman a man would want late on a Saturday night anywhere in the world.'

A quick glance in the window of the massage parlour showed her what he meant. The smeared lipstick made her look as if she was ready to be passed around the boys. She looked cheap and worthless. All the fight went out of her then. She allowed him to pull her the last few metres to the massage parlour and when he opened the door she surrendered and followed meekly. Nana stepped in behind her, closing the door, sealing them into the small reception area.

A woman of thirty or so sat behind a Formica counter watching a soap opera on a TV perched on a high shelf to her left. The sound was bad and the characters squawked like parrots. The woman didn't turn immediately and all that Giselle could see was stiff blonde hair emerging from her head like a static discharge. Charles went to the counter and leant over. His body must have cut off the signal and the screen crackled and blinked. The woman leant back a little, so that Giselle could see her face – a mask of boredom, no longer young, but never destined to be wise. She examined Charles with a torpid disinterest; Charles smiled a fireproof smile.

'Hi,' he said.

The way that he spoke – quietly but forcefully – made Giselle realise that he would soon be angry.

The woman tried to look over Charles's shoulder at the flickering screen but Charles moved a little so that her view was blocked. Eventually she gave up and swivelled round in her seat. It was only then that she saw Giselle, who avoided the woman's eye in embarrassment.

'What can I do you for then?' she asked, trying to be cheery.

'A sauna maybe, a massage. The full works,' Charles told her.

'The full works?' repeated the woman.

'For the ladies.'

The woman looked at Giselle and Nana in turn, not troubling to hide her surprise.

'We don't get many ladies here,' she said apologetically. 'I mean our masseurs are . . . well, you know what I mean.'

234

'Your masseurs are ladies?'

'Real ladies,' she said sharply, as if some kind of loyalty had been touched. 'But our customers . . .'

'Are usually men?'

'Right.'

Charles glanced in Giselle's direction. She could feel her cheeks burning. In the close atmosphere of the reception area she could hardly breathe.

'You must have somebody who likes to work on women,' Charles persisted, 'someone with a natural inclination in that direction.'

The blonde took his meaning, then thought for a moment before pressing a button on a white plastic box in front of her.

After a few moments there was a squawk, vaguely human, from the box. The woman pressed the button again and leant forward a little.

'Is Sheri in?' she asked.

A thin female voice crackled an answer.

'Sheri?'

'Yeah, Sheri.'

'I'll check.'

The box went dead and the woman looked up at Charles.

'Sheri might suit you,' she said non-committally.

Charles stepped over to Giselle and ran his fingers through her hair. She flinched away, not wanting to be touched while the woman was watching. When he looked at her coolly, questioningly, she surrendered and allowed him to do as he chose. His fingers searched through her hair again and when he brought his hand away he was grasping a fragment of dry leaf. He dropped it into a half-full ash tray on the counter.

'We took a turn around Regents Park,' Charles explained.

'Nice this time of year.'

'Very.'

235

Giselle wondered if the woman knew what time of year it was. It was hard to imagine her outside this tiny space. The brittle structure of her hair could never have survived a breath of wind. The absurdly long finger nails would have made her hands useless for any normal task.

The box crackled, making Giselle jump. The woman looked at her.

'Are you all right, lovey?'

Giselle felt her throat swell and knew that she wouldn't be able to reply. There were too many conflicting feelings. Tears weren't far away.

'She's fine,' Charles said, smiling.

'There are other places you know, places for kinky stuff,' the woman said sourly.

'But we like it here,' Charles told her, laying a fifty-pound note on the counter. 'For you.'

She looked at the red and white rectangle, then at Giselle, giving a poor imitation of a woman who didn't like to be bought. After a moment, her hand slipped across the counter and palmed the money. The box squawked again and the woman pressed a button before replying.

'Yeah?' she asked.

'Twenty minutes. She's in with a punter.'

'OK. Tell her to buzz me when she's finished.'

'Yeah.'

The box went dead.

'Sheri's in with someone,' the woman said unnecessarily. 'Do you want to wait?'

Charles glanced at Nana, then Giselle. Nana shrugged. Giselle shook her head. She wanted to be anywhere but that place. If her will had been all powerful, she would have dissolved through the wall to materialise in the deserted street and make a run for sanity.

'We have plenty of time. We can try the sauna,' Charles said.

236

'There's nothing separate for the ladies, you know. And we've only got one changing room.'

'It wouldn't be as interesting if you did.'

The woman shrugged, then gave Giselle a pitying glance. For Nana there was a look of mild contempt, as if the girl's ease, her relaxed posture as she leant against the wall, were evidence of moral depravity.

'As you like.'

The final efforts to dissuade Charles seemed to have exhausted the blonde woman. Wearily, she hauled a calculator from her desk drawer and clumsily pressed the keys, listing the various charges as she went. Giselle listened in horror as the price of her humiliation mounted. At the end, Charles laid four more red and white notes on the counter.

'I don't have change for fifties,' the woman told him with the glibness of a practised liar.

She ignored his derisive laughter and held up each of the notes to the light before casually dropping them into the drawer. She then swivelled in her seat and pointed to a door at the back of the reception.

'Through there.'

As soon as she finished speaking, her eyes turned back to the TV. They had been processed and no longer existed, it seemed. When Charles pushed at the door, the bottom caught on the vinyl floor and bent as if it might break. The corridor that they found themselves in was narrow – not much more than shoulder width – and made of the same material as the door. The walls flexed uncertainly as Giselle leant against them to steady herself. The whole building seemed as insubstantial and transitory as one of Charles's sets. In a sense, it had become one of his sets. He had commandeered the flimsy construction, and the people who worked in it, for one of his scenarios. Only the cameras were missing.

As they went on down the narrow corridor, the atmosphere became hotter and more humid, thick with the presence of bodies. There was a smell of cheaply perfumed oil and the floor glistened with it. Giselle imagined the flesh that the oil had clung to before being trodden out here. She shuddered. Nana laid a reassuring hand on her shoulder but Giselle shrugged it off. The feeling of separation from her sister had become profound. They had fought often enough when they were growing up but this was different. Giselle had always protected and cared for the younger Nana. Now that Nana was acquiring power through Charles, there was no evidence of protection. Nana seemed keen only to aid Charles, to make his fantasies come true, whatever the cost.

At the end of the corridor was a door marked CHANGING ROOM. Charles opened this, looked inside, and gestured for them to follow.

Here the smell was of talcum powder and damp towels. Giselle was relieved to find the long, narrow room empty.

Half a dozen grey steel lockers stood against one wall. The furthest one leant crazily and looked as if it might fall at any moment. There was a pile of neatly folded towels on a bench, each one marked with the words Pharo Spa Health Club. Giselle wondered if they had been stolen or whether this massage parlour was one of a string of grubby ventures. Charles pulled at the door of the nearest locker but it wouldn't open. He stooped to read the instructions.

'You even have to put money in these,' he said with a note of pleasure, as if he was enjoying being ripped off. She imagined him tipping the receptionist extravagantly on the way out. The pleasure of showing her that he could waste money on her. The pleasure of wasting money on his whores.

Charles fished some coins out of his pocket and slipped them into a slot on the door. He pulled at the handle a few times and eventually it yielded. He opened

238

the two neighbouring lockers for Nana and Giselle, then began to undress. Nana followed suit. Giselle could only watch them.

'OK?' he asked.

It wasn't OK. She stared at him for a moment as if he were utterly alien.

'Let me help,' Nana said, stepping forward. She had already stripped off her top and was naked to the waist. Her heavy breasts swayed; her feigned concern appalled.

'Why are you doing this?' Giselle asked.

Nana halted, obviously puzzled.

'You'll get into it,' Charles told her. 'It will be an experience.'

A few weeks before, she would have thought that he was right. But too much had changed. She didn't want to get into it.

As they gazed at her, it all became too much. Tears began to flow. Her body shook and Nana enfolded her softly, wordlessly.

'I want to go home,' was all that Giselle could say. 'I don't want these games anymore.' The plaintive, childish note surprised her. The rush of feeling made her feel dizzy. All that had happened in the previous weeks suddenly came to her: the remembering, the reliving of her time at the quarry; the telling of her story, first to Greta, then to Nana; the loss of her sister to Charles. Whatever had happened while Charles and Nana were in China seemed irrevocable.

They let her weep. The warmth of Nana's body softened her a little – the power of sisterhood hadn't been completely dissipated. Charles sat on the bench and waited patiently. When Giselle was quiet, he stood and kissed the side of her neck.

'Give me this,' he whispered, 'and tomorrow we'll talk about it.'

'I want to go home,' she said again, her voice a flat monotone.

'You will. But not now. Not tonight.'

239

He kissed her full on the lips. His tongue slipped into her mouth and, against her will, she felt herself melting. Nana stroked her hair. The girl's naked breasts were soft against her arms. It was hopeless to struggle anymore. The hopelessness brought more tears, the tongue an arousal that she didn't want.

When they finally let her go, she stood in the centre of the room with her head down and tears dripping from the tip of her nose. Because it was inevitable, she reached for the buttons of her blouse and slowly undid them. Nana helped to pull the arms free for her, then undid the zip on her own dress.

'The prettiest girl in all of France,' Nana said and kissed her forehead.

'In all of Europe,' Charles added.

There was a low wooden bench in the middle of the room and Giselle sat down to unpeel her stockings.

'Better?' Nana asked.

Giselle smiled weakly. 'A little.'

Charles draped his jacket over a steel coat hanger that sagged with the weight, then pulled his shirt out of his trousers. His broad torso made the room seem even narrower. The perfect tone of his muscles made the crazily leaning locker seem even more pitiful.

The marks on her behind and the front of her thighs were a fierce red when Giselle bared her legs. In the pitiless fluorescent lighting her flesh seemed pale. There were hints of blue where venous blood showed through the taut skin.

Charles finished stripping and hung the remainder of his clothes in the locker, then stepped aside so that she could hang hers.

When she was finished he pushed her back against the coldness of the steel.

'Don't,' she said.

His mouth clamped on to a trembling breast. The lips sucked.

'No,' she said, squirming. His hand rested on her hip and pressed her back hard.

There was something mechanical in the way that he went about arousing her. He opened her thighs and worked two fingers into her sex. She was still wet from the beating, but not wet enough for him to explore her easily. He made her moisten his fingers with her tongue and then went into her again. She couldn't respond. Nana's eyes examined her coolly, as if she were a mechanism that was malfunctioning. The gaze chilled her as much as the steel of the locker against her back and the clinical dispassion of Charles's fingers. He turned her to face the locker, pressed her firmly to its surface and told her to raise her arms and hold the rimmed top.

'You look good,' he told her, but there was no desire in his voice – the appreciation was aesthetic. She knew how she would look draped over the lockers, her slender arms and legs against the cold steel. She had come to understand the fantasies of men. This was an extension of the cheerleader scenario, except that this time it was her, not Nana, cast in the starring role.

When Charles was ready he slapped her behind sharply, half a dozen times, working over the area that had been whipped. The sound was deafening – the receptionist at her desk would surely hear it above her beloved TV. Then he spread her legs and worked on her sex from behind. His thumb pushed inside and his fingers rubbed at the apex of the lips. She gasped, then groaned and, finally, she felt her sex flood. He kept working until her hips thrust back to meet his hand and her mouth was wide with wanting. Then he stepped back.

'OK, that will do,' he said.

She turned slowly. Her flesh was now pink, infused with arterial blood. There was a pulsing in her ears. She noticed that his sex was soft and she blushed.

241

Nana touched her arm. 'Beautiful,' the girl whispered. She approved now. The mechanism was working again.

Charles picked up a towel from the pile on the bench and wrapped it around his waist. Giselle reached for one then hesitated.

'Can I?' she asked.

'Of course.'

She took the towel and tied it beneath her arms. The bottom just covered her sex, but not the mucus that gleamed on the inside of her thighs, nor the red marks on the backs of her thighs where she had been whipped.

'Take your bag,' he told Nana, 'and this.' He handed the girl his wallet and she slipped it in beside the whip.

Through the door at the end of the changing room they followed the signs for the sauna. The thought of a small, hot room didn't appeal to Giselle. She was already too warm, too dizzy. Sweat was running from her skin in the humid atmosphere. It gathered in the depressions above her elegant collar bones and spilt across her breasts in rivulets.

Beyond the changing rooms, the space opened out and they walked side by side down a brightly lit corridor.

She caught sight of herself in one of the mirrors placed along the walls. Her face was red and her eyes were overly bright. The smeared make-up made her look debauched. She remembered Xavier's descriptions of demonic succubi, phantasms that came to men's beds in the fever of the night.

A young woman in a white overall passed them, carrying a bucket and mop. She stared at Giselle open-mouthed. Charles stepped aside for her and said hi. The woman laughed in embarrassment.

'The village idiot,' Charles whispered unkindly.

Giselle glanced back along the corridor. The woman was standing, staring. Giselle smiled, tried to reassure her with that smile. The woman flushed and hurried away.

242

Eventually, they came to a little lobby with a desk. A middle-aged woman, plump, homely and unnervingly wholesome, was sitting there working on a crossword. She looked up and smiled easily as the group approached.

'Sauna?' she asked.

Charles nodded.

'It's through there.'

The woman pointed to a pine door with a small window in it.

'Call if you need anything.'

Charles thanked her.

'All right, lovey?' the woman asked as Giselle passed, echoing the receptionist's words, as if she were one of a series of gatekeepers in this mini-hell.

Giselle nodded stiffly. She recognised the woman's voice as the one from the intercom in the reception room. Without the electrical distortion there was a weary warmth in her tortured vowels. Her eyes were curious, envious even.

'Sheri won't be long. I'll tell you when she's ready.'

Charles had already reached the door to the sauna and was looking through the window.

'Fine,' he called to the woman and opened the door.

There was a blast of hot, dry air. Charles stepped aside to allow Giselle and Nana to go first. There was a shock for Giselle as she realised that they wouldn't be alone. In one corner, a man sat with a towel across his lap. His eyes were closed and he didn't notice the girls immediately. Giselle took in his large belly and shiny bald head with horror. Nana smiled, amused, it seemed, by the shapeless flesh.

The sound of the door closing must have disturbed the man. His eyes half opened and drifted slowly in the girls' direction then, seeing them, opened fully. The thick neck and the large, surprised eyes made him seem like an owl perched on the slatted bench. He turned further to look at Charles and nodded, as if the man were real and the girls were not. Giselle was grateful to go unacknowledged, grateful to be a fiction in the owl man's eyes. Charles pressed his hand into the small of her back and pushed her gently to the far corner of the pine-walled cell. She sat awkwardly and pressed her thighs together tightly, defensively. Charles took a seat on one side of her, Nana on the other. Giselle found the courage to look at the owl man again. He was smiling now that the surprise was gone. His eyes had become mere ovals – languid and hooded. In the heat and gloom of the little room he seemed to be melting, flowing from one indistinct form into another.

'Hot enough?' the man asked, his voice tougher than Giselle would have expected, the 'h' from hot almost disappearing in the Cockney growl.

Charles smiled. 'Plenty.'

'Tell me if you want more.'

The man indicated a lever to his side with a plus and minus sign at either end of its run. Charles nodded again.

Giselle noticed the man's feet and hands as he spoke – large flipper-like organs attached to short, chubby limbs. Now he seemed more like a frog. She almost smiled. Half owl, half frog, he was like a chimera hallucinated by a medieval monk, one of the Albigensians perhaps, heretics and ghosts that Xavier had taught her about. Then her eyes closed of their own accord as the heat penetrated and sapped her energy. One by one her muscles succumbed and went slack. The darkness behind her closed eyelids was a velvet black-red. For a while there was silence. She almost forgot where they were as the tension drained away with the sweat that seeped though every pore in her skin. Then she felt fingers trailing down her neck and across her naked shoulder. She opened her eyes to see Charles leaning towards her. A sudden shyness made her turn

244

away. She felt a row of soft kisses where the fingers had been, then a long lingering kiss on her ear lobe. A sound from across the room – a sudden sigh of expelled breath – made her turn to the stranger. He was looking at her intently, the smile gone from his lips. He was the owl now, the predator of the dark woods. But he was far away and she closed her eyes, accepting Charles's kisses, giving herself to his protection, relaxing even further.

'More heat,' Charles said, and Giselle heard a grating sound of metal on metal.

Lips surrounded hers and she was kissed deeply, a tongue finding its way inside her mouth and firing all the nerves in her body. She was sinking deliciously in the heat – the heat of the room and the heat of her body as it responded to the caresses. She was almost grateful when Charles began to undo the folds of the towel above her breasts but tensed as the towel was opened and laid aside. Her arms were too heavy to raise in defence and her mouth was full again with his tongue as she went to speak and say no. She struggled to find the strength to keep her legs closed tight as a hand came to rest on her stomach. She recognised Nana's lightness of touch and part of her wanted to open, part of her wanted that hand on her sex. Her mouth was plundered again and again. The hand circled. She jerked as her nipples were flicked, once, twice, three times in succession.

Then the hands and lips were gone and there was a void of feeling. There was only the heat, the heat inside and out. And silence. She wanted to be touched again but couldn't ask, not in that room, not with an audience.

'That is some lady,' growled the cockney voice. 'What about the other one?'

She heard Charles laugh, a short snort of amusement that suddenly made her feel cheap. Her eyes opened briefly to see Nana undoing her towel, smiling at the stranger as she bared herself.

Then there was a finger in her mouth.

'Suck,' Charles told her. She wanted to suck but not while she was being watched. 'Suck,' Charles said again. The finger explored her, running across the soft insides of her cheeks. Still she couldn't suck. The fingers disappeared and her nipples were flicked again – hard, sharp flicks like a barrage of hailstones. Her belly melted under that assault, melted and flowed like warm butter to her sex, oiling her inside and making her ready for him – but not here she prayed, not on this bench, with this spectator. When the finger returned to her mouth, all reservations dissolved. The second invasion undid her. She groaned and surrendered, sucking without prompting. She didn't care about the owl man now and sucked as if it were a teat between her lips. Her thighs relaxed, opened a little. The finger slipped in and out of her mouth like a man's sex. The wickedness that had invaded her with the finger made her feel like a whore, made her want to feel that way, and she sucked harder.

It was so good to fall, so good to fall from goodness. Xavier had shown her how to fall gracefully, how to be an angelic whore. Her thighs opened a fraction and she longed for the courage to open them fully. There was the desire to abase herself, to writhe and revel. The monsters of desire, perverse and undoing, surrounded her and goaded her. Then it ended. There was a knock at the door and the finger disappeared – a sudden, cruel loss. Reason returned with all of its cruel denials. Before the disappointment could fully register, she was being pulled to her feet. The towel stayed behind on the bench as Charles led her out. Her eyes opened to take in the livid face of the stranger who had shared her excitement. He touched her behind as she passed and she shivered when she realised that her body had welcomed the touch.

'She likes you,' Nana told the stranger.

'Tell her to come back later,' he growled, 'when you've finished with her.'

Nana laughed again. 'Maybe.'

Then they were outside and the middle-aged woman from the lobby was leading them along the corridor. One of the doors was open. Inside, a tall Indian girl was waiting for them. She was very pretty in a delicate way, with skin the colour of shellac and hair like a black waterfall reaching to her shoulders. Through the haze of heat and arousal, Giselle felt the woman examining her, appraising her body. Giselle felt shy again, weak in the face of a woman's interest.

As they stepped into the room the masseuse smiled broadly. The whiteness of her gleaming teeth competed with the whiteness of her crisp overall.

'Hi,' she said. Her voice had faint accents of the East – India and the Mile End Road mixing easily on her palate. 'I'm Sheri.' She seemed like a hostess at a smart party: bright, kind and attentive. Not at all the sort of woman that Giselle was expecting.

'Hi,' Charles said in return, looking around the room.

Behind the woman was a leather-topped massage table. In the far corner was a shower enclosed by glass doors.

'So hot,' said the Indian girl, laying her hand on Giselle's arm. 'It is dangerous to get so hot.' Giselle looked down at her naked breasts and realised how red they were.

Sheri went to the shower and, reaching inside, turned a tap. Water hissed from stainless steel.

Giselle had to be helped inside. The water was like a torrent from a mountain stream: glacial, sudden. Her mind cleared with the shock and she spluttered. She saw Charles and the girl through the glass doors. They were laughing.

'That has woken her up,' said Sheri, her voice muffled by the sound of rushing water.

The heat stored in Giselle's body and the coldness of the water contended. As she cooled so there came a feeling of freshness and peace. Before catharsis could become a freezing displeasure, Sheri opened the door and, smiling, turned the water to warm. They allowed her to wash. Nana and Charles were talking together, Nana holding Charles's sex as if it were a pet, her thumb stroking the crown and bringing him to erection. Giselle turned away when they looked at her with calculation in their eyes. Then the cubicle door opened again and the Indian woman took her arm.

'Better?' she asked.

Giselle nodded and stepped out of the cubicle into the towel that the woman was holding. Shellac-coloured hands rubbed her dry as Charles turned the shower setting back to cold and stepped in. His eyes opened wide and he let out a whoop as the water hit him. Nana slipped in too and they splashed each other furiously, like children in a swimming pool.

As the Indian woman knelt to dry Giselle's legs, she saw the marks of the whip. She stopped and sat back on her heels. Her eyes swept from the bruising flesh to Giselle's face and back again.

'Did he do this?' she asked.

Giselle nodded.

The woman frowned and stood.

'You need another girl,' she said. 'It's not my kind of thing.'

Giselle laid her hand on the girl's arm.

'It's OK. I wasn't forced. I didn't want it, but I could have said no.'

The woman stepped back. She looked puzzled.

'If you didn't want it, why did you let him?'

'Because sometimes I do want it,' Giselle replied, feeling lame. It seemed impossible to explain. 'Please, don't let it bother you.'

The Indian woman still seemed uneasy. Giselle

thought quickly, thought of what she could offer the girl. Charles would be angry if she let her go.

'You like women?' Giselle asked.

'Yes.'

She stepped forward and took the girl's hands. 'Am I not attractive enough?'

Sheri smiled. 'I wouldn't make you pay,' she said softly.

'And my sister?' Giselle asked, glancing into the shower cubicle.

'Your sister!'

'Is she attractive enough?'

'Your sister!' The woman repeated, then laughed.

At that moment Charles stepped out of the shower and snatched up a towel. He rubbed himself furiously. The water flying from his hair was cold and stung Giselle's back, making her jump. She stepped away, still holding the woman's hands.

'Stay,' she said to Sheri quickly.

'For sisters I will stay.' There was a musical note in her laughter, a glint in her eye.

Charles finished drying his hair and looked at them curiously. He had heard nothing but seemed to sense that something had happened.

He took hold of the Indian woman's hand and drew her aside. After a minute's whispered discussion, Charles took his wallet from Nana's bag. The woman looked uncertain as she took the notes that he offered. She glanced at Giselle and a shadow of guilt passed across her delicate features. Then she shrugged and tucked the money into the breast pocket of her overalls.

'If she says no . . .'

'Then it's over,' Charles assured her.

This had been said loud enough for Giselle to hear and Sheri glanced at Giselle, obviously concerned to make sure that all was understood. Giselle locked her eyes into the other woman's and nodded.

249

Nana emerged from the shower during these exchanges, her eyes as bright as stars. Sheri patted the leather couch.

'So, who is to be first?'

Charles looked at Giselle. She shrugged and climbed on to the couch. Sheri told her to lie on her front as she worked oil into her hands. The woman's touch was gentle and sure. Where the fingers needed to go deep, they went deep; where a sweeping caress was sufficient, they obliged. Giselle's resistance faded. The mood of the sauna crept back over her. Her eyes closed. She sank into the pleasure of being touched.

When her back had been thoroughly softened, when every muscle was as pliant as Giselle's will, Sheri told her to turn over. Giselle's eyes opened as she did so. Nana was on her knees, Charles's sex deep in her mouth. There was the familiar stab of guilt as desires gathered in the pit of Giselle's belly, desires that centred on her sister as much as on Charles. Then Sheri's hands were sweeping along the inside of her thighs, squeezing away all tensions, shaping the guilt into a fine spear that smoothly entered her sex and was consumed.

'The full service,' she heard Charles say.

'Of course,' Sheri murmured.

The hands finished her legs and went to Giselle's belly. There, they found her gathered desires and swept the feelings upwards, into her breasts, so that the soft tissues became alive and the tips hardened. Hands took her ankles, lifted and spread. Her feet were placed next to her hips. Her sex felt the caress of the humid air. Lips moved along the inside of her thighs. A tongue entered her, retreated, returned. Then there was a hand beneath her head, lifting, and Charles telling her to open her eyes. Sheri's head was still between her thighs. Nana was pressed against the wall beside the shower, caressing herself. The touch of Giselle's eyes froze her for a moment, then Sheri found Giselle's clitoris and made

250

her groan. That sound – the longing, the pathos – seemed to give her sister the permission that she needed. Her fingers dug deeper into her sex. Her behind ground into the wall. Giselle watched entranced as her sister's mouth opened and she slid down the wall into an open-legged squat.

Then Giselle's mouth was filled by Charles and she lost sight of Nana. He fucked her slowly, easing himself deep into her throat, withdrawing, trailing the tip of his sex around her lips, then plunging back in. All the time that he enjoyed her, Sheri's tongue worked and Nana's groans mingled with her own. Finally, Charles let her head return to the couch. He reached for Nana, taking her hand and pulling her upright. Then, telling Sheri to step aside, he pushed Nana to the place vacated. The sisters looked at each other. In the studio, when Nana had worn the cheerleader outfit, it had been Giselle who had called the shots. Now it was for Nana to take that role, but she hesitated. Charles took her hand and rested it on Giselle's mound. It felt good – as good as Jean's had been; as wrong too – wrong and good, the two going together as they had on the island.

'Taste her,' Sheri said softly in encouragement.

Nana looked at the woman and blushed.

Charles came to stand behind her and Giselle watched as his arms circled her sister's waist and his hands sought her sex. Soon Nana was gasping.

'Shall I whip her first?' Charles asked. 'Would it be sweeter if she was weeping?'

Nana frowned and groaned. It might have been a no. It might have been a yes.

'Pass the bag,' Charles said to Sheri. Sheri glanced at Giselle, a question in her eyes. When Giselle turned away – unable to agree, but unwilling to dissent – Sheri shrugged and passed the bag to Charles. The blade of the whip, laid across Giselle's belly, brought her attention to a sharp focus. Charles still had one hand in

Nana's sex. The girl was close to coming. Giselle could feel it – the weight of the brimming pleasure that swirled in her heaving belly. But then Charles withdrew his hand and left Nana on the brink. He stood to Giselle's left, lifted his arm and struck. The whip curled across Giselle's upper thighs and drew a shriek.

'Put your hand over her mouth,' Charles commanded Nana.

She moved quickly, sealing Giselle's mouth as the whip struck for a second time. This time Giselle convulsed. The whip had caught the under surface of her breasts. It was an effort not to bite into her sister's flesh. The whip fell twice more before Giselle surrendered to the tears. Then the hand came away from her mouth and she was left for a moment to gasp and moan.

Charles slipped his hand into Nana's sex again. After the whipping she was visibly more excited. Giselle felt the extra dimension of arousal as her ankles were taken and lifted again. When she was fully splayed, a tongue took possession of her sex. She knew that it was Nana's but refused to look. The sensation was too sweet to risk losing; the sense of wrongness acute enough without confirming it with her eyes. The tongue took her to the edge and then withdrew. She heard whispered words, then the opening of a door. Charles stroked her forehead and told her to kneel up. It was an effort – the couch was too comfortable and the arousal too beguiling. No sooner had she taken the position that he wanted, bottom high in the air, breasts pressed to the leather, than the door opened again. She didn't want to open her eyes, didn't want her worst fears confirmed.

Charles wouldn't allow her such an easy escape. He lifted her chin and told her to look. When she did, she saw the owl man. His towel was gone and his sex was thick and hard.

'Help yourself,' Charles told him.

The man smiled and presented his sex to Giselle's mouth. She didn't want it but it slipped in as easily as a knife. The man's paunch rested against her forehead.

'Is that just a toy?' he growled. Giselle didn't understand what he meant until the whip came into view, Charles's hand delivering it to the questioner.

'Get the girl to use it.'

A few moments later she felt a burning stripe across the back of her thighs. There were three strokes, each delivered as the owl man was lodged deep in her throat, blocking her screams. Nana's face appeared.

'I'm sorry,' she whispered as her lips rained kisses on Giselle's cheeks. Then she watched as Giselle's mouth was fucked with long deep strokes. A woman's lips, Sheri's, sucked on Giselle's burning sex, quickly bringing the indignity of orgasm while the stranger callously plundered her throat.

It took an hour to exhaust all the possibilities. Nana wasn't spared the whip. The owl man enjoyed sex and anus with equal ruthlessness. Charles was content to watch for the most part. When he decided to come he used Giselle's behind but cast his seed in Nana's mouth.

14

Cynicism

The following week was the hardest of Giselle's life. From the moment the Eurostar pulled into Paris, Charles became a tyrant. The Takitsua collection, with her as the sole model, was one of his single biggest commissions. They worked twelve hours a day and, at the end of each, the scent of latex was buried deep in her skin.

Nana helped around the set for most of the week but then, one day, there was a different woman. She was black, tall, swan-necked and possessed the grace and indolence of a well-fed leopard. It was her name that shocked Giselle. She was introduced as Katarina and, with that word, Giselle knew that her sister's fate had been decided. If Charles had Katarina then Gustave had Nana.

Charles made no secret of his desire for the woman. Despite the Takitsua deadline he photographed her in preference to Giselle. Giselle was obliged to wait in her exotic costumes while Katarina sprawled naked in a director's chair or crouched in the glare of the lights and opened the lips of her sex. He used her mouth openly as Odette attended to Giselle's make-up. He took her regularly into the darkroom and emerged flushed and feverish, inflamed rather than sated. Part of Giselle understood the exchange. Katarina had a quality that would have drawn any man. She seemed bred for sex, awake and aware only when a man wanted her. The narrowness of her waist – artificial perhaps, the result of long training with corsets and restraints – made her seem as sinuous as a snake. Her skin glowed like polished bronze. Her eyes were as lustrous as horse chestnuts, fresh on the autumn ground. Yet if Giselle understood Charles's desire, she couldn't forgive his betrayal of Nana. She had moulded herself to Charles's desires as willingly as wax. Now, after less than a month, she had been traded in, swopped for a whore.

As Giselle watched him use Katarina's mouth for the third time in as many hours, she was finally aware of the depth of his cynicism. Once he was finished, as soon as his seed had sprayed the black girl's lips and cheeks, Charles was reaching for his camera and turning his attention back to Giselle. She realised that, for him, neither Katarina nor Nana had any real meaning, that sex was a mere tube – throat or sex or anus. The packaging was clearly important – the face that surrounded the lips, the sculptural beauty of the behind that opened to his prying hands. But, beyond that, beyond the signs and surfaces, he had no interest. He was the post-modern lover, incapable of attachment and contemptuous of meaning. Only the arrangement and rearrangement of motifs – oral, anal, vaginal – had any appeal. The whip set his mind on fire, not the body. The marks on a girl's flesh signified not loyalty or love, but were mere additions to his library of images. She remembered how he had examined the bruises on Nana's behind the night that she had lost her virginity. He had commented on the colours that deepened before their eyes, the contrast between the blues and greens, how the shadow of Nana's cleft transformed all to black. He had pinched the bruises to introduce a new red and told her to be still when she writhed with the assault. The tears which had touched Giselle's heart were, to him, merely an opportunity to view the sweetness of Nana's eyes through a new lens.

Giselle realised that she had always been aware of this cynicism. She remembered his skilled manipulation of the models on the beach at Pleneuf-Val-Andre. His own treatment of her while Greta waited for him to come to bed. Now, fully conscious of the depth of his contempt, she recalled Greta's advice in the bar on the left bank and hardened her heart. It was all a matter of money. She would become a professional. She would no longer store up her rewards in heaven, but in Credit Lyonnaise.

Nana, too, was becoming a material girl. At the end of her first day with Gustave she was pale and drawn. She brushed aside Giselle's concern with an emphatic rebuff. With Charles, there was a distance and a sense of something irrevocably changed. He hardly seemed to notice. For all the time that Nana worked for Gustave, Katarina attended to him with the devotion of a dog.

By the end of the week, Nana had undergone yet another metamorphosis. She was no longer pale. She went out to work with the focus of any career girl. That Saturday she went shopping. She chose retro-sixties clothes and bedecked herself with kitsch accessories. It wasn't Charles's kind of thing, or Greta's, or even Giselle's – it was her own, bought with her own money. Porn paid pretty well for some, it seemed. Even the obscenity of her language as she described the films that Gustave made had a newness and Giselle welcomed it. There were so many things unnamed in their lives and any names were better than none.

In the evenings, Nana began to find her own pleasures. Giselle felt a sort of pride in her sister as she tottered out into the Parisian streets on three-inch heels, a boa flapping from her neck, her hair a mess of beads. It was a sort of independence, bravely won. Money was making her and if she was becoming brittle and hard – a coating only, Giselle sensed – she was also becoming her own creature.

Charles still visited Giselle at night. He was cruel and

efficient in the darkness of her bedroom but he rarely looked at her. Except for his brisk instructions, they would climax without speaking. Their flesh and nerves shared a common language and that was enough.

The *Takitsua Catalogue* was due to be published in the autumn but *Femmes* picked up some of the pre-launch publicity photographs and suddenly Giselle was a star. The week that saw the images of her bared behind and latexed torso spread across its pages brought a string of offers. In April, astonishingly, she was on the cover of *Vogue*. Charles had done everything that he said he would. He had made her a star. He was making her rich.

With each franc that flowed into Giselle's bank account, she took a step closer to home. If she allowed herself to dream, it was of a house in the hills that overlooked Avignon. Nearby would be a flooded quarry and, in the sparkling blue waters, a grey-stone island.

It was still Greta who held everything together. Her tireless goodness was the foundation of everything that Charles did. Giselle still talked about her time in Avignon; still repeated her stories. With each telling they became more real. It was Greta's understanding that allowed what had happened to become bearable. She steadied Giselle, confirmed her thoughts and feelings. Black-and-white facts became full-colour experiences.

It was a long time before Giselle told Greta what had happened to Jean on that last night together. When she did, she insisted on telling the story in the third person as if it had happened to someone else. 'I knew a girl who had a brother called Jean,' she began. They were sitting in the Tuileries in the brave spring sunshine. Greta listened and was shocked. She listened in silence, absolutely motionless, as the story of what had happened on the bedroom balcony unfolded. She listened to the joining of brother and sister, sex to sex.

She listened to the discovery, to the struggle of enraged father and son, the breaking of the balustrade and the plunge to the concrete below.

'He died in the ambulance,' Giselle concluded. 'The boy's father lay beside him, crippled for life. It was very melodramatic.'

It was these final words that shocked Greta the most. She took Giselle's frozen hands and squeezed.

'It was not a melodrama. It was not a story. It happened to you,' she insisted. 'You can't get away from it. You can't pretend that it happened to someone else.'

Giselle shrugged.

'It happened. But I don't really believe it.'

'Then you will have to go home. Perhaps then you will believe it. Only when you believe in your own story can you have a life.'

Giselle shrugged and closed her eyes. The Parisian sun was too weak to warm her and she shivered. She would go home soon – as soon as she felt that she would survive it.

NEW BOOKS

Coming up from Nexus, Sapphire and Black Lace

In For a Penny by **Penny Birch**
November 1999   £5.99   ISBN: 0 352 33449 5
Penny Birch is back, as naughty as ever. *In for a Penny* continues the
story of her outrageous sex life and also the equally rude behaviour
of her friends. From stories of old-fashioned spankings, through
strip-wrestling in baked beans, to a girl with six breasts, it's all there.
Each scene is described in loving detail, with no holding back and a
level of realism that comes from a great deal of practical experience.

Maiden by **Aishling Morgan**
November 1999   £5.99   ISBN: 0 352 33466 5
When Elethrine, Princess Talithea and their maid, Aisla, threaten to
spank the sorceress Ea, they are punished by being transported to a
distant part of their world. *Maiden* charts their journey home through
a series of erotic indignities and humiliations, throughout all of which
Elethrine is determined to retain her virginity. What she doesn't
realise is that this will involve far more humiliating encounters for her
than for her companions.

Bound to Submit by **Amanda Ware**
November 1999   £5.99   ISBN: 0 352 33451 7
The beautiful and submissive Caroline is married to her new master
and the love of her life, James, at a bizarre fetishistic ceremony in the
USA. He is keen to turn his new wife into a star of explicit movies
and Caroline is auditioned without delay for a film of bondage and
domination. Little do they know that the project is being financed by
James' business rival and Caroline's former master, the cruel Clive.
Clive intends to fulfil a long-held desire – to permanently mark
Caroline as his property. Can her husband save her from his
mesmeric influence? A Nexus Classic.

Sandra's New School by Yolanda Celbridge

December 1999   £5.99   ISBN: 0 352 33454 1

Nude sunbathing and spanking with a lesbian, submissive girlfriend lead hedonistic Sandra Shanks to the rigours of Quirke's school, where adult schoolgirls are taught old-fashioned submission, in the stern modesty of too-tight uniforms. In a school without males, the dormitory fun of 'all girls together' is as deliciously naughty as Sandra imagined – until she learns sadistic Miss Quirke's own guilty secret.

Tiger, Tiger by Aishling Morgan

December 1999   £5.99   ISBN: 0 352 33455 X

Aishling Morgan's third novel is a study in gothic eroticism. Her world is populated by strange half-human creatures, like Tian-Sha, the tigranthrope, a beautiful blend of girl and tiger. In this bizarre fantasy world a complex plot of erotic intrigue is played out against a background of arcane ritual and nightmare symmetry.

Sisterhood of the Institute by Maria del Rey

December 1999   £5.99   ISBN: 0 352 33456 8

The strict Mistress Shirer has always kept the residents of the Institute on a tight rein. Her charges are girls whose behaviour is apt to get out of hand and who need special discipline. Now they've opened a male dormitory and all manner of strange goings-on have come to her attention. Determined to restore order, Mistress Shirer sends Jaki, her cross-dressing slave, into the dormitories to find out exactly what is going on. A Nexus Classic.

A new imprint of lesbian fiction

Getaway by Suzanne Blaylock
October 1999   Price £6.99   ISBN: 0 352 33443 6
Brilliantly talented Polly Sayers had made two big life shifts
concurrently. She's had her first affair with a woman, and she's also
stolen the code of an important new piece of software and made her
break, doing a runner all the way to a seemingly peaceful coastal
community. But things aren't as tranquil as they appear in the haven,
as Polly becomes immersed in an insular group of mysterious but
very attractive women.

No Angel by Marian Malone
November 1999   £6.99   ISBN 0 352 33462 2
Sally longs to test her limits and sample forbidden pleasures, yet she's
frightened by the depth of her yearnings. Her journey of self-
discovery begins in the fetish clubs of Brighton and ultimately leads
to an encounter with an enigmatic female stranger. And now that
she's tasted freedom, there's no way she's going back.

Bound by Contract by Helena Ravenscroft
November 1999   Price £5.99   ISBN: 0 352 33447 9
Samantha and Ross have been an illicit item for years –
rivals as children, and passionate lovers as adults. When Ross
becomes involved with the submissive Dr Louisa Richmond, Sam
senses his waning interest in her own dominating ways. Reading the
classic *Venus in Furs* inspires her to sign a contract to be Ross's slave
for a month. She imagines it will rekindle the spark in their
relationship – but it becomes altogether more erotic, and totally out
of her control.

Velvet Glove by Emma Holly
November 1999   Price £5.99   ISBN: 0 352 33448 7
At the ripe young age of 22, Audrey is an SM Goldilocks in search
of the perfect master. Her first candidate, an icy-eyed international
banker, is far too hard. Her second, a childhood playmate, is far too
soft. A charismatic bar owner seems just right, especially when he
saves her from a watcher the bank has set on her trail. But can
Audrey trust the man behind the charm? Or will Patrick drag her
deeper into submission than even she would care to go?

The Best of Black Lace edited by Kerri Sharp
December 1999   £5.99   ISBN: 0 352 33452 5
This diverse collection of sizzling erotic texts is an 'editor's choice'
compilation of extracts from Black Lace books with a contemporary
theme. The accent is on female characters who know what they want –
in bed and in the workplace – and who have a sense of sexual adventure
above and beyond the heroines of romantic fiction. These girls kick ass!

Stripped to the Bone by Jasmine Stone
December 1999   £5.99   ISBN: 0 352 33463 0
Annie is a fun-loving, free-thinking American woman who sets
herself the mission of changing everything in her life. The only snag
is, she doesn't know when to stop changing things. Every man she
encounters is determined to find out what makes her tick, but her
playful personality means that no one can get a hold on her. Her sexual
magnetism is electrifying, and her capacity for the unusual and experi-
mental sides of sex play have her lovers in a spin of erotic confusion.

NEXUS BACKLIST

All books are priced £5.99 unless another price is given. If a date is supplied, the book in question will not be available until that month in 1999.

CONTEMPORARY EROTICA

THE ACADEMY	Arabella Knight	
AMANDA IN THE PRIVATE HOUSE	Esme Ombreux	
BAD PENNY	Penny Birch	
THE BLACK MASQUE	Lisette Ashton	
THE BLACK WIDOW	Lisette Ashton	
BOUND TO OBEY	Amanda Ware	
BRAT	Penny Birch	
DANCE OF SUBMISSION	Lisette Ashton	Nov
DARK DELIGHTS	Maria del Rey	
DARK DESIRES	Maria del Rey	
DARLINE DOMINANT	Tania d'Alanis	
DISCIPLES OF SHAME	Stephanie Calvin	
THE DISCIPLINE OF NURSE RIDING	Yolanda Celbridge	
DISPLAYS OF INNOCENTS	Lucy Golden	
EMMA'S SECRET DOMINATION	Hilary James	
EXPOSING LOUISA	Jean Aveline	
FAIRGROUND ATTRACTIONS	Lisette Ashton	
GISELLE	Jean Aveline	Oct
HEART OF DESIRE	Maria del Rey	
HOUSE RULES	G.C. Scott	Oct
IN FOR A PENNY	Penny Birch	Nov
JULIE AT THE REFORMATORY	Angela Elgar	
LINGERING LESSONS	Sarah Veitch	

THE MISTRESS OF STERNWOOD GRANGE	Arabella Knight		
ONE WEEK IN THE PRIVATE HOUSE	Esme Ombreux		
THE PALACE OF EROS	Delver Maddingley		
PENNY IN HARNESS	Penny Birch		
THE PLEASURE CHAMBER	Brigitte Markham		
THE RELUCTANT VIRGIN	Kendal Grahame		
RITES OF OBEDIENCE	Lindsay Gordon		
RUE MARQUIS DE SADE	Morgana Baron		
'S' – A JOURNEY INTO SERVITUDE	Philippa Masters		
SANDRA'S NEW SCHOOL	Yolanda Celbridge		Dec
THE SCHOOLING OF STELLA	Yolanda Celbridge		
THE SUBMISSION OF STELLA	Yolanda Celbridge		
THE SUBMISSION GALLERY	Lindsay Gordon		
SUSIE IN SERVITUDE	Arabella Knight		
TAKING PAINS TO PLEASE	Arabella Knight		
A TASTE OF AMBER	Penny Birch		
THE TEST	Nadine Somers		
THE TRAINING OF FALLEN ANGELS	Kendal Grahame		
VIRGINIA'S QUEST	Katrina Young	£4.99	

ANCIENT & FANTASY SETTINGS

THE CASTLE OF MALDONA	Yolanda Celbridge		
THE FOREST OF BONDAGE	Aran Ashe		
NYMPHS OF DIONYSUS	Susan Tinoff	£4.99	
TIGER, TIGER	Aishling Morgan		Dec
THE WARRIOR QUEEN	Kendal Grahame		

EDWARDIAN, VICTORIAN & OLDER EROTICA

ANNIE	Evelyn Culber		
ANNIE AND THE COUNTESS	Evelyn Culber		
BEATRICE	Anonymous		
CONFESSIONS OF AN ENGLISH SLAVE	Yolanda Celbridge		Sep
THE CORRECTION OF AN ESSEX MAID	Yolanda Celbridge		

THE GOVERNESS AT ST AGATHA'S	Yolanda Celbridge	
THE MASTER OF CASTLELEIGH	Jacqueline Bellevois	Aug
PRIVATE MEMOIRS OF A KENTISH HEADMISTRESS	Yolanda Celbridge	£4.99
THE RAKE	Aishling Morgan	Sep
THE TRAINING OF AN ENGLISH GENTLEMAN	Yolanda Celbridge	

SAMPLERS & COLLECTIONS

EROTICON 4	Various	
THE FIESTA LETTERS	ed. Chris Lloyd	£4.99
NEW EROTICA 3		
NEW EROTICA 4	Various	
A DOZEN STROKES	Various	Aug

NEXUS CLASSICS
A new imprint dedicated to putting the finest works of erotic fiction back in print

THE IMAGE	Jean de Berg	
CHOOSING LOVERS FOR JUSTINE	Aran Ashe	
THE INSTITUTE	Maria del Rey	
AGONY AUNT	G. C. Scott	
THE HANDMAIDENS	Aran Ashe	
OBSESSION	Maria del Rey	
HIS MASTER'S VOICE	G.C. Scott	Aug
CITADEL OF SERVITUDE	Aran Ashe	Sep
BOUND TO SERVE	Amanda Ware	Oct
BOUND TO SUBMIT	Amanda Ware	Nov
SISTERHOOD OF THE INSTITUTE	Maria del Rey	Dec

Please send me the books I have ticked above.

Name   ....

Address   ....

                   ....

                   ....

                   .... Post code.......................

Send to: **Cash Sales, Nexus Books, Thames Wharf Studios, Rainville Road, London W6 9HT**

US customers: for prices and details of how to order books for delivery by mail, call 1-800-805-1083.

Please enclose a cheque or postal order, made payable to **Nexus Books**, to the value of the books you have ordered plus postage and packing costs as follows:

UK and BFPO – £1.00 for the first book, 50p for the second book and 30p for each subsequent book to a maximum of £3.00;

Overseas (including Republic of Ireland) – £2.00 for the first book, £1.00 for the second book and 50p for each subsequent book.

We accept all major credit cards, including VISA, ACCESS/MASTERCARD, AMEX, DINERS CLUB, SWITCH, SOLO, and DELTA. Please write your card number and expiry date here:

....

Please allow up to 28 days for delivery.

Signature ....